Totally Bound Publishing books by Sierra Cartwright

Mastered
With This Collar
On His Terms
Over the Line
In His Cuffs
For the Sub
In the Den

The Donovan Dynasty
Bind
Brand
Boss

I0611258

Mastered

ON HIS TERMS
THE 10TH ANNIVERSARY EDITION

SIERRA CARTWRIGHT

On His Terms: The 10th Anniversary Edition
ISBN # 978-1-80250-577-1
©Copyright Sierra Cartwright 2023
Cover Art by Kelly Martin ©Copyright September 2023
Interior text design by Claire Siemaszkiewicz
Totally Bound Publishing

ON HIS TERMS

Dedication

For BAB and long nights and lots of coffee.
Shayla, your support and inspiration means the world.
For the sprint group that helps keep me going!
And especially for YOU! Thank you for spending time at
the Den.

Chapter One

"There he is."

"Where?" Chelsea Barton craned her head to get a look at Master Alexander Monahan.

"Near the fireplace," her friend Sara said.

Chelsea glanced in that direction. Dressed in blue jeans, a long-sleeved, Western-style shirt, a black leather vest, a silver bolo tie, and a cowboy hat, he didn't fit her image of a BDSM trainer. His height, though—over six feet tall—was definitely what she'd expected. The billionaire Dominant was as gorgeous as he was unapproachable.

"Quit staring!" Sara cautioned. "Good submissives don't behave that way."

That didn't stop Chelsea. Rules were helpful for other people. As for her, she ruthlessly pursued what she wanted. And she'd decided that Master Alexander would help her become the perfect sub—or at least passable enough that no one would notice if she wasn't really all that into it. That was step one in Project Snag Evan C.

Master Evan C was a rocker whose band was climbing the charts. With the right PR firm — *hers* — he could become a megastar. As a double bonus, her company would gain real credibility by signing the celebrity, which would in turn bring her the success she dreamed of...the success that would prove she was worthwhile, despite what she'd been told her entire life.

So far, her efforts to ensnare his attention had been a dismal failure.

Six months ago, she'd met him at a party and had developed a certifiable fangirl crush on him. She fantasized about him tying her up and fucking her hard.

Chelsea wanted him. And not just as a client, but also as a Dominant and lover. What could be more fabulous than career success and having a sexy man to boot?

Sara, always the unwelcome pragmatist, had advised Chelsea to forget her ideas. Master Evan C liked well-trained submissives, women who subjugated their needs to suit his. Which, as Sara pointed out, really wasn't Chelsea. Chelsea was headstrong and determined, a driven achiever who chewed antacid for breakfast, suffered from rampant insomnia, and hadn't taken a vacation in over two years. That Master Evan C discarded women like the scarves he wore while performing made her even more resolved to succeed.

That was where Master Alexander came in.

According to Sara, he used to be a trainer, and he was still well respected in the community. He didn't get emotionally involved with subs, and he was one of the best.

"He's looking this way," Sara whispered.

"And he's alone, finally." When Chelsea had learned that Sara and Lyle—her Dom—had been invited to Master Alexander's birthday party at the Den, Master Damien's luxury Colorado mountain retreat, Chelsea had begged, pleaded, and cajoled for an invitation.

At first, Sara had refused. She hadn't wanted to be part of any more of Chelsea's shenanigans. While Chelsea didn't blame her friend—after all, their last escapade had earned Sara a punishment from Lyle—Chelsea refused to be deterred. "If you'll excuse me…?"

"Remember, you don't know me."

She gave her friend a false smile. "Have we met?" After setting her shoulders, Chelsea headed straight for Master Alexander.

A couple stopped to talk to him. Foiled, she paused to grab a glass of sparkling water from a passing server. She was woman enough to appreciate the hottie. He wore a bow tie, but no shirt, and it looked as if he could have been poured into his dress slacks. The material revealed his muscular thighs as well as his hot rear. And she supposed it was possible he had oil rubbed on his bare chest.

With a nod, he said, "Enjoy your evening, ma'am."

Maybe she'd hire this crew for her next event. It would certainly be a shocker and earn her some much-appreciated publicity.

Rather than taking a drink, she rolled the glass between her palms and waited for her chance to approach Master Alexander. Finally, the couple moved off.

After putting down her drink she walked toward him. Damn, his cowboy hat made him look like an outlaw.

He rested his forearm on the mantelpiece and studied her intently as she approached. Even from several feet away, he exuded power.

Calling on the bravado that she suddenly needed, she continued on.

When she stopped near him, he swept his gaze over her, from the toes of her pumps to the top of the shiny clips she'd placed in her short hair.

He didn't greet her. Instead, he waited. That didn't surprise her. She'd done plenty of research on him and learned he was inflexible, a formidable foe in the business arena despite his recent setbacks.

"Mr. Monahan, I'm Chelsea Barton." She extended her hand and gave him her most dazzling smile. The look was practiced. She could charm anyone with it. "I wanted to wish you a very happy birthday."

"Did you?" Finally, he dropped his arm to accept her hand.

His grip was warm, firm, reassuring. Electricity shimmied up her spine. This close, he was even more gorgeous. Small lines were etched next to his captivating green eyes, and his lips were firm and full. The crazy notion of kissing him skipped through her mind before she ruthlessly shoved it away. She had a business proposition for him, nothing more.

When he released her, she felt strangely bereft. "Who are you here with, Ms. Barton?"

"Uh...a friend," she hedged.

"Are you always evasive?"

"Are you always so direct?"

He folded his arms across his magnificent chest. "Save us both some time and cut through the bullshit. It's my birthday, my party, and I approved the guest list. I saw you speaking with Sara. As she is pretending not to look at us, I assume you wanted to meet me for a specific reason. Because I'm feeling generous, I'll give you thirty seconds. Start talking."

Suddenly she wished she'd taken a drink of that water. "You're right," she confessed. Because he was direct, she responded in kind. "I came here specifically to meet you." Quickly she added, "But not for the reason you might think." She hoped that comment was intriguing enough to buy her an extra minute of his time. "I own a company named You're The Star. We do PR."

"Monahan Capital has a PR firm."

"Who should have done a better job of spinning the Bartholomew deal initially, but they've been passable since then." When all he did was arch an eyebrow, she pushed on. "However, if you did a couple of events in the community, such as a fundraiser, your positive press would shove the other headlines from the first page of the search engines. But that's not my point." Since he was still listening, she kept talking. "I sought you out because I want you to train me as a submissive, and I understand that you're the best."

"At one time that was true."

From his mouth, his flat statement didn't sound arrogant.

"But I'm quite sure you've heard I don't train anymore."

She pushed back the trepidation that had started doing the backstroke in her veins. The years had taught her a valuable lesson—when she wasn't getting what she wanted, she needed to turn up the charm.

Gently, she placed her hand on his arm. When he didn't react, she continued, "I'm sure a man as discerning as you has high expectations and demands excellence. I understand that it comes at a cost. Name your price, and I'll write you a check."

He didn't respond to her tactics. In fact, his jawline could have been chiseled from granite. "I'm not for sale, Ms. Barton."

She gave up on charm and dropped her hand.

From the corner of her eye, she noticed Evan C and a woman were heading toward the stairs. Although she hadn't seen it, she understood Master Damien had a dungeon with some private play rooms. Seeing Evan C with someone who should have been her only increased her resolve. "You're a businessman. Better than anyone, you understand that everyone has a price."

"What's yours?" Master Alexander countered. "Selling your soul for success?"

"That's harsh." Chelsea blinked. "You don't know anything about me."

"On the contrary. I know you will use manipulation in order to get what you want."

She pulled back.

"If you want this conversation to continue, be honest." His tone was as icy as a cold front that raged down from the Arctic.

Chelsea hadn't expected this to be so difficult. She'd figured most Doms would love to have a sub begging for their attention. Her offer of money should have sealed the deal. "I want Evan C to hire my company and accept me as his submissive."

"And you think some training will intrigue him?"

"It will."

"You sound convinced."

She recalled the party they'd been at. "He snubbed me once because I was too new." Seeing him toss his scarf over his shoulder as he'd walked away had stung.

"What kind of experience do you have?" Master Alexander asked.

"Not much," she admitted reluctantly.

"Be specific."

"How much information do you want?"

He captured her chin, ignoring the way she'd tipped it stubbornly.

She was tall, especially in her spiked fuck-me heels, but he still towered over her by several inches. Since she was accustomed to looking men in the eye as they spoke, having to look up was a little disconcerting. For one of the first times in her life, she felt small, overpowered.

His fingers were strong and firm, as unrelenting as the glint of steel in his eyes. "I'll tell you when I've heard enough."

She tried, and failed, to hide her shiver. For the first time in her life, she wondered if she'd set her sights too high. He'd seen her subterfuge and cut through it — despite the fact she'd become a master at it.

Once she exhaled, he released his grip.

When one of the servers came near, she signaled for a glass of wine, needing the fortification. She had no problem at all promoting others or her firm. But exposing her secrets? That required courage.

She took a long drink of her wine, then held on to the stem as if it were a lifeline. "I didn't know I liked kink until one of my boyfriends blindfolded me."

"What did you like about the experience?"

Several Doms and subs moved into the living room, and she looked around nervously.

"Eyes on me," he instructed.

You're relentless. She caught a glimpse of what he might be like as a trainer, and it terrified her as much as it intrigued her.

"Or excuse yourself now."

She looked up from where she'd been staring into the depths of her wine.

He missed nothing.

"I liked that I had no idea what would happen next. My hearing seemed heightened. And when he touched me, the sensation was magnified."

"Go on."

"One guy would sometimes swat my bottom when I passed him." She had no idea this would be so embarrassing. There was nothing sexual about the conversation, rather, the facts were somewhat clinical. But that didn't stop her from blushing. "Last Halloween, I attended a BDSM party. Compared to this..." She swept her hand around. The gathering at Master Damien's house was for people who lived the lifestyle. "It's clear now that most of us were just dabbling. We wore outfits we bought at the costume store, but afterward my date tied me up for the first time. It was just to his bed, and he used a light whip on my ass. I liked it. Well, enough to explore more, but he said it really hadn't worked for him all that well. He didn't like hurting me. Even though I promised him he hadn't."

"You're telling me most vanilla guys aren't interested in spanking an ass like that?"

She blinked.

"I noticed you when you first came in, and you wore that skirt hoping I would."

"Yes," she admitted. "I did." It was one size smaller than she bought for business meetings, and she'd never wear it out in public. The material hugged her rear so tight she was nervous about sitting down.

"So show me."

"I beg your pardon?"

"Lift your skirt to your waist, turn around, spread your legs as far as you can, then bend over and grab your ankles."

For a moment she could hardly breathe. He said nothing further and he looked unconcerned, as if it didn't matter to him one way or another whether she did as he said. She recognized the order as his first test.

He extended his hand to take her glass. That was probably for the best—she was suddenly afraid of dropping it. He slid the stemware onto the mantel, then used his thumb to tip back his cowboy hat.

She pulled up her skirt and she was grateful she'd worn a thong. Exposing herself to a stranger was far different from playing with a man she'd been dating.

Master Alexander continued to say nothing. She realized then that he was a man of few words, and he didn't repeat himself. There was no cajoling from him, no teasing, no 'Oh, come on, Chelsea, have a little fun.' This man was a Dominant all the way to his core.

Mouth dry, she turned away from him and followed the rest of his instructions. For at least sixty interminable seconds, he said nothing. Her heart thundered. The tops of her shoes dug into her ankles, and blood rushed to her head.

"This is the ass you've had a difficult time convincing men to spank?"

"Yes," she said. Then she wondered what the protocol was for addressing him. Sir? Mr. Monahan? Master? Alex? Alexander?

He caressed both her bare butt cheeks.

Slowly, she began to relax.

Other people continued to move through the rooms, and a man stopped to talk to him. He removed one hand and continued to rub her with the other.

This was awful, humiliating. She wasn't accustomed to being exposed, unseen, completely ignored.

Horrified, she started to stand, but, saying nothing, he pinched her upper thigh.

Though she yelped, she forced herself to stay in position, fighting off her instinct to stand, drop her skirt, and get the hell away from him.

Instead, she drew on the determination that had seen her work two jobs through college. Now, like then, she kept her eyes on the goal.

Eventually, the man moved off. Although he kept one hand on her, Master Alexander still didn't speak, leaving her with no idea what to do.

Right then, he slapped her left buttock, hard. She cried out, more from shock than because it had hurt.

"You did well for a beginner. Stand, pull your skirt down, then face me."

As she followed his instructions, her legs quivered. In the last three minutes, she'd had a bigger taste of BDSM than she'd had in the last six months. She wasn't sure she liked it.

"Tell me about your thoughts while you were bent over."

"I felt nervous and exposed."

"And how did you feel when I smacked you?"

"I was startled, I suppose. And I didn't like how impersonal your touch was. I could have been anyone."

"Was it difficult for you to remain in position?"

She reached for her glass of wine and took a deep drink. "Yes."

"Why?"

The question vexed her, and she snapped her answer. "This isn't supposed to be an exploration into my psyche."

"Anyone who engages in BDSM with me opens every part of themselves. It's your choice." He shrugged. "Leave at any time."

Chelsea had spent years shielding herself from criticism, so much so that she rarely shared her innermost thoughts with anyone, even close friends. But this man was demanding access to her emotions, requiring vulnerability that made her shake. Since she had no other option, she opened up a little. "I don't like to be left out. When you ignored me like that? Frankly it pissed me off."

"Yet you stayed in position. Why?"

"Because I want you to train me. And I wanted to show you I can do it."

"Very good. By the way, you have a very spankable ass. It turned bright red with my handprint."

No doubt the color matched her face.

"Being a submissive is very different from being tied up, wearing a blindfold, or even getting a spanking. What you just experienced is a sample of what my submissives endure."

Wildly, she wondered if she had any idea what she was asking for.

"Doms typically adore and cherish their subs. Some couples, as you may have ascertained, indulge like you and your previous boyfriends, just with a few more rules and a bit more regularity. They may even use the words Dominant and submissive. To me, submission comes with strict protocols, with service, along with delicate body movements."

"What you just showed me... I didn't know it would be that hard core."

"Go on."

"The whole being submissive thing..." She worried her lower lip. Once she realized she was doing it, she stopped immediately. Her mother had spent years reinforcing what an awful habit that was. How would Chelsea ever capture a husband if she couldn't be more elegant? "I guess I thought it was mostly about getting spankings and being tied up."

"It's more a state of mind," he informed her. "What you're talking about falls under the broad umbrella of bondage and discipline. And it could just be added kink in an otherwise vanilla relationship. But submission is about putting someone else's needs before your own. And you do it from a genuine desire to serve, not because you see it as a means to an end. Most of all, it's about mutual trust."

His words landed like a chastisement.

"I appreciate your honesty," he said. "I'm sure you will be able to find a man to spank you."

Realizing he was dismissing her, she made a desperate offer. "Are you interested? I mean, it is your birthday, and someone should get a spanking, and I'm guessing you won't be baring your butt."

"Quite correct."

She wished he'd tip his sexy cowboy hat back once more so she could read his expression better. "You could consider it a birthday present."

"I'm not interested in giving you a spanking. And it has nothing to do with your delectable derrière. As I mentioned, my subs have a desire to serve. Which you do not."

While she hadn't liked being ignored, or the nasty little pinch, she had liked his firm command and the way he'd so masterfully swatted her. It had stung. But it had also warmed her skin, leaving her turned on.

"Please, I implore you to reconsider." After all, she could do anything she set her mind to. "You won't be disappointed in me. I promise you that."

Just then, Master Damien called for everyone's attention.

Standing next to each other, she and Alexander turned.

Sara had told Chelsea that the Den's owner could have been a movie star. He had long, dark hair that was secured at his nape. Leather pants highlighted his strong muscles, and a short-sleeved black T-shirt revealed a tattoo she couldn't quite make out.

Some Doms and Dommes urged their subs to their knees for the announcement. Those instructed verbally or through hand commands knelt without complaint.

Now she understood Master Alexander's point. No one else appeared to rebel against the indignity the way she instinctively had.

When the crowd fell silent, Master Damien went on. "We're celebrating Master Alexander's birthday tonight." He beckoned to a woman who pushed a rolling cart into the living room. A half-sheet cake was ablaze with dozens of candles.

He began to sing the happy birthday song—too bad Master Evan C wasn't in the room—and others joined in.

When the terrible rendition ended and the guests applauded, Master Alexander blew out the candles. And because she figured he wouldn't make a wish, she made one of her own.

"Thank you all! Being back is the best gift of all."

Once more, everyone cheered enthusiastically.

"Chelsea here will be helping to serve the cake," Master Alexander announced.

What? Furiously, stomach plunging, she scowled at him.

He leaned down to whisper in her ear. "Let's see how much you really want to be a sub."

No way could she do this. Cake cutting wasn't one of her skills. She could never get the pieces to stand up, and she always ended up with frosting all over her hands.

"You're going to help Brandy."

Be a server, as if she were his submissive?

"Follow her instructions." The command in his tone left no room for arguing. "And, Chelsea? You're going to do it with a smile."

To get her going, he placed his fingers against the small of her back and gave her a gentle nudge.

Left with no other option, Chelsea accepted the pearlescent handle from Brandy.

"You do that while I remove the candles," Brandy suggested.

The same man who'd brought her wine earlier carried over a stack of plates.

After cutting a bunch of jagged lines, she picked up the cake spatula and transferred the corner piece onto a plate.

"Since it's his birthday, go ahead and take the first slice to Master Alexander," Brandy said kindly.

"*Me?*"

"I get the idea that would be his preference. I'll take care of Master Damien, then the hired staff will help us with everyone else."

Chelsea took the plate to him, hiding her internal snarl behind a smile.

"Not good enough. Try again," he said.

Are you serious right now? "Excuse me?"

"Watch Brandy."

As she moved toward Master Damien, she kept her head dipped. She extended the plate and, when he accepted, she offered the fork and napkin as one package.

Chelsea scowled. Considering the ridiculous number of etiquette classes her mother had made her take, she should have noticed. Of course, Mother had anticipated Chelsea would go on to be an executive's wife. As such, she'd need to be able to be his hostess. Never in a million years would Marjorie have expected her only daughter to bare her rear in front of a roomful of people.

"Watch what I do." Brandy gave a brief, perfectly executed curtsy.

Chelsea's mouth opened as she rounded on Master Alexander. "You expect me to do *that*?"

"You would receive this kind of instruction as part of your training." He studied her. "If you'd like to proceed, return to the cart and try again. This time with much more decorum."

Cheeks burning with frustration, she carried the plate back.

A tall, good-looking man with the air of a pirate was standing near the tray, arms folded across his chest. His shoulders and chest were massive, and she wouldn't have been surprised to learn he played professional football. Or maybe he made a living as a bouncer.

"No one is looking at you."

"I beg your pardon?"

"Almost everyone here is with a sub, or they've been around the lifestyle for years. All subs have their behavior corrected from time to time. It's totally natural." He smiled and set her at ease. "I'm Gregorio," he explained. "I work with Master Damien here and I take care of the Den."

"And that includes reassuring wannabe subs?"

His silver earring winked in the overhead light. "My jobs are many and varied."

"I'm not even his sub. I just want him to train me."

"So, he's seeing if you're worth the effort?"

"He turned me down."

"Did he?" Skepticism edged his voice. "I'd say he's intrigued. You found a way to get an invite to a private party to meet him. So don't give up yet, unless you've decided it's not for you. In that case, move on and find someone who shares your kink."

She nodded.

"Are you planning to take the cake back to him?"

After thinking about it for a few seconds, she softly sighed. "Yes."

"Are you right-handed?"

"I am."

"In that case, I recommend you carry the plate in your left hand. Wrap the napkin around the fork and carry those in your right hand. Keep your head down, gaze lowered. At this point, he won't be expecting you to kneel. Concentrate on the pleasure he will receive from your actions. Offer the fork and napkin first, and then seamlessly transfer the plate to your right hand so you have no awkwardness. The most important thing with service is to think about things ahead of time, plan them out, but have the room to be flexible if your Dom desires it."

No doubt Gregorio was correct. Master Alexander had already said that—service was part of submission. "What about that little curtsy thing?"

"You can manage something, I'm sure. Bonus points if you use the term Sir or Master Alexander when you address him."

"Right now, I'm not sure I can remember my own name."

"That's why you need to concentrate on him, not yourself. Don't overthink," he added. "Try to be natural. You will screw up. Everyone does. Just accept the correction without taking it personally. As I'm sure Master Alexander has already advised, give yourself over to the experience of pleasing your Dom. Get out of your own way, allow someone else to be the center of your universe. If you're a submissive, pleasing him will fulfill you. It's not for everyone. In fact, it's not for most people."

Before she could thank him, he had moved off. Surreptitiously, she watched another server. Cake was offered one way to Doms, and a little less formally to subs. Some Doms accepted a piece for themselves but refused one for their submissives. A male sub was hand-fed.

One server was directed to place a plate on the floor. The blonde didn't hesitate before lowering herself to all fours and starting to eat. Her Domme placed the spiked heel of her boot on the girl's shoulder while tasting her own dessert and conversing with another Domme.

As Gregorio had observed, no one seemed to notice.

But the more she saw, the more she questioned the path she'd set for herself.

At that moment, Master Evan C entered the room, electrifying the atmosphere with his energy. The woman he'd been to the dungeon with looked radiant, smiling, with tear tracks staining her cheeks. She walked over to the tray and carefully selected a plate for him, and she looked happy to do so. If others could find pleasure in this, so could Chelsea.

Doubly resolved, she straightened her spine, picked up Master Alexander's plate, along with the utensils. As she moved toward him once more, she focused on the act of serving him, ignoring the little voice protesting what she was doing. "Happy birthday, Sir."

"Thank you," he replied. "But I've changed my mind about having cake."

Aggravation flared. Just in time, she bit back her instinctive curse. "Of course, Sir."

"I've decided I'd rather give you a birthday spanking after all."

Chapter Two

Chelsea lost her grip on the plate, almost dropping it.

Alex had unnerved her, and he wasn't sure anything had pleased him more.

Without saying anything, she turned and hurried back to the serving cart, her sensual hips swaying provocatively.

What the hell am I thinking? He'd stopped training over two years ago. Even when he'd done a fair amount of it, he'd only worked with subs with prior experience who needed minor refinement. In her heart, her soul, every part of her being, Liz had said she was committed to the lifestyle, but she'd really been more of a masochist. Training had been a constant—and wearing—battle. Eventually he'd learned that she hadn't wanted to be a perfect sub, she'd wanted his punishment. The harder, the better. Though he'd fallen in love with her, her constant misbehavior had destroyed their relationship. Recently he'd heard she'd married a man who was much more extreme than he was.

Still, the dissolution of their bond had devastated him. Maybe it had even contributed to the failure of his business, something he hadn't looked closely at.

In the past two years, he'd been selective about who he'd played with. He took no one home and refused to form physical or emotional attachments. Not that he would have had the time, even if he'd had the inclination.

Rebuilding after the Bartholomew scandal had consumed his life and focus. Along with his younger brother and business partner, Gavin, and their team, he'd performed months of due diligence. But one of their attorneys had been paid to overlook some contractual details at the final negotiating table, leading to devastating results for Monahan's clients.

Tonight was the first time he'd been at the Den in perhaps eighteen months, and he wouldn't have come if Damien hadn't organized the party and presented it as a fait accompli.

Damien wasn't just a friend, he was one of the investors who had lost big in the scandal, but he insisted there were no hard feelings. Business was business. Sometimes a deal went south.

Now that he'd met Chelsea, he was grateful for his friend's generosity. The pretend sub was refreshing. Bold. Brazen. Unable to comprehend the word no. She made him forget the disaster that had become his life. Time with her might be exactly what he needed.

She was at least five foot seven, even taller with the heels on. Her short blonde hair had chunks of dark lowlights, and the few curls that had escaped their clips lay on her forehead. But her blue eyes snared and kept his interest. They were wide and expressive, and he could see her emotions revealed there.

The way she sometimes betrayed her inner turmoil by worrying her lower lip charmed him. In the time they'd been talking, she'd worked off most of her lipstick, making her appear a little more vulnerable. He doubted she'd appreciate that observation.

Although he had no intention of seeing her after tonight, he could give her a taste of what she was really in for if she pursued her course of action. He understood why she'd want Evan C as a client, but frankly he thought the self-absorbed rocker was a wannabe and a never-gonnabe. Evan C lacked discipline and vision, though he demanded both of the subs he played with. Still, the man had a modicum of talent that might sustain him as a cover vocalist.

Her challenge would be the fact she wasn't a true submissive, and her behavior proved it. As sure as sunrise, she hadn't liked being bent over, her pert rear exposed to the world, while he'd greeted guests. Though he admired her commitment, his money was on her failing, no matter who she found to train her. She might enjoy whips, bondage, and blindfolds, but subjugating her will would be impossible.

Twisting her hands in front of her, she returned to him.

"Before we go any further, we need to get a few formalities out of the way."

Around them, the party began in earnest. Evan C and his band moved into the sunroom and picked up microphones and the instruments that had been set up earlier. People spilled out onto the patios. One had a fire burning in a brick pit, another was warmed by propane heaters. Several people headed for the dungeon. And that left him all but alone in the living room with the headstrong Chelsea Barton.

"Does this mean you're agreeing to train me?" she asked.

"Not at all." He shook his head. "But I'm taking you up on the offer of spanking you, and we'll go from there."

"Just know that I'll be trying to change your mind."

Persistent. He grinned. "And I'll be trying to convince you to give up your quest. You're not a sub."

"Deal." She stuck out her hand.

The gesture startled him, but he accepted. As they shook, he noted the focused gleam in her blue eyes, making them steely. "First of all, you will address me as Sir. You may call me Master Alexander, but not Master."

"What's wrong with calling you Master?"

"It's too confusing for someone as new as you. I'm not your Master. That speaks to a level of relationship we don't have."

"You underestimate how fast I learn."

"Perhaps," he conceded. "But that's part of being a good sub."

She scowled. "What is?"

"Following my rules, whether you like them or not, whether you agree with them or not."

"So I have to do everything you want?"

"Of course."

She swallowed hard.

"Within reason," he amended with a grin. "We'll use a safe word, and I need to be aware of your limits."

"I really don't know much about my limits," she admitted. "No permanent scars or markings, I suppose."

He respected that she hadn't looked away. "Understood. We'll learn about the rest of your limits together, then, through your safe word. Do you have one?"

"Parsley."

He raised his eyebrows.

"I hate the stuff."

"And you'll remember that during distress?"

"I remember to request it be left off my plate when I go out to eat. So yes, I'll remember."

"Very well. And if it works for you, we'll use the word 'slow' if things are too much and you need a break."

She nodded.

"The Den also has a safe word. *Halt.* Master Damien, Gregorio, or any guest will intervene if you use that word. Are you clear?"

"Mmm-hmm."

"Yes, Sir," he corrected, voice a whiplash. "Or 'yes, Master Alexander.' From this moment forward, I am the Dom. You are the sub. And you will remember to acknowledge that. After all, you're a fast learner. Or so you've said."

She took a little breath. "Yes, Sir."

"Any physical limitations I need to be aware of?"

"No, Sir."

"In that case, about my birthday spanking…"

"Yes?" Then she tried again. "Yes, Sir?"

"We'll go to the dungeon." He pointed toward the stairs. "After you."

Chelsea grabbed her wine, and he closed his hand around her wrist.

"Sober, or not at all." One of his few hard, inflexible rules.

She hesitated, then nodded. He released her, and her hand shook as she returned the glass to the mantel. Their gazes met, and she glanced away first.

Cautiously, she moved down the stairs, likely gripping the banister as much to settle her nerves as for balance.

Speakers blasted Evan C's music through the space. In the dungeon, lighting was dim, and the conversation was loud to compete with the band. "Give me your wrist."

She frowned, as if not understanding the instruction, but offered her right hand. Since his last visit, several hooks had been attached to the walls. He'd heard a rumor that Damien had had them installed after one sub expressed shock that the dungeon didn't have shackles. Of course, Damien had said, a slave should be able to be chained to the walls.

Alexander used a thoughtfully provided leather strap to attach her to the hook.

"I..."

He spoke into her ear. "Obviously you can undo that as I only secured one of your hands." It would take her some time to unfasten the buckle, but it was doable if she panicked. "However, it's my desire that you remain in place while I go to the bar."

Frantically she glanced around. "But I'm the only one tied up like this."

"Yes," he agreed. "You are." His little sub drew her eyebrows together. Was she going to fail her first test? "And I'm so proud of you being my good girl."

A pulse beat in her throat. "I find that statement a bit insulting."

"Do you? They aren't meant as anything other than an expression of my approval. Until you can see that, bask in it..." He left the rest of his sentence unfinished.

"If you prefer, I could attach you to the wall by your neck. In fact—"

"This is fine, Sir."

"You may want to thank me for my kindness."

"What? Seriously."

In silence, he regarded her.

"I mean... Thank you, Sir." Her words held a snarl.

"The fact I had to coach you to use your manners informs me how unschooled you really are."

"In future I'll do better." She took a breath. "Sir."

"See that you do." Without a backward glance, he walked to the bar to order two bottles of water.

While there, pretending an interest in the festivities, he kept a close eye on Chelsea. A waiter carrying a tray of wine walked past her, ignoring her completely. With her lips pursed, she watched him go.

Rather than engaging in conversation with other attendees, Alex returned to Chelsea. One minute had probably seemed like an eternity to her. "Well-trained subs are unconcerned when they're ignored. Instead they concentrate on pleasing their Dominant. I secured you to the wall because I wanted to, not because you were being punished. What would the experience be like if you had just centered yourself and thought about my imminent return?"

"This is difficult, Sir."

"You may safe word at any time and admit I was right."

Though she smiled, it was clear her back teeth were clenched. "Hard doesn't mean impossible, Sir."

"In that case, next time I'll place you naked in the stocks. They're portable and can be moved to the middle of the room. Completely adjustable so I can have you standing, sitting, kneeling, bent over, or even squatting. Depends on what part of your body I want exposed."

Color drained from her face.

"And I'll expect you to thank me for the experience."

"I..." She blinked. "What?"

"Your lack of gratitude for my attention is a bit off-putting."

"I'm confused," she said.

"My time is valuable. Especially since it's my birthday, I could find someone a little more agreeable to play with." Brandy, who'd helped out with the cake, was standing near a wall, carefully watching all the goings-on, in case she was needed.

He signaled to her, and she hurried over. Though she moved with purpose and speed, her motions were graceful.

"Master Alexander." She smiled. "May I be of service?"

"Are you available for a short demonstration?"

"Of course, Sir."

"Do you have a safe word?"

"Red, Sir."

"Anything else I need to know, Brandy?"

"Thank you for asking, Sir. Nothing else you need to know."

"Any issues with corporal punishment?"

"No, Sir."

He turned back to Chelsea. "Observe. Relax. This isn't about me pointing out your shortcomings, it's simply a part of your instruction."

Though her lips were set in a tight line, she said nothing.

"Remove your garment," he instructed Brandy.

Within moments, she stood in front of him, naked.

"Please present your breasts."

"Certainly, Master Alexander." Gaze downcast, Brandy cupped the abundant globes in her palms. She lifted her breasts and drew them together.

"Thank you," he said. "I'm going to squeeze your nipples hard."

"Of course, Sir."

He gave her a couple of gentle squeezes, preparing her for what was coming. When she leaned toward him, wordlessly indicating she was ready for more, he increased the pressure.

When she moaned, he backed off.

She exhaled. "Thank you, Sir."

He repeated the process, but this time he added more pressure.

Brandy closed her eyes and made soft purring sounds.

When he released her, she kept her eyes closed. From her position, it was obvious she liked what he was doing and wanted more. Still, moments later, she opened her eyes again and softly said, "I appreciate your attentions, Sir."

"You're very welcome, pet." Then he directed his attention back to Chelsea. Her gaze was transfixed on Brandy.

"Didn't that hurt?" she asked the submissive.

Before responding, Brandy looked at him for approval.

After he nodded, she replied to Chelsea. "It did. But Master Alexander knows what he is doing. He stopped before it became too uncomfortable, but I always have a safe word if I can't tolerate something."

Gregorio walked over to them.

"Kneel," Alex instructed Brandy.

Instantly, she complied, her legs spread wide, resting her bare buttocks on her calves. He preferred a slightly different stance, and before sunrise, he'd teach Chelsea several positions.

The difference in the two women was remarkable. Brandy turned her palms up, cast her gaze down, and drew long, deep breaths. Although she seemed at ease, he knew she was ready to respond to any command, no matter how subtle.

Chelsea was a different story. She was straining against the strap so hard he was afraid she was going to bruise. Though she looked at the floor as he spoke to Gregorio, she kept glancing back up. Alex understood her confusion.

Earlier she'd been talking to Gregorio as an equal. The man was a switch, meaning he could sub or he could dominate. He related to subs and often helped them navigate their way through unfamiliar situations, but he wielded a wicked single tail, gave demonstrations, was an expert rigger, and the few times he'd been in relationships, he'd clearly been in charge.

What she needed to learn was that unless Alex said otherwise, she was to act as a sub to everyone. "Brandy, get on all fours and show your asshole to Gregorio."

"Of course, Sir." She placed her forehead on the cold tile floor, arched her back, and reached back to spread her buttocks.

The two men continued their conversation, ignoring both women.

Finally, Gregorio excused himself.

"Very nice, Brandy. Thank you for your assistance. You may get up and dress."

"Thank you, Sir."

She donned her short dress, then returned to her duties.

He faced Chelsea again. "That kind of behavior, flawless service, is what I expect, what any Dom will expect from you. Would you like to continue your lesson, or shall we have a drink and listen to some of Master Evan C's music?" He left her attached to the wall while she considered her options.

"I'd like to continue on, Sir."

"Even if it means dropping to your knees and showing your anus to the world?"

Shaking slightly, she met his eyes. "Even if, Sir."

"Brave girl."

Surprisingly, she didn't protest his praise.

As he unfastened her, he was forced to admit grudging respect. She was either committed to her course, or she was incredibly stubborn. Either way, he'd expected her to run before now.

When he had been a trainer, he'd often waited weeks or a month before asking a sub to practice in public. Fighting emotions was more difficult when you weren't alone with your Dom. Yet she'd approached him here. "As you heard, Gregorio said that we can use the second space down the hall on the left. Before we go, you need to know there's a screen for privacy, but there's no door. If you cry or scream, as you will, others may hear you." Evan's unintelligible music was still chipping the paint off the walls, so her sounds would be muffled. "And others may walk by and see you. You will be naked. The humiliation you've experienced so far will be nothing compared to what you'll endure over the next hour or so."

As he rubbed her wrist, she tipped her head back.

"Would you like me to follow you, Sir?"

I would indeed. He grabbed their water bottles and started down the hall, not checking to see whether or not she followed — the choice was entirely hers.

Once he'd entered their assigned space, he moved toward the side wall. As he familiarized himself with the paraphernalia and apparatus, on the wall and in drawers, he said, "Please strip." He didn't look over his shoulder as he spoke to her. "Then kneel in the center of the room. Some Doms will permit you to use a mat. I will not."

As always, Master Damien had ensured each room in the dungeon was well stocked. Damien was not only a gracious host, but a shrewd businessman. A production company often filmed at the Den and on its surrounding acreage. Not only that, but the facilities were available for rental.

A few of the rooms had themes, but this one was multi-purpose. A padded, massage-type table was off to one side. Hooks had been strategically attached, but he doubted he'd be using them this evening.

After placing the water bottles on a shelf, he opened drawers, set out a container of disinfectant wipes, tossed a condom on the counter, laid out several pairs of surgical gloves, then pulled out a bottle of lube.

Alex studied the assorted floggers, spankers, and other implements hanging on the wall. As he did so, the soft sounds of her reached him.

Finally he selected a thick flogger—crafted from deer hide, if his guess was correct. It should provide a nice thud, but nothing too intense for her creamy skin.

When he faced her, she was in the same position Brandy had been in earlier. Chelsea was even looking at the floor. *A nice start.* Her skirt and shirt were folded precisely. If she had removed all her clothes, he would have been elated. "What instructions were you given, girl?"

She looked up. "To strip and to kneel, Sir."

"What part of that was open to interpretation?"

"I..." She sighed and rolled her hands into tight fists.

He wasn't sure if she was anxious or whether she was frustrated with him. "Was your thong expensive?"

"No, Sir."

"Good." He took out a pair of emergency scissors and approached her. He crouched in front of her and snipped the material. "And the bra?"

"Uh...I'm happy to remove it, Sir."

"You had the opportunity." When she didn't argue, he went on, "You understood my command. Did the bra cost a week's salary?"

"No, Sir."

He moved behind her to release the hooks, then he squatted in front of her to cut through the shoulder straps. After the ruined scrap of lace had fallen to the floor, near her thong, he caught her chin. "Lesson learned?"

"Yes, Sir." Her eyes were wide and unblinking. "When you tell me to strip, that means I am to be naked."

"You have ten seconds to remove your shoes. Remain on your knees."

He stood and worked the pulleys on the wall that would lower an overhead hook. Then he took out a small stool that was stored in a corner. Once things were prepared, he returned to her. Her shoes were laid alongside her neatly folded pile of discarded clothing. "The position you are in is what I call kneeling back. It's a fairly comfortable position for a sub. But you should place your hands palms up on your thighs."

When she did, he added, "However, that's not my preferred position. I prefer to have my subs kneeling up."

He took a cane from the wall. She couldn't know that he didn't intend to punish her with it, but rather, he would use it to correct flaws in her posture. He didn't explain it to her. It was fine with him if she had some questions, even better if she had some concerns.

He tapped the rattan against his open palm. "When I instruct you to kneel, you can assume it means I want you in the kneel up position. This means placing your hands behind your neck." When she did so, he added, "Spine straight, and no more resting on your calves. Thrust out your breasts. Keep your knees far apart. Farther." He tapped the insides of her thighs with the rattan. "Even more." When he was satisfied, he nodded. "This makes it possible to punish your pussy if I desire."

"I... Yeah. That scares me."

"No need to be. Yet."

"You're doing this on purpose, aren't you? A cane on the pussy is most definitely on my limits list."

"Acknowledged. However, it doesn't have to be wicked, if you ever want to try it."

In obvious disbelief, she flicked her gaze at the implement.

"Now stand so I can inspect your naked body."

She hesitated for a moment.

"Many Doms like to ensure their subs have complied with their grooming rules. And sometimes they simply enjoy touching while she or he is unable to move. For others, it's simply a perfunctory part of the relationship."

Like most novices, she stood awkwardly, putting a hand down to steady herself.

"We'll try that again, shall we? This time, keep your hands behind your neck. Use your abdominal muscles. It's tricky with shoes on, but since you're barefoot, it's easier to find your balance." He forced her to rise and kneel ten times before she was a bit out of breath. The altitude of Damien's mountain club might also have something to do with it. "If you want to hold your Dom's interest, you'll practice that dozens of times a day. With heels, barefoot, holding a tray, hands in various positions. Your movements should be beautiful…poetry in motion."

"Yes, Sir."

"For a standing inspection, I require you to keep your head up, looking straight ahead. Of course, others have different expectations, but if you're with someone for the first time and no other orders have been issued, this is a fairly safe default position. Of course, that doesn't mean you won't be punished for your assumption." He flashed her a wicked grin. "I'll show you a lying down variation after we're done here. Now, push your elbows out farther so that your breasts are more prominently displayed. Bring your shoulder blades together."

"Oh my God. More trips to the gym are in order."

"I have a tongue clamp if you can't keep your mouth shut."

Wisely, she said nothing.

He tapped the insides of her ankles with the rattan and she spread her legs wider in response. "Good. Now, I intend to inspect you. Your mental state matters here. You can see this as a humiliating exposure, or you can see it as part of the procedure, or you can know you're pleasing your Dom. You can even enjoy the experience. It's all up to you." He walked around her. "You have a lovely body, Chelsea." When she remained silent, he prompted, "You may thank me for the compliment."

"Thank you, Sir."

"Lovely breasts, with long, thick pink nipples."

When she remained silent, he tapped her forearm with the cane to prompt her. "What do you say?"

"Thank you, Sir."

"Do you have sensitive nipples, girl?"

"Uhm…not overly so, Sir."

"Mind if I find out for myself?"

Her hesitation was so slight that he might have missed it had he not been watching her so carefully. "Please do, Sir."

Before cupping her breasts, he returned the cane to its place. "Stay in position." He lifted her breasts slightly then tightened his grip on the firm flesh.

Though the speed of her breathing increased, she didn't protest.

He moved his hands to gently squeeze her nipples. Her mouth was slightly parted, and she continued to look ahead. He released her, then did it again, and again slightly harder. "How's that?"

"It's…" She blinked then met his gaze. "Amazing."

"And yet I don't hear any gratitude."

"Thank you, Sir!"

"Much better. What are you thanking me for?"

She wrinkled her nose, and said, "For your attention to me, Sir."

"Now your pretty pussy." He used his left hand to part her labia and he skimmed the inside of the tender flesh. "Many Doms will want you clean shaven there. If you were my sub, I'd use a pair of tweezers to get every stray hair that you missed."

She swallowed hard.

"Lucky for you, you're not my sub." He stroked her clit, then slid a finger inside her. She was nicely damp, responsive. He moved behind her and swatted her rear on both sides with an upward motion of his hand.

She lost her balance momentarily before immediately getting back into position.

After putting on a pair of surgical gloves, he said, "Open your mouth."

For a moment she looked so mutinous that he was betting she'd use her safe word. But eventually she yielded. He found it interesting that many subs didn't protest him probing any other orifice, but they didn't like him sticking his fingers in their mouths. "Wider. I mean it," he added when she didn't comply. "Good. Now stick out your tongue." He grasped the end of her tongue and pulled on it.

After he'd released it, he ran his finger around the inside of her mouth. He did this part to reinforce the totality of submissiveness. Once he was finished with that part, he said, "Now get on all fours like Brandy did, forehead on the floor, and then reach back to part your ass cheeks."

"Sir…"

"You can use a safe word, or you can ask me to slow down so we can talk about it. Communication is essential to your success. But if you're merely stalling, that will try my patience, and you won't get the most out of this experience tonight. I'm sure you're aware that many Doms use all their sub's holes."

"Oh my God."

"Too real?"

"It's…" She shook her head. "Just a lot of new experiences all at once."

Even though it took her a ridiculous amount of time, she complied with his request.

"How much anal experience have you had?" Alex crossed to the counter and pumped a dollop of lube onto two fingers.

"Very little…maybe twice." Warily, she watched him. "I've never had more than one finger up there, Sir."

"Until today," he amended, returning to her.

"Right. Until today."

"Are you ready?" He crouched behind her.

She clenched her buttocks. "Not sure I ever will be."

"In that case, we might as well proceed." He stroked her spine. "It will be easier for you if you relax."

"I'm not sure I can, Sir."

"There's always a hard way and an easy way. The choice is up to you." He started slowly, inserting the tip of a finger and then pulling back. He did that several times, going a bit deeper each time. "Feel this ring of muscle?"

"You're embarrassing me," she muttered, swaying.

He was glad she couldn't see his smile. "No embarrassment needed. It's totally natural. Bearing down will make it easier for me to get past the muscle, and it will be much more pleasant."

"Pleasant?"

Her legs quivered, no doubt from the strain as much as her natural apprehension. Still, she did as instructed. Soon he had two fingers inside her. "Well done," he said approvingly as he finished up and removed the gloves. While she situated herself, he disposed of them. "Return to your previous standing position and tell me what you thought of your first inspection?"

Not meeting his gaze, she looked straight ahead. "I suppose it was okay, Sir. I did what you said and tried not to feel humiliated. I didn't like the mouth part for some reason, but having your fingers up my ass wasn't as painful as I thought it might be."

"Do you recall my earlier conversation about gratitude? I've yet to hear your manners, girl."

She went still, as if oxygen had been sucked from the room.

The pounding from Evan's music suddenly ceased, leaving everything silent.

"I... *Hell.* I mean, thank you. Thank you, Sir."

"Being inspected like that is a privilege, girl."

"I'm not sure I understand, Sir."

"I'm happy to show you. If you don't want another demonstration, afterward you'll remember your manners." He cupped her breasts and squeezed mercilessly.

"Oh, God! I understand. I'm sorry, Sir!" she gasped. "Thank you! Thank you!"

"That's better. Now your nipples." He pinched her, quick and hard before releasing her.

To catch herself, she had to lock her knees.

"Nothing to say?" He repeated the process, this time using a ridiculous amount of pressure.

"Argh!" Tears welled in her eyes. "Thank you, Sir."

To drive home his lesson, he slapped between her legs. "I could use an implement." He leaned toward her, keeping her gaze trained on him. "It would hurt much worse than my hand."

"Thank you for your kindness, Sir."

He fingered her beautiful pussy without bringing her any pleasure. When she didn't thank him quickly enough, he spanked her again. "Now open your mouth." He donned a new pair of gloves while she watched and waited, wavering back and forth.

As he repeated what he'd done earlier, but without tenderness, she squeezed her eyes shut.

When he gave her a moment's reprieve, she muttered her gratitude. Then he went on, "Now show me that ass." Because he'd already stretched her anus, and because her rear passage had already been lubed, he squirted only a small amount of gel onto his fingertips before entering her with no prior verbal warning. This time, he finger-fucked her as she whimpered her gratitude. "Now, girl, kneel back and think about the differences in those experiences and how thankful you are that I was so lenient with you the first time."

Chapter Three

Emotion, regret, resolve, and the residual pain from his demonstration overwhelmed her. Chelsea had begged him to train her, but she had to admit that he was right. She'd really had no idea what she'd been asking for. It was a long way from kink that made her giggle to...this.

She struggled into the position he'd said, fighting for breath as she placed her upturned hands on her thighs. He draped a blanket around her shoulders.

With resounding clarity, she realized she'd never been with a true Dom before. At the parties she'd attended, she'd observed a couple of scenes. Even here, tonight, she'd observed interactions, and still, she hadn't understood.

The last ten minutes with Alexander had changed everything for her. She finally understood that being a sub wasn't just about getting an occasional mind-blowing spanking. It was about transcending or transforming your perceptions. Whips and cuffs might be part of it, but they weren't all of it.

As she tried to steady the rollercoaster of thoughts and feelings deep inside her, she drank in a few breaths.

"Please look at me," Master Alexander said in a soft and reassuring voice. He didn't sound like the same person she'd just been with.

She glanced up to see him standing in front of her, holding an uncapped bottle of water.

Somewhere along the line, he'd removed the cowboy hat. Now that she saw his whole face, he looked even more implacable. His short, dark hair was swept back from his deeply lined forehead. His gaze seemed to penetrate her, as if he saw past the outer facade that almost everyone, including her family, knew, and into the inner depths she'd never revealed to anyone. Maybe not even herself.

"Drink some of this." He extended the bottle.

Her hand shook as she accepted. Several drops of water splashed over the side. After managing a few sips, she offered it back and swiped her hand across her mouth before resuming the correct position.

"Parsley?" he asked.

Chelsea rose to the challenge in his tone. "No chance, Sir."

"There's no shame in stopping this," he said. "Many people find they want something lighter, that they're not cut out for anything other than an occasional scene. That's a perfectly viable option."

"Even if people rarely indulge, aren't there still expectations?"

"There are. But not all Doms are as firm as I am about inspections and impeccable service. As long as you're somewhat well behaved, you'll satisfy most Tops."

"But right now I will not satisfy the most discerning Doms, Sir." *Like Master Evan C.*

"True. But plenty of people just want a little kink, and maybe get their cock sucked or pussy licked."

While they'd been talking, her heart rate had returned to normal. Sweat had dried on her body. And she'd mostly managed to corral her galloping thoughts.

"Do you want to continue on?"

"I may be a slow learner, Sir, but I am learning. You won't have to repeat that lesson. Yes, please. I'd like to continue on. Thank you for the water, and for the two inspection examples."

"If you'd had more experience, girl, I wouldn't have gone so easy on you."

That was easy?

"It could have involved a spanking, perhaps an oversize plug or dildo in your anus, clamps on your cunt to hold the labia apart, having your mouth opened with a dental gag. You could have been manhandled considerably worse."

Couples actually play that way? Despite the blanket, she shivered. "In that case, thank you, thank you, thank you for going easy on me, Sir."

"When you're ready, lie down on that table for a supine inspection."

In her life she'd often found that things that seemed easy at first turned out to be more difficult than she could have imagined. But she'd also discovered the things she worked hardest for were the most rewarding in the end.

Drawing on her inner resolve, she shrugged off the blanket and offered it to him before climbing up onto the table, with far less elegance than she would have liked.

"On your back, hands at your sides. Knees upraised. Feet flat on the surface about shoulder-width apart. Some Doms may do this on the floor, or a bed, or a tabletop. A kitchen counter is perfect if he or she has company."

She blinked. *Company?* She wasn't sure she was that brave.

"It can be enjoyable to have others observe the inspection. A bit of voyeurism. Some Doms allow someone else to perform the inspections while he or she observes. For now, we'll keep it between us."

"Thank you, Sir."

This time she knew what to expect, so that had to make things easier.

As she'd seen Brandy do, Chelsea took a few deep breaths to center herself.

Master Alexander squeezed and kneaded her breasts, and she moaned. "Thank you, Sir," she whispered.

But then, instead of releasing her, he changed his grip so that he could flatten her nipples between his thumb and forefinger. It was as if the nubs were trapped in an awful vice.

She'd been wrong.

Knowing what to expect hadn't made it easier. Even though he was doing essentially the same things, he was doing them differently.

Gasping, she arched her back, trying to relieve some of the pressure, but he was relentless, watching her, a small smile flirting with his sensual lips.

Bastard was enjoying her suffering.

"Very nice nipples."

"Thank you, Sir."

"How high can I tug them before you beg for mercy?"

"Is this part of an inspection, Sir?"

"Certainly, girl. Gauging your responses, capabilities, and obedience is the biggest part of it."

"Thank you for explaining that, Sir." *God.* How much more could she endure?

"Back flat on the surface, keep your legs apart. Understand?"

The man was merciless. "Yes, Sir."

"Feel free to cry or whimper or moan. Screaming is okay, too. You have your slow word and safe word."

Which she didn't want to use. "Yes, Sir."

His grip was excruciating. But then he began to pull, as well.

She curled her hands into fists. Looking at her, he continued on. Hungrily, she gazed into his eyes, knowing she could drown in their depths.

The pain ratcheted up, making her want to close her eyes, but connecting with him gave her strength.

"Can you take more for me?" his voice encouraged and soothed.

Can I? In that moment, recognition rocked her world. This was no longer about her. She wanted to please the man standing above her. "Yes, Sir."

"Good girl."

This time he sounded approving, rather than patronizing. Had his tone changed or had her attitude?

He pulled harder, and she whimpered, digging her heels into the table cushion. The amount of pain she was enduring wasn't possible.

Gasping for breath, she panted. But then, shockingly, even as the agony increased, she started to become turned on.

"Ah. That exquisite line between pain and pleasure," he told her. "You're there. Endorphins and arousal. I can smell your muskiness, see the haze in your eyes."

Yes.

Chelsea wanted…something. Something out of reach, maybe unattainable. But there was a raw, demanding need deep inside her.

He increased his threshold even more. Desperate, she squeezed her eyes shut and cried out, "Slow."

"Well done," he said. "I'm going to release you a bit at a time, so it hurts less."

"Thank you," she said, while desperately wishing he'd just let go. Still, when he finally did, she whimpered. As blood surged back into the abused tips, the momentary pain was excruciating.

"Now I know where this limit is, so I can, with your permission, push you further in future."

She wasn't sure anyone was going near her nipples again. Ever.

"Stay in position."

She opened her eyes in terror when he returned. He had several items with him, including a towel and more of those damn blue gloves, but the metal contraption that he held up riveted her attention.

"This is a dental gag."

It resembled a medieval torture device. It was quite wide, with two metal pieces running parallel and a ratchet on either side, presumably to keep the teeth apart.

"As you can see, the bits are dipped in rubber, so it's quite safe. A lot of Doms like them because they restrict speech and keep the mouth open for insertion of any number of items, including a cock."

Her tummy twisted in fear. "This is for educational purposes, right, Sir?"

"Instructional. Once it's inserted, and you get a feel for it, I'll remove it. When I inspected you earlier, I noticed how far you could comfortably open your jaw. Some subs find this kind of gag rather pleasant. They don't have to remember their manners and they can surrender to the scene. In lieu of a safe word, we'll use a safe signal. Simply raise your right hand, and I'll remove it."

Never, even in her kinkiest thoughts or readings, had she imagined enduring anything like this.

"Open wide."

For a moment, she simply stared. She wasn't stalling, she was considering whether to stop him, this…madness.

"Chelsea, safe word or open your mouth."

Her fingernails gouging into her palms, she opened her mouth.

Though she tried, she couldn't look away. He was entirely focused on what he was doing as he began to adjust the ratchets. Just when she thought she couldn't take any more and was ready to raise her hand, he stopped.

"I pay very close attention to you, girl. You're safe with me. I want you to breathe and accept the gag for about two minutes. It will feel like an interminable amount of time. But I will not leave your side."

He smoothed the hair back from her forehead. Because of that and the way he looked into her eyes, she vowed to do as he asked.

"Fifteen seconds," he announced.

She was sure it had been four times that.

"You really are stunning in your submission, Chelsea. There's something alluring about a woman who knows her power and isn't afraid of it. And when she surrenders it, it's magnificent. You doing okay?"

She nodded.

"Your shoulders are tense. Try to relax."

It wasn't just her shoulders — it was her entire body.

"Uncurl your hands."

When she didn't, he simply took her left hand and opened it, very, very gently.

"You're still okay. Now try with the other."

Reluctantly, she did.

"I promise, some subs find this experience sublime. It's easier to let go when you're not required to speak. You've got a minute left. Give up the struggle. Match my breathing."

He continued to hold her hand. She looked at him. How could he be both her salvation and her damnation?

"That's it. Breathe with me."

As she stopped fighting the experience, she realized they were communicating silently, on a deep, intimate level. She'd never felt more attuned to another human being.

"Good," he said. "Time's up." He pulled away his hand. "You should be proud of yourself. I'm proud of you. I'm just going to give you a quick demonstration of how an oral inspection might work with the gag in place."

She nodded again.

"It would probably be a little farther open, but I won't do that at this time." He inserted a finger into her mouth and swept around, pushed on her teeth, pressed against the inside of her cheeks.

"Makes you very much aware of giving up control, doesn't it?"

Transfixed, she nodded. He was standing above her, totally in control, large, uncompromising, a Dom sure of his power.

He overwhelmed her.

"You can imagine how this probe could be much more degrading and uncomfortable."

She blinked.

"This, Chelsea, is submission. Subjugation of your will for another's." He removed the dam and wiped her mouth with the towel. "No worse for wear?"

Since she wasn't able to find her voice, she shook her head and hoped she wouldn't be in trouble.

His patience seemed infinite as he helped her to sit up. After she'd flexed her jaw and taken a couple of grateful sips of water, she managed to thank him for the experience.

Once she had regained her equilibrium, he helped her to lie down, and he resumed his inspection. This time he pulled back the hood of her clitoris to play with the nub. Most men she'd been with only had a passing acquaintance with her clit, but he plumped it, tweaked it, stroked it, fondled it then, making her scream, licked it. She grabbed the table and lewdly pushed her pussy into his face.

"You have a very responsive body," he said, moving on.

"Thank you, Sir."

He inserted one finger inside of her. "Your G-spot should be about..." He felt around a bit. "Here."

She arched and struggled, wanting more, wanting him to stop.

"Do you want an orgasm, girl?"

"Yes! Yes, please, Sir."

He continued his relentless motions. She was on the edge. The treatment of her nipples, the crashing emotion that the surrender to his gag had caused, then the way he touched her clit, the way her ass had been stretched wider than ever before, and now...heaven help her, he slipped a second finger into her and pressed his thumb to her anus... "Sir!" She thrashed her head about. In this moment, he owned her reactions.

"Please." She gasped. "I need... I can't, I can't." Her legs shook. "Please, slow..."

"Come."

To ensure her compliance, he ate her out as he finger-fucked her pussy and ass.

Chelsea had never had a man command her to orgasm, but she came, hard, fast, completely, screaming his name.

When the world stopped spinning, he was standing next to her, stroking her cheekbone.

"Thank you, Sir."

He grinned — the gesture filled with triumph. "If I were training you, we would work on orgasm control."

"Yes, Sir," she lied. Flat-out lied. There wasn't a chance on this earth that she would deny herself that kind of shattering experience, even at the expense of any diabolical punishment he might devise.

Once more, he helped her into a sitting position, encouraged her to drink another sip of water, then said, "If a sub passes inspection, and the Dom doesn't need to punish her for something or have her correct something in her grooming, they move on to the next thing."

The next thing? There's more after that?

"For example, the Dom's birthday present."

She blinked. At some point, she'd forgotten she'd volunteered to accept a spanking from him.

"Assuming you still want to continue?"

Even if she wasn't able to convince him to train her, the things she'd already learned would help her attract Master Evan C's attentions. "Yes, Sir."

"Have you ever played with a flogger?"

"At the parties I attended, yes. But I'm betting it was nothing like you mean."

She watched as he moved a small stool to the middle of the floor. Then he went to the far wall and lowered a pulley. It didn't take her long to add up the facts. She was going to be standing on the stool and attached to the hook. As she'd guessed, this was nothing like the playtime she'd had with others.

Her nerves skittered when he removed his bolo tie and hung it on the wall. His vest and shirt followed, and when he turned back toward her, she was even more aware of him as a man and as a formidable Dom. His chest was broad, and his biceps well defined. He had a small amount of dark chest hair that gave him a sexy edge. When she had fantasies, this was the type of guy who showed up center stage.

She vehemently disagreed with the little voice suddenly nagging her, informing her that he, rather than Evan C, was the right kind of man for her. Master Alexander was too brash and demanding. Besides, she definitely wasn't the type of woman he would be attracted to.

He helped her from the table. For a moment she was close, far too close, to his chest, to being in his arms.

When he had been fully dressed, the atmosphere had felt somewhat instructional. Now sensuality simmered on the surface. He'd brought her to a rocking orgasm, and it wasn't just because of what he'd done to her body. It was because of the connection that arced between them. She liked the touch of his strong fingers on her skin. His commanding tone of voice made her want to bend her knees in abject submission.

Music began to blare again, shattering the intimate air. She was grateful. It would be easy to forget she wanted to learn about submission so she could ensnare a different Dom.

"I'm going to bind your wrists together and then attach you to that hook."

As his words confirmed what she suspected, she nodded bravely.

"I want you flat on your feet, so there's no compromising your safety." Once she nodded, he went on. "Since today is my thirty-third birthday, and you graciously offered to accept my spanking on my behalf, I'm going to flog you thirty-three times. This is a fairly lightweight implement, perfect for a light, sensual experience."

That, she wasn't sure about.

Could she do this? When she'd made her desperate suggestion, she'd thought maybe he'd pull her over his lap. But to be on a stool, arms stretched, naked, subjected to his lash...?

"Chelsea? Are you still with me?"

Bravely she met his eyes. Maybe it was bravado, but she wasn't backing down. "Yes, Sir."

He studied her for a moment before nodding. He selected a pair of cuffs — thankfully they were fabric, rather than metal — then fastened them around her wrists.

"Onto the stool when you're ready."

Filled with trepidation, she accepted his hand and took the small step up.

Movements sure and efficient, he attached the cuffs to the hook, then slowly hoisted it up a few inches, stretching her, crashing tension through her body.

"How's that?" he asked.

Closing her eyes, she took a breath. "It's fine, Sir."

"Good." He double-checked all the rigging. "Parsley?"

"Sir is a dreamer." She expected the flogging to begin immediately, but he shocked her by vigorously rubbing her legs, then her buttocks and arms. He used a much gentler pressure on her front, but he covered her entire body. "That's nice, Sir."

"You're welcome, sub."

The soft growl of approval in his voice, sent skitters of awareness through her.

He picked up a flogger, and it felt as if the room temperature dropped by at least ten degrees. It had been one thing to discuss it theoretically, another to have him approach with the wicked-looking strands dangling from his hand.

"Ready?"

"Yes, Sir," she lied. She wasn't, but probably never would be.

The first landed on her buttocks. It was light, almost delicious.

"How are you doing?"

"Good. Shockingly."

Then he began in earnest, back and forth, catching her buttocks, thighs, upper body, and the sensitive area beneath her ass cheeks. Within moments, she was lost to the thuddy, amazing experience.

Then suddenly, he stopped. *Is that fifteen?*

"Your back is red." He traced lines where the strands had fallen. "It looks magnificent."

"Thank you, Sir."

"I'm glad you remembered your manners so we didn't have to begin again." He moved in front of her and shook out the strands. "Are you ready to continue?"

She nodded. Watching him was so different from having him behind her. Seeing his eyes narrow as he selected the spot he intended to strike was frightening. The man was more focused and intent than anyone she'd ever met.

When the strands connected with her belly, she closed her eyes. She was more relaxed when she couldn't see what was going on.

The leather licked at her breasts and curled around her sides. Her breathing became deeper as she surrendered.

"You're doing so well."

She drank in his crooning words of approval.

"Continue to let go."

She opened her eyes to find him studying her intently, and that helped deepen her trust.

He continued his blissful motions, and shockingly, she relaxed completely.

"Good, girl," he said.

Earlier, similar words had annoyed her, but now, they were a soothing balm. As he crisscrossed her with the strands, she suddenly understood why Sara sounded euphoric when she talked about her Dom flogging her.

Moments later, he eased a finger down her cheekbone. Without her being aware of it, he'd stopped his motions.

"That's it. Come back to me."

She blinked as awareness returned. "Are you finished, Sir?"

"Those fifteen are, yes."

"Oh. Thank you." Her body was dotted with perspiration, and a raw hunger uncurled in her. "I enjoyed that more than I thought possible."

"This was a sensual experiment," he informed her. "I assure you, the flogger, especially crafted from something such as buffalo, feels quite different from this. The number of strands, their length and the way the Top wields it changes the intensity, as well. If you're being punished, it will not be like that."

"Thank you for clarifying that." She was getting the hang of the right verbiage. When he stood there, still flicking his wrist rather than letting her down, she frowned. Then she remembered. "You're thirty-three today, Sir." And he'd only given her thirty strokes.

"Ask for your last three."

"May I have them on my breasts, Sir?"

"You may not. Spread your legs."

Goose bumps chased up her arms. He couldn't mean…?

He stooped and moved her feet apart. *Now* she was frightened.

"Give me a birthday present to remember."

Her tongue felt too big for her mouth. But she also knew that drawing this out wouldn't help. The sooner it was over, the better. "Please, Sir, give me the last three on my pussy."

"My pleasure, girl. And if you draw your thighs together, we'll start over until we get three good ones in a row. Are you clear?"

"That's diabolical."

He grinned, in a not-reassuring way. "It is indeed." In anticipation, she curled her toes slightly. Whatever he dished out, she'd take. After all, a lot was at stake.

The first was mild — a kiss more than anything.

The second scorched. As she cried out, she was tempted to press her thighs together to find release.

"What did you think of that?"

She forced back her instinctive reply, "*Fuck off.*" But as the moments progressed and the burning sensation receded, her clit started to throb. Stunning her, the stroke had turned her on. "Wow."

"Another like that?"

Dare I?

"Are you brave enough?"

The initial pain would be awful, but the aftermath...? "Yes," she whispered.

"I didn't hear you."

As she nodded, she clenched her hands. "Yes, Master Alexander."

He flicked his wrist, and before she'd fully registered his motion, the stroke landed, searing into her.

Desperately, the edges of a climax building, she started to draw her legs together, only for him to press his palms to her inner thighs, forcing her to comply with his orders.

"Sir!" Heavy with demand, her pussy throbbed.

"When you're with me, your orgasms are mine to give or withhold."

Desire became a physical need, and tears sprang to her eyes.

"I'm waiting for your response."

He was awful, a master in every way. "I understand." *Even if I hate it.*

"You took those well."

His casual conversation brought her back from edge, from the dangerously seductive place inside her mind. "Thank you, Sir."

"I'm going to lower you, and when I do, I want you to move slowly."

He didn't have to tell her twice. Her body felt heavy, leaden, and she wasn't sure she'd be able to move at all.

But he was there, rubbing circulation back into her shoulders and arms. Then he scooped her up from the stool and carried her to a chair, where he held her in his lap.

Frustratingly, the tension inside her didn't go away.

For long moments, she stayed where she was, resting her face on his chest, listening to the reassuring thud of his heart, inhaling his primal, masculine scent.

Once her breathing returned to normal, she pressed away from him to look up and meet his gaze. "Happy birthday, Master Alexander," she said. "And thank you for giving me the gift."

"The gift was all mine."

The sound of his voice, the memory of his hands on her, all of it was too much. She was restless and incomplete. "This…"

He waited.

Her hand trembling, she pushed a stray lock of hair back from her forehead. "I'm not sure how to ask, but…" She took a breath of courage and prayed she wasn't rejected. "Will you fuck me?"

"It's not a good idea to confuse training that way."

"But you're not my trainer," she pointed out. And she wanted to be taken hard, by a man as uncompromising as he was. He knew her body better than she did. "Sir."

He unfastened her wrists. "Chelsea—"

"You're the one who made me horny, Sir."

"Get on the table."

His gruff order made her heart leap. "Yes, Sir."

After wiggling from his lap and finding her footing, she made her way across the small space and perched on the edge of the table to watch him undress.

Deliciously, he was commando beneath the jeans. His pubic hair was well trimmed, and his cock jutted out. She'd been so caught up in her own sensations that she hadn't seen how hard he'd gotten.

And his dick was glorious—big, thick, and pulsing. The sight of a man's penis had never made her salivate before. But then, she'd never wanted sex this badly, either.

"Lie down," he instructed while sheathing himself in a condom. "But keep your legs where they are. You're going to be wrapping them around my waist."

There would be no doubt he'd be fucking her, rather than making love. His way of keeping emotional distance between them? Regardless, that was fine with her. She wanted it raw.

In silent invitation, she lay back and spread her legs.

"Is your pussy hot, girl?"

It is now. His coarse language heightened the energy in her raging hormones.

He moistened his thumb pad and pressed it against her clit. She arched up, wordlessly begging for more. And he gave it to her, rubbing her gently, then with more vigor before backing off again. "Yes, please, Sir."

Instead of taking her to completion, he guided his cockhead toward her entrance.

As he wanted, she wrapped her legs around him, then, forcefully, he took her.

"Play with your breasts while I fuck you. I want to see your expression. Make sure you squeeze your nipples hard, or I'll put a pair of clamps on them and yank on the chain with so much force you'll see stars."

It didn't matter whether or not he'd actually do that. Just the threat was enough to make her delirious.

In a single thrust, he drove into her.

There was nothing sweet or reserved about his claiming. She gasped from the depth of his penetration. "Damn, Sir."

"Is this what you wanted, girl?"

"It is!" He filled her and satisfied her.

"You're getting to me, Chelsea."

His confession increased her ardor. She wanted to be owned by him. "Do me, Sir." Her request was both a demand and a plea.

Repeatedly he took her, and her body jerked from the force. She played with her breasts and pinched her nipples. From the way he'd used her earlier, the tips were still swollen and sensitive, and that only heightened her arousal. "Oh, Sir!" She closed her eyes as they fell into a frenetic rhythm.

When she was on the verge of an orgasm, he stopped, and she cried out her frustration.

"Give me more. Knees over my shoulders, girl." Grabbing her ankles, he adjusted her until she was in his preferred position. "That's better."

Leaning forward, he made her take his weight. It stretched her hamstrings unbelievably, and it permitted him in so deep she couldn't draw a full breath. "*Sir!*"

"All of me, girl. Take all of me."

In full command, he pistoned his hips. He was so powerful, amazing…

The climax claimed her so hard and fast, and she screamed her pleasure.

"My beautiful little submissive."

From somewhere distant, she was aware that he sounded proud.

"There's more." He released his grip on her ankles and brushed her hands aside and pinched her nipples as he continued to fuck her.

The exquisite agony he inflicted, combined with the relentless pounding, made her come again.

Even as she rode crest after crest of pleasure, he continued to fuck her.

He was impossibly masterful, and so very, very sexy.

For a moment, their gazes collided, and she saw raw desire there.

"*Fuck.*" Then he closed his eyes and tipped his head back. "Chelsea..." With a raw, guttural moan, he ejaculated, spilling inside her.

That she had that kind of power over him intoxicated her, and she sucked in breath after breath, trying to steady her pulse.

Long moments later, he released his grip on her nipples, then laved them with his tongue to soothe the ache. Then, in a wonderfully unselfish move, he played with her clit to bring her off one more time.

She couldn't remember ever being this devastated, this complete.

"Stay there," he said, withdrawing from her.

As if she could move.

He lifted her and moved her higher on the table so that she was fully on her back.

When she shivered from a slight chill, he draped his shirt over her. In this moment, it would take maybe thirty seconds for her to drift off to sleep.

After disposing of the condom, he returned, carrying a washcloth. With a soft word of gratitude, she reached for it.

"I'll bathe your pussy."

His statement surprised her. She hadn't expected this kind of compassion in a BDSM experience. But from the beginning of the evening, nothing had gone as she'd expected. She was dazed.

He pressed the coolness against her, taking away some of the tenderness from the sex as well as the flogging. With a tiny moan, she arched her back.

When he was finished, he offered a hand to help her sit up. "You've made this a memorable birthday. Thank *you.*"

She was satiated, and anxious to have another experience with him. More than ever, Chelsea was determined to convince him to train her. She just needed a plan.

Chapter Four

"She fucking did *what?*" Alex demanded, fury soaring. Pushing back from the desk in his office, he strode to the window, seeking to harness his flare of temper.

"Chelsea called Niles," Damien repeated unnecessarily.

He balled his hand into a fist and stared out at the foothills as his mind raced.

He'd spent one evening with Chelsea and he had no claim on her. In fact, he'd told her he didn't want to train her.

On the surface, her reaching out to Niles Malloy made sense. At one point, the other Dom had been well-known in the community. And he still garnered respect. But since the death of his wife had left him brokenhearted, he'd become somewhat of a recluse. He participated in some scenes filmed at the Den, but he saw no one beyond professional models and actresses.

And just like Alex, Niles had an edge to him. But Niles was rougher, more remote. Some now wondered if he was even capable of emotional attachment. Alex shoved away the unwelcome idea that the same description could apply to him.

"Niles turned her down," Damien continued. "But he gave her several recommendations."

Of course she refused to be deterred. Alex should have realized that and not ended the evening the way he had, by wishing her well in her endeavors. She wanted to snag Evan C's attention, and so would recklessly pursue any path that got her there. And not every Top could be trusted. *Foolish girl.* "Thanks for the heads-up."

While he had Damien on the line, Alex updated him on their investments. One was doing as well as anticipated, but another was outperforming even their wildest projections. Neither made up for the colossal failure of the Bartholomew deal, but it was a start. He was pursuing other opportunities, but before he said anything, he and his brother Gavin would be triple-checking all the details.

After ending the call, Alex stared at the late afternoon clouds. At least the view was one good thing about their recent move to the less expensive address. Their Cherry Creek offices had been swanky, but nothing rivaled looking at the mountains.

Restless, he paced the room and dropped his phone onto the desk.

His wayward thoughts once more returned to Chelsea.

What the fuck was up with him?

He hadn't allowed himself to be obsessed with a woman, even a sub, in years.

But now…?

Ever since the night at the Den, he hadn't been able to stop thinking about the saucy, sexy submissive. He'd enjoyed introducing her to things she'd never tried before, seeing what made her nervous, then pushing her past those fears.

And fucking her…?

She was unbelievably responsive, and he couldn't get enough of her.

Now, the idea of her calling every Dominant in Denver pissed him the hell off.

It shouldn't matter. He told himself it didn't.

But goddamn it, it did.

Someone with less skill than him might crush her innocence and joy of discovery. Worse, she could be physically or emotionally hurt.

He dragged his hand through his hair. Alex wanted to be the one to watch her blue eyes open wide, to soothe her when she was frightened, to teach her proper decorum.

Fuck it.

If she was so desperate to be trained, he'd be the one to do it.

Resolute, he strode back to his desk, snatched up his phone, then scrolled through the contacts list until he found the number for Lyle, Sara's Dom.

As Alex expected, and hoped, Sara refused to give him Chelsea's contact information. Instead, Sara asked for Alex's number and said Chelsea would contact him, if she wanted to.

Wanted to?

It took all of his restraint to be polite instead of slamming down the phone.

He paced, continually checked his phone, and fumed before finally getting back to work.

Before leaving for the night, Gavin knocked on the doorframe, then entered without an invitation and dropped into the chair on the far side of his desk. "How'd it go at the Den?"

Gavin's question seemed casual, but it wasn't. Returning to the club after an extended absence had been significant, both because of the crash of the Bartholemew deal and because of Liz. "Small party. No one seemed to give a shit about the past."

"Good to hear." He drummed his fingers on his thigh. "Anything interesting happen?"

Alex narrowed his gaze. "Who'd you talk to?" After his regrettable drunkfest so long ago, Gregorio had placed him in the guest quarters, and Damien had given Gavin a heads-up. Appreciated, but not needed.

"No one." Gavin grinned. "I'm fishing. But it seems I landed something. Shall I reel it in?"

Though he was tempted to tell his only sibling to fuck off, Gavin wouldn't give up.

"Yeah. Name's Chelsea. Wants me to train her."

Gavin stopped drumming his fingers. "Bro —"

"I know."

"You going to do it?"

"She's going through every Top in the club trying to find someone."

"And you don't trust most of them?"

"Yeah. And she wants Evan C."

He scowled furiously. "That cocksucker?"

Good to know Alex wasn't the only one with that opinion.

"He doesn't deserve subs."

And there was part of the conundrum. At least if she spent time with him, she'd understand more about submission and learn to draw some boundaries. "Agree."

"Which is why you're going to do it." Gavin's tone was fatalistic, and his words weren't a question. "Be careful."

He'd say he knew what he was doing. But he'd thought he had with Liz, as well.

Gavin stood. "Gonna hit the gym, if you want to meet me there."

"I'll consider it." Working off some of the energy churning inside him was better than brooding.

Which was what he did for the next couple of hours.

Finally, she called him. "Round one to you," he said, voice clipped as he answered.

"Excuse me?"

"You win," he conceded.

"Does this mean you're agreeable to training me?" Excitement laced her tone, leaving it breathless. It wasn't triumph, but honest enthusiasm. "Are you serious…? You've made me the happiest person on the planet, Sir."

That soothed him, somewhat. "I'll give you two weeks. Are you available in the evenings and on the weekends?"

"There are a couple of events that I need to attend, but mostly I can rearrange my schedule, Sir."

"I recommend we start tomorrow."

"That sounds reasonable."

"Dinner? Six o'clock."

"*Dinner?*"

Lesson one. Keep her guessing. No doubt she'd expected him to suggest a club or one of their homes.

He named a restaurant near his office. "Wear a short skirt or dress, heels, no undergarments. And pack an overnight bag in case you decide to stay. Any questions?"

There was silence. "How much will your training cost me?"

"I don't charge."

"In that case, I'll make a donation to your favorite charity in the name of Monahan Capital."

He exhaled. She might not be a masochist like Liz had been, but that didn't mean he would have the patience he needed to deal with her annoying persistence. "Don't be late."

"I never am. Sir."

He'd half-expected her to call and try to change the arrangements and he was pleasantly surprised when she didn't. He arrived at the restaurant five minutes early, and she was already there. Impressive. She was sitting on a bench, her impossibly long legs crossed. Her back was hunched slightly, as if she were trying to hide the fact her breasts were bare beneath the loose-knit sweater. Her beauty was startling, and he was man enough to notice and savor it.

He'd prefer to see her present her body more proudly, and they'd be working on that. The next time they dined in public, her behavior would be different.

With the artificial, calculating expression he recognized from the first time she'd approached him at the Den, she stood and offered her hand, as if he were a business associate. He ignored her hand and said, "I'd prefer you to kiss my cheek."

She blinked. "Uhm... If you say so," she said, leaning toward him.

"If you say so, Sir," he corrected. "You're in training. And don't forget it for one moment."

"I apologize." With her eyebrows furrowed slightly, she kissed his cheek.

"How does it feel to have skipped undergarments?"

"Strange," she admitted. "Unnatural."

"Aware of your submission?"

"I suppose you could say that, Sir. It's uncomfortable."

"Good. Be glad you're not going to be sitting on a massive butt plug or filled with a dildo." He tipped his head to the side. "This time."

Her mouth opened momentarily before she snapped it shut.

"Please," he said, indicating she should precede him. When she did, he placed his fingers against the small of her back. "Stand up straighter. Pull your shoulders back so your breasts stick out. Tonight, you're mine. I'm proud of you, and I want you to own the fact you're pleasing me." Though she sucked in a sharp breath, she complied. "Reservations for Monahan," he told the hostess.

After they were seated, with menus in hand, he asked Chelsea, "Any preference?"

She looked at the entrées. "Probably just a salad. With sirloin. Maybe some wine."

"How do you like your steak cooked?"

Over the top of the menu, she scowled at him.

"I'll be ordering your food," he told her.

"I'm capable of doing that myself."

"Of course you are, but this is about your willingness to allow me to handle the details."

She put down the menu.

"A good Dom always takes his sub's desires into account. A good sub in turn trusts he will make good decisions on her behalf. If you have any preferences, now is a good time to express them."

"I'm not sure I like this dynamic," she admitted.

"Over the next two weeks, there will be plenty of things you won't like. You have a choice to deal with it or end your training. Your safe word will be honored."

She drummed her fingers on the table.

"This isn't as easy as you'd anticipated, is it?"

The waiter stopped by, and Alex refused wine, and instead ordered them each a glass of sparkling water. She set her chin mutinously but said nothing.

"You may find my dominance irritating. Or you could decide it's nice to have someone take care of you for a change. It can be a struggle, or not. But understand this, bad behavior will be corrected and perhaps punished. So, Chelsea, shall we proceed as submissive and trainer, or would you like to have dinner as friends?"

"Do you expect me to address you as Sir, even in public?"

"When we are out as a Dom and sub, yes. If we were at a business event, that would be discussed and rules agreed to beforehand."

She was silent for so long he wasn't sure if she was going to answer. Finally, she said, "In that case, I prefer my steak medium-rare, Sir."

He nodded. "Now sit up straight. I don't want to tell you again."

"As I mentioned, not wearing a bra is uncomfortable."

"Be that as it may. I like to see your nipples. And visualizing them with clamps on."

"I'm not sure I've recovered from last weekend."

"Ah."

"I'm not hearing any sympathy, Sir."

"No. You're not." The waiter returned with the sparkling water, and Alex ordered their meals and remembered to say, "Please ensure there is no parsley anywhere near the lady's plate."

The man nodded.

When they were alone again, Alex asked her, "Rather painless, wasn't it?"

"Yes, Sir. It wasn't nearly as bad as I'd made it in my mind."

"Did it take away from your empowerment?"

She sank against the back of her chair. "No." She picked up her water. "It didn't change who I am, Sir, or the fact I'm capable of ordering my own food at any other time."

He nodded. "First lesson. Being submissive doesn't take away anything from you as a person or as a woman. You'll enjoy the meal you wanted, cooked the way you like, and you delighted me in the process."

"Yes, Sir."

"Not all Doms order for their subs, but many do. Take your lead from him or her, and don't argue in the process."

"I understand," she said.

As they relaxed, he asked about her background and her desire to succeed.

"You don't leave much uncharted territory, do you?"

"Understanding you will make me a better trainer."

"You take this seriously."

"I do. Which is one of the reasons I no longer deal with neophytes."

"It's time consuming."

"This is about you, Chelsea. I won't allow you to redirect the conversation." *But nice try.*

"No one really knows this, except my closest friends..."

"Your secrets are safe with me." He topped off her glass. "I don't discuss my trainees with anyone. Whatever you choose to share is up to you, but I will reveal nothing."

"That helps." She traced tiny circles on the tablecloth before sitting back. "My father didn't have much use for a daughter."

Fuck that.

"Neither did my mom, for that matter. According to them, boys are more intelligent."

"They're not." *That* he knew from his business dealings.

"My brothers—one younger, one older—both received great educations, cars the moment they were old enough to drive, and they were indulged with every whim and interest. Even when Ian—the baby of the family—went to jail, my father said that boys will be boys." She shrugged. "They each have positions at Dad's firm. I was told I needed to get married. When I didn't want to enroll at the college they selected—where I'd presumably meet my future husband—they withheld the funds they'd set aside for me. Instead of getting to play soccer like I wanted, I took modeling classes then was sent to charm school." She flashed an overly bright smile. "Clearly it worked."

"Clearly."

They both laughed, a shared moment unlike any he'd had in years.

"Can you believe they called it that? *Charm school.*" She toyed with her knife and fork. "To them, nothing was more important than learning the correct etiquette to attract the right man. I'm a huge disappointment to them."

"Despite your success?"

"If I find a man they approve of, I'll be welcome back in the fold and they'll release the money they've set aside for my wedding. Of course, they'll be in control of the purse strings, selecting the venue, the dress, even the food."

"Another reason me ordering for you was difficult?"

"My entire life, I've struggled against everyone's expectations — or lack thereof. I've learned to fight for what I want, advocate for myself because no one else will."

"It has to have been challenging."

She brought up her chin.

"And lonely."

For a moment she looked away and didn't respond. Had he hit a nerve?

When she once again looked him in the eyes, she had regained her composure. "It's also been rewarding."

"Always being your own cheerleader?"

"In charge of my own decisions. Answerable to no one."

"Which makes me even more curious about why you're interested in submission."

Their meals arrived, saving her from having to respond. But he bookmarked his question and circled back to it when they were once again alone.

"Honestly? The experience with you at the Den left me feeling alive in a way I haven't before. Excited."

"It was a novelty, perhaps?"

"Potentially." She shrugged. "But I think it's something more."

He'd wait and see, when the thrill wore off and the only thing she was left with was her decision to capture an unworthy Top's attention.

When the server checked back to be sure everything was satisfactory, Alex glanced at Chelsea.

"It's fabulous, Sir."

"Another sparkling water?" he suggested.

"That would be lovely. Thank you." This time, her smile wasn't the hundred-watt fake one she usually gave him.

"Well done," he told her when the server moved off.

"Much as I hate to admit it, you were right," she said. "Not just tonight, but the other night. If I think about what my Dom wants, the struggle isn't as difficult."

"Lesson two," he said. "At this rate, we'll be done in three days."

"Do you think so?" she asked, holding a fork poised near her mouth.

"No." He grinned when her shoulders fell again. "You're still slouching, despite the fact I've already corrected you twice."

She put down the fork and sat up. "Sorry, Sir. Clearly charm school wasn't as effective as my parents hoped."

"I have just the thing to help reinforce my will. I'll show you when we get to my house." He cut a piece of steak. "Eat up."

She left part of her salad and refused dessert and coffee.

Then, as he paid the bill, she protested.

"Chelsea, if I want you to pay, I'll let you know. This changes nothing between us and takes nothing away from your feminine power. So give up the fight."

"In that case, thank you, Sir."

He nodded, wishing all arguments with her were this easy to end. "Did you bring an overnight bag?"

"I did. But I'd prefer not to stay, Sir."

"That's up to you. I have a guest room. My bed is comfortable. There's also a hook attached to the footboard if you prefer to be chained to it, along with a nice pile of blankets on the floor, if you prefer."

Color drained from her face, and she pushed away her wineglass.

"Some Doms expect their subs to sleep on the floor."

As if choosing her words with great care, she asked, "Is that your expectation, Sir?"

"No." He'd had the chain installed for Liz when he'd trained her, and he'd done it at her request. He was happy to snuggle after a session, and there were nights when he wanted his woman to sleep in his arms. Liz had never wanted to do that. Even if he hadn't taken the time to chain her and arrange her bedding, he would wake up to find her on the floor, cocooned with her pillow and a single blanket, her collar affixed to the chain. "I had a sub once who preferred it that way. It helped her."

"I don't understand."

He had never discussed intimate details of his relationship with anyone other than Damien. "Liz was a masochist. Being in my bed would have been a luxury she didn't want."

She folded her hands on the tablecloth. "Is she the reason you're no longer a trainer?"

"She has a lot to do with it, yes."

"And you loved her?"

"Yeah," he admitted. "I did." *Deeply. Painfully.*

For a moment, she was quiet, but she pushed forward, despite the fact his tone had been cold and final.

"Did she end it, or did you?"

He sighed. "I suppose if I don't answer you, you'll continue to ask again and again."

Interestedly, she leaned forward. "And again, Sir."

"Liz ended it." Except for Damien, no one knew how devastated he'd been and how long the anguish had lasted.

Months after she'd walked away after finding a Top much more extreme than he was, he and Damien had stayed up almost an entire night at the Den, drinking a bottle of Bonds's finest single malt.

The next day, hating what he saw in the mirror, Alex had vowed never to look back.

"You haven't gotten involved with anyone since?"

"No. And I'm not planning to." A warning to her? Or perhaps to himself? "D/s relationships can be more complex than ordinary ones. Be careful what you wish for."

"Why is that? I thought they might be better."

"For many people they are," he agreed.

Eyebrows knitted together as she studied him, she waited.

His answer was going to reveal more than he was comfortable with. "If—when—it ends…" *Fuck*. "There can be significant emotional fallout."

"Are you speaking from personal experience, Sir?"

He didn't owe her an answer. He was her trainer, nothing more. Still, he couldn't resist her. "A sub—a Dom—can fill a lot of roles, not just the kink, but as life partner, and a lover. When that ends, there can be a gulf in multiple areas."

She shuddered. "Warning heeded."

"Ready?" Done with the conversation, wanting to put the brooding behind him, he stood and offered his hand. "This time, follow me. Stay back about two feet. No more. No less."

Though she didn't reply, she didn't protest. He knew his behavior kept her off-balance, and that was his intention.

He walked her to her car and waited while she programmed his address, that was near Golden, into her navigation system. He intended to drive so that she could follow, but he would expect her at his house again, and he didn't want to hear that she'd got lost.

It took less than fifteen minutes to arrive at his home. "I never expected you to live in a place like this," she said when he opened her door and offered his hand to help her out.

Her comment intrigued him. "Like...?"

"Homey." She studied the house and him. "I guess I thought you might have a loft or something modern. But this is amazing. How old is it?"

"It's considered Victorian style, even though it was built after 1940," he responded. "It was on the market for a steal because of the extensive amount of work it required—electric, plumbing, everything, basically. You may have heard of Master Marcus from the Den. His company oversaw the restoration. It took about eight months, but I think it was a good investment."

"It's charming."

He didn't add that he'd bought it with the expectation that he and Liz would live out their days together, maybe have children. So she was right that it was homey. Nice garage, yard, plenty of space. Not that he needed it. But he'd been so busy rebuilding after the

Bartholemew deal that he hadn't gotten around to listing it and moving on to someplace better suited to his bachelor lifestyle.

"The grounds are spectacular." Standing together on the sidewalk, she took in the trees and flowers.

"Landscaping company," he explained. "I wouldn't know a pansy from a petunia."

"You have both."

"Do I?"

"In those pots." She pointed.

"I'll take your word for it." He led the way to the three steps leading up to the wraparound porch.

As he unlocked the heavy wooden door, she wrapped her arms around her middle, despite the mild evening weather.

"After you." He held out his hand, palm up, indicating she should precede him.

Inside, she gasped. "Oh my God. It's even better than I imagined. Do you mind if I have a look around? This would be a perfect location for a charity fundraiser."

He shook his head, as bemused as he was enchanted. "Do you ever stop?"

"Are you kidding me?" she countered. "This house was designed for entertaining."

When he'd outlined his vision to Marcus, Alex had envisioned hosting parties for business associates, along with an occasional lifestyle function. That she saw the same potential that he did pleased him. "You can place your purse on the side table."

"Would you like me to take off my shoes?"

"It's not necessary. Yet." But he appreciated her consideration.

He showed her the study, then the great room with its gas fireplace and stone hearth. Next he showed her the dining room, then the kitchen.

The largest chunk of his funds had been spent on this part of the house, ripping down walls, opening the space, adding a glassed-in breakfast nook. Since he didn't eat at home much, he'd taken Marcus's word that the appliances were a chef's dream.

"I love the combination of classic and contemporary throughout the whole place," she said, running her fingers over the marble counters. "It really works. Seriously, Sir, you have to let me plan a party here."

Alex enjoyed her enthusiasm. What he wouldn't have given for Liz to have fallen in love with the house like Chelsea seemed to. "There's a media center downstairs," he said. "And the bedrooms are upstairs."

As if she were a guest rather than a sub who'd be screaming within half an hour, he gave her a tour of the upper story, including the guest room, home gym, and his suite.

"You weren't kidding about the hook in the footboard of your bed." As she stared at it, she rubbed her forearms.

Shock? Intrigue? "I don't joke about things like that." He regarded her.

Her breath caught as she met his gaze. Was she ready for a Dominant like him?

"Have a look around."

He had two enormous closets. His was only half filled. The other was empty. "You don't think I'm being too nosy?"

"Since you'll be using it at some point, you should know your way around the place."

In the en suite, she looked around. "Wow. You made some really bold choices here."

She was right. The black-and-white floor tiles were art deco in style. "My decorator was inspired." A claw-foot tub stood off to one side, and an extra-large shower had built in benches and dual showerheads on poles.

The water closet was behind another door, and there were two sinks with tall, arched faucets. A couple of shelves held candles, while a skylight completed the space.

"This is truly impressive, Sir."

"I'm glad you approve. Would you like to see the play room?"

"The…?" She tipped her head, as if trying to discern whether or not he was joking.

"After Liz left, I got rid of almost everything. But for our purposes, it will suffice."

She followed him to a closed door. When he opened it, she peeked inside but didn't enter.

At one time, the place had been packed, but he no longer saw the point.

Gigantic mirrors adorned one wall, and there was a Saint Andrew's cross off to one side. A large chair, a rolling cart, and some sort of storage unit were the only other furnishings.

"That you have a dungeon is a little unnerving."

"All the ways I can torment you…" And more occurred to him by the minute. "Now that you're familiar with the house, please go down to the great room and strip. Leave your clothing on the couch. If the room is cold, there's a switch on the wall for the fireplace. I want you kneeling, facing the window."

She looked up at him, and the air seemed to sizzle.

"Questions?"

"Won't the neighbors be able to see me?"

Instead of responding, he captured her chin. "If you're in a relationship with a Top who you trust implicitly, you can be assured he or she has considered that."

Alex watched emotion play out in her pretty blue eyes.

"Does that mean you might want people to watch me?"

"I'm all about consent, Chelsea. Though you and I may be voyeurs, I cannot make that decision for others. Rest assured, no one will be able to see you. Landscaping and window coverings will provide plenty of privacy."

Still she remained rooted in place. "I didn't notice curtains or blinds."

"You're wearing me out, girl. I'll give you the same choice I offered you earlier. Use a safe word, and we can have a glass of wine together on the deck. But if you want a BDSM trainer, time is ticking."

She wrapped her fingers around his wrist, and the act was so unbelievably intimate that it caught him off guard, shook him.

"Thank you for your reassurances."

"You're smart to ask questions. I'd be disappointed if you didn't."

"Yes, Sir."

He cleared his throat, seeking to regain his emotional distance. "Now unless you want to earn a punishment, you'll get on with it."

"Of course."

He released his grip on her chin and eased his hand away from her, severing their connection. "I'll meet you downstairs, at my leisure." Maybe after he jacked off.

"Yes, Sir," she whispered, submissive trust dancing through her words.

At the doorway, she paused and looked back at him. Her lips parted, as if she wanted to say something. He waited. Then, with a tiny shake of her head, she left — the floral, feminine scent of her lingering on the air.

What the fuck had he gotten himself into?

Jesus.

From the moment he'd first seen her, she'd bewitched him. It would require self-control to keep himself physically and mentally at a distance from her.

Shaking off his unwelcome introspection, he ordered his home computer to close the main floor blinds. Then he crossed to a drawer in his closet where he selected two instructional pieces, along with a tawse designed by Master Marcus. Fancifully, Marcus had etched a dollar symbol into the leather, in honor of the first multimillion-dollar deal Alex had brokered.

Once he no longer heard distant sounds, he walked down the stairs.

Chelsea was exactly where he'd ordered, kneeling up per his preference. She'd remembered, and that pleased him.

After placing his toys on an end table, he swept a cursory glance over her, but said nothing. Instead, he folded his arms, waiting, watching, testing her resolve. "Very nice," he eventually approved.

"Thank you, Sir."

"Louder."

She took a breath. "Thank you, Sir."

"Inspect." He was pleased when she stood, her head up, looking straight ahead to the window. She placed her hands behind her head and thrust out her breasts. Finally, she spread her legs. "You remembered."

"Yes, Sir."

Even as he closed the distance, she continued to look ahead.

He circled her a couple of times, and she remained perfectly in position. "You shaved your pussy."

"I did, Sir."

Everything he'd asked for, she'd delivered. "Mind if I see how good of a job you did?"

"Please go ahead, Sir."

He ran his hand over her bare mound, then slipped a finger between her folds. "Smooth."

Already damp from desire, she jerked against his hand. Could she be any more perfect?

"You won't be needing your tweezers after all, Sir?"

"Pity."

She gasped a little.

Alex dropped his hand. Because of their previous play, she likely had expectations about how the rest of this procedure would work, so he changed it up. "Turn around and show me your ass."

"Do you want me on all fours, Sir?"

Obviously she'd recalled his instruction to Brandy. "Not necessary."

With a small nod, legs wide apart, she bent and grabbed her ankles.

"Spread your cheeks."

Struggling a bit for balance, she complied.

"Every morning before you go to work, you are required to insert a small butt plug that will remain in place all day."

"You—?" She started to break position, and he delivered a quick spank to her right buttock.

"Try your response again."

She exhaled a frustrated breath. "Yes, Sir."

"Still waiting for gratitude."

Her knuckles whitened where she gripped her ankles. "I have to thank you for ordering me to do something I don't want to?"

"Not at all." He scraped his thumbnail down the tiny mark left by his hand. "You're thanking me for thinking of you, being considerate enough to find a way to remind you of your training even when we're apart."

"Considerate?" she scoffed.

"Safe word or cease your arguing." He was grateful she couldn't see his mirth.

It took several seconds for her to respond. "Thank you, Sir."

"In fact, you should send a message every morning, letting me know when it's in place and expressing how thankful you are for my attention."

She didn't reply.

"And for the fact I'm not requiring a large-size one."

She gulped.

Yet.

"Yes, Sir. Of course. Once again, please accept my thanks."

"When those statements happen faster and with more authenticity, I'll know the training has been effective." He dug his fingers into her butt cheeks. "Don't think I'm not paying attention to your tone, in addition to your words. And you can be assured that your obstinance is being noted and will be corrected."

For a moment she released her ankles before clearly remembering she was supposed to stay in place. "I'm sure that's what makes Sir an excellent trainer. Your attention to detail."

This time, her tone was so neutral he couldn't ascertain her sincerity. *Clever girl.* "Kneel up."

Her motions were slow and somewhat exaggerated. "You're struggling to do things, which tells me you need daily practice, something I mentioned at the Den. Along with other Dominants, I expect your motions be flawless and elegant."

"I apologize, Sir."

"No need. Since you're an absolute beginner, I anticipated you'd be rather awkward."

Because he was looking at her, she couldn't hide the way she pursed her lips. No doubt she didn't like the criticism — not that he blamed her.

"You'll be going through your paces daily, and we'll begin now so that I'm sure you're doing things correctly."

Her nipples were hard, and the heady scent of her arousal reached him. She might protest that she didn't like it, but her feminine responses were sexily submissive. And fuck it all, that summoned his raw, dominant instincts.

She will belong to another.

How many times would he need to remind himself of that fact?

"Return to your former position, where you were showing me your ass, and then kneel up. Then go from kneel up to showing me your ass. We'll begin with twelve repetitions." He took a seat in a wingback armchair and watched.

She'd turned on the fireplace, so a fine sheen of perspiration began to dot her back as she moved through the exercise.

"Stop thinking and judging. Allow yourself to flow from one move to the other."

A few minutes later, she seemed more natural. "That's much better. Do you feel the difference?"

"Yes, Sir. I do."

It wasn't long until her form suffered again. Her breathing grew labored, and she had to steady herself, no doubt from fatigue.

"At the end of our two weeks together, you'll be able to move with ease, from standing to kneeling, or from lying to kneeling, or any possible combination thereof. As you practice — I recommend several times a day — mix it up. Listen to your body, become comfortable and fluid."

Though she nodded, she added, "This is more difficult than it seems."

"Hmm... I'm sure it is."

He stood. "We discussed your posture several times."

Her blue eyes were wide, and a bit of fear danced in them. "Am I going to be punished, Sir?"

"I prefer to punish you for flagrant disregard of my requirements. For example, skipping these exercises. However, if it's something I haven't trained you on, you can't be expected to be perfect."

"Is that the expectation? Perfection, Sir?"

"Flawless actions, yes." He picked up one of the items from the side table and showed it to her. "This is called a posture collar. It will keep your head and shoulders straight at all times. For the rest of our time together this evening, you will wear this. Going forward, anytime you need correction, you'll fetch it for me."

Though she didn't utter a protest, she kept her gaze on the collar.

"Please stand with your hands behind your back. Feet shoulder-width apart."

His little sub didn't blink as she stood in position.

"This is one of my favorites. It's strict, but not terribly uncomfortable." He showed her the wide collar. "This is padded, for your chin to rest on." Once more, she remained silent. "Ready?"

"Yes, Sir."

He wrapped the stiff leather around her throat then moved behind her to secure its two metal buckles. He checked the fit before tightening it more. "How is that?"

"Fine."

"Look down."

She attempted to lower her head, but the leather piece restricted her movement.

"And now?" he asked.

"Effective, Sir."

"There's a mirror over there. Go look at yourself. See how beautiful you are."

As she walked, she reached up to touch the collar's three D-rings.

"I can attach a leash, secure your wrists, or tie you to any number of things." That thought hardened his cock.

Clenching his hands, Alex fought back the all-too-real reaction—something he'd never had with another sub, even Liz.

"It's...it's a bit frightening, Sir."

To reassure her, give her a connection, he came to stand behind her and placed his hands on her gently shaking shoulders. In the mirror, he watched her looking at herself. "Please tell me your safe word."

"Parsley."

"Even during training, you may stop the scene at any time. If you're just a bit scared, you are welcome to ask to talk or use the word slow." Intentionally, he turned her to face him.

Her eyes hid nothing, a vulnerable layer of concern and trust. Her exquisite beauty set him on fire. He craved her with the kind of ferocity that had overcome him at the Den.

But he wouldn't be fucking her tonight, or ever again for that matter. More than anything, he was a man of honor. And sex had no part in what they were doing.

Reminding himself of that fact didn't make self-control any easier. "Return to the center of the room and practice kneeling up from the inspect position." His voice was gruffer than necessary. "Do it ten times." But then, fighting himself, he added, "You may use the rug."

"Thank you, Sir."

"You recalled your manners." Ridiculously, her sensual whisper pleased him. To hide that, he donned his Dominant facade. "Kneeling on the hardwood was uncomfortable, wasn't it?"

"Yes, Sir."

"So you understand that a rug is a luxury."

"I do."

"I'm glad you recognize that." He forced himself to release her shoulders before he was no longer capable of it. "Get on with it."

As she made her way to the rug, her hips swayed. The wide collar made her gait more sensual. Having her use it all the time was a definite consideration.

Barefooted, she crossed the room. At the Den, her toenails had been a creamy peach color. Tonight, they were a fire-engine red. Though his preference was for mile-high heels, this might be one of the sexiest things he'd ever seen.

Refocusing, he picked up the rattan cane.

She stumbled when she saw his approach.

"Just like at the Den, I do not intend to use this for punishment. I prefer canes for instruction or for sensual play."

"I'm relieved to hear that, Sir."

"However, begin your movements again. The idea is for you to be able to do what you need to, despite distractions." He stood close to her, inhaling the scent that had haunted him for almost a week—vanilla, and something else that was light and innocent.

Once she had finished the entire sequence, he said, "Extend your hands." He attached fabric cuffs to her wrists then fastened those to the D-rings on her collar. "Another dozen."

"Uhm…" Frantically she blinked. "But I won't be able to balance as well, and my legs are getting a bit cramped."

"In that case, you'll need more practice. Make it two dozen," he amended.

"I…"

He cocked one eyebrow.

She set her jaw and glared. "No."

The cane he dropped clattered to the floor. In a single swift motion, he pulled her to her feet and swept her from the floor.

She squirmed and squealed as he carried her to the chair. Since her arms were confined, maneuvering her was more tricky than normal, but he managed to sit and get her body across his lap.

"Sir!"

"Stay still. The use of your safe word and slow word is encouraged, but flat-out willfulness...? That will be dealt with immediately." He trapped her lower body with his legs. "You'll receive eight spanks for your insolence and you'll be grateful it isn't more."

Rubbing her rear, he waited, giving her the chance to opt out of his upcoming punishment. "Tell me when you're ready."

"Get it over with, Sir."

Insolent still, but she was facing the consequences.

She yelped when he blazed the first spank into the back of her thigh. Rather than giving her time to absorb the action, he went on, making her skin red.

By the time he was finished, her rear and thighs pink, her apologies were continuous.

Much better. "Lesson learned?"

"Yes, Sir."

"Any questions? Or are you ready to perform your three dozen exercises?"

"Three dozen?" she echoed, shock in her tone.

He helped her from his lap and onto her knees. "Surely you didn't expect the spanking to erase your bad behavior?"

She blinked back sudden tears.

The display of raw emotion from her reached him in a way nothing else could. "Talk to me, Chelsea."

"I hated that." Her confession was soft, plaintive.

God save me. Her reaction was so different from what Liz's had been that he was gutted. "Please continue."

An internal struggle played across her face, and she worried her lower lip before finally speaking, her angelic voice soft, the words broken. "You were impersonal. As if I don't matter."

"I assure you, my brave sub, that you do matter. I wouldn't be spending my time with you if you didn't."

She exhaled, eyes wide as she studied him.

"That said, my punishments are meant to be instructive, a way to correct unwanted behavior. I hope they're not enjoyable."

"It was miserable."

Again, he was struck by how different she was from his ex.

"It wasn't at all like our night at the Den."

"Which seemed more sensual?"

"Yes." She blinked, and a single tear escaped to leave a track down her cheek. "And…" Her voice cracked as she faltered.

"Take your time."

"This collar, and the way my wrists are attached…"

"I'm listening."

"It just…" She looked up at him.

The sheen of moisture in her eyes made the blue even more startling.

She attempted to reach her hands toward her face, but the bondage restricted her movements. This woman bore little resemblance to the one who'd approached him so confidently at the Den. She was humbled, more vulnerable, but he also saw her internal confusion about what that meant to her.

"You were right. I wasn't prepared for it to be this difficult."

He nodded. "It takes a tremendous strength to subject yourself to someone else's will. As I've said, it's not for everyone. Probably not for most people." At times, being a Dom, especially a trainer, wasn't easy, either. It could be an emotional minefield, and he sure as hell wasn't perfect and didn't always make the right choices. "Remember that you always have the power. I can only act based on the parameters you outline. You never have to do anything you don't want to. Safe words will always be honored, and you can walk away from me at any time." Suddenly he didn't want her to.

"That's not..." She sighed.

"Go on. Whenever you're ready."

"I've never felt more humiliated, less connected."

"You've never looked more attractive, with your red bottom and your honest tears. And since you've been here, you've been the center of my attention."

Slowly, she nodded, but he didn't see the dawning of understanding, meaning she was lost somewhere inside her own thoughts.

Alex stood, then extended a hand toward her, helping her up. He drew her toward the couch where he sat with her in his lap.

She curled into him.

"It was a true taste of submission. Not a fun spanking, a little kink."

Though she tried to nod, the rigid leather around her neck wouldn't let her.

"I get that." She swallowed deeply. "At least I think I do. Until now, no one has ever seen me cry."

He believed that. "I'm honored that you're not hiding that."

"I'm freaking trying to, Sir."

"So honest."

"I can't get rid of the sensation of humiliation."

"So not being able to wipe your eyes is as difficult as the tears themselves, and maybe harder than being spanked?"

"I'm not sure how you know that, but yes."

He smoothed a lock of her hair back from her forehead. "Your emotion, your struggle, is real. At any rate, it may mean you're going to have a profound shift, perhaps toward submission, maybe away from it. Or maybe it's just a cathartic release that you need."

She remained silent.

"You can embrace the tears or pretend they don't matter. I assure you they do. You're not the same person who walked in here." He studied her as he stroked her cheeks. "And what's happening right now is important."

"I'm feeling a little overwhelmed, Sir."

Immediately he released her bondage. "We'll end today's training early."

"But... I didn't use a safe word."

"I'm making the decision on your behalf. On *our* behalf. Let's get you dressed, then we'll talk."

She nodded.

After unbuckling the collar, he feathered his fingers across her unblemished skin. "You did well."

Shaking her head, Chelsea finally wiped her face and inhaled deeply. "I feel like a failure."

"Not at all. You learned a lot, and it would be prudent to take some time to think about whether you're doing this for yourself or whether you're doing it simply to hook a man whose attentions you seek. Also ask yourself whether he deserves this kind of sacrifice."

She brought her chin up. "I know what I'm doing."

"Do you?" Had he ever met a more stubborn woman?

"It seems as if you're disappointed in me, Sir." She swallowed again.

"You will never disappoint me." He shook his head. "I promise you." Chelsea's reaction proved that she was totally different from Liz. When Liz found something he couldn't tolerate, she repeated the act over. "Now, please get dressed, and I'll be right back with you."

After helping her to stand, he walked to the powder room to grab a tube of arnica. When he returned, she was curled up on the couch, and he asked her to stand and bend over for a moment.

Once she had, he flipped up the hem of her dress to examine her. "You have a couple of minor marks on the backs of your thighs." Aware that she needed connection, he took his time as he rubbed some cream onto each mark.

He recapped the tube and offered it to her. "Take this home with you and reapply it before you go to bed."

"Thank you for doing that, and for the instruction, Sir."

"My pleasure," he told her as he smoothed her garment back into place. Then he dropped the tube of arnica next to her purse before walking to the kitchen for bottled water.

As he returned, she covered herself with a blanket despite the night's warmth.

"Thank you." With a shaky hand, she uncapped the bottle and took a small sip.

As he once again sat in the nearby wingback chair, she spoke. "Questioning myself isn't something I'm familiar with."

"BDSM is, above all, a journey, as I said at the Den."

A moment later, after apparently being lost in thought, she nodded. "I hate to admit it, but you're right. I have some thinking to do."

He pressed his palms together. "Take as much time as you need."

"We have a two-week agreement, though."

"It can begin again when you're ready. And if you want to end our arrangement" — *which might be my smartest move* — "there's no need to contact me again."

"I just…"

With infinite patience, watching the confusion in her eyes, he waited.

"I don't know what I want."

"Understandable."

"Would you be open, I mean… God." She wrapped her arms around her. "This uncertainty is so unlike me."

The version of Chelsea in front of him — so captivating, so tiny — was completely different from any she'd revealed before. Right now, her air of vulnerability reached him on a deep, protective level.

As much as he was getting to her, she was getting to him.

"I may want to talk some more."

"My door is always open."

"Thank you…" She hesitated, as if not sure whether to add an honorific. If the relationship were over, there was no need. "You're being very patient and understanding."

Despite the gravity of the emotional situation, he couldn't help but nod, pleased. She'd remembered her manners.

When she stood, he followed suit. "I'll walk you to your car."

"Thanks, but I can see myself out. Your path is well lit."

He wouldn't hear of it. "The gentleman in me insists that I see to your safety."

Softly, she sighed. "In that case, I accept." Though her words were calm and in control, her face was pale, and her voice lacked its usual enthusiasm.

She led the way to the front door, where she picked up her purse and slung it over her shoulder — fastening her hand on the strap in a death grip.

Outside, they walked down the path — past the pansies and petunias — and to her car. She used a key fob to unlock it, and he opened the door for her.

Before getting inside, she hesitated. "Thank you again for dinner. And for the learning experience. I'm not sure I'll ever be the same again."

He reached to smooth back escaped strands of her short blonde hair, but he dropped his hand to his side before he touched her. With the distance between them, he didn't have the right. "It's been an honor. A pleasure."

Her expression appeared fragile enough to shatter the moment she was out of sight.

She climbed behind the steering wheel, and he closed her inside the vehicle.

Less than a minute later, after starting the engine and pulling away from the curb, she drove off without looking back.

Alex watched her go, not knowing if he'd ever see her again…something that suddenly wasn't okay with him.

A plan formed. But it had risks. Lots of them. And he wasn't sure she'd thank him if he pursued it.

Chapter Five

With breaths threatening to strangle her, Chelsea pulled into the parking lot of the shopping mall at Denver West, found an empty spot, then shut off the engine before sinking against the seatback and exhaling.

As she'd driven, she'd struggled to understand what had happened at Master Alex's home, and emotion and memories had pummeled her, making concentration impossible.

Now she sought solace in the evening sky.

How had he gotten to her so completely? So deeply? She squeezed her eyes shut.

After the night she'd scened with Master Alexander at the Den, she had wanted him to call her. Almost a week later, when he hadn't, she'd begged Sara to put her in touch with some other Dominants, gambling that Master Alexander would hear about her inquiries, and more, that he wouldn't like that.

Unless she was mistaken, he'd been as intrigued by her as she'd been fascinated by him.

Chelsea has done a small jig around her office when Sara had finally provided Chelsea with his contact information following her call to Master Niles. *Mission accomplished.*

But seeing him this evening had upended her entire world.

His invitation to join him for dinner had shocked her — no doubt as he'd intended. But she should have known it wouldn't be an ordinary dinner.

From the beginning, when he'd instructed her to skip her undergarments, to ordering her food, to choosing difficult topics of conversation where he'd sifted through her carefully stored childhood memories, the evening had been a challenge.

And then...

At his home, the scene had been intense for her. Having her motions restricted was difficult, but she hadn't expressed that, instead, she'd tested him with her defiance. His retribution had been swift and sure. And because he'd been so impersonal, he'd chipped away at her emotional armor, leaving her drowning in her tears.

Even then, he'd been tender, seeking to understand, and maybe even more importantly, helping her understand her own reactions.

She'd never met anyone like him, and that unnerved her.

Her cell phone chimed with an incoming text message, and she checked it.

Master Alexander.

Please let me know when you're safe. If you wish to call, I'm available.

Had she ever known a man who was more considerate than he was? His thoughtfulness steadied her, restoring her self-confidence enough to start the car and finish the drive home. Once she arrived, she dutifully texted that she'd arrived but said nothing more.

Even though she was feeling more stable, she had too much energy to sleep, so she changed into a swimsuit.

Her apartment complex had some niceties, including indoor and outdoor pool facilities. She found water to be relaxing as well as restorative, and she did a lot of her best thinking in the bath as well as the outdoor hot tub. But as she was leaving her unit, she caught sight of a couple of pink stripes on her upper thighs.

They took her back in time, to the Den, to his home. How fascinating that she could have such monumentally different experiences, both where she'd been spanked.

Chelsea went back to her bedroom for a long, flowing swimsuit coverup. But with luck, no one else would be using the hot tub.

Other than a couple of teenage boys who were horsing around in the deep end of the pool, she had the area to herself.

After turning on the jets to drown out their noise, she removed the outer garment and sank in deep, letting the water bubble around her chest. Eventually, she closed her eyes and leaned her head back, wishing the earlier experience had been less confusing.

When she'd set her sights on landing Master Alexander as a trainer, she'd known it wouldn't be easy, but she'd expected to at least enjoy the experience. During their two weeks together, she'd thought she'd have orgasms and thrilling sex, learn some useful skills, maybe get tied up, enjoy a few sexy spankings.

But she hadn't expected the whole experience to be so much work, mentally as well as physically. Holding up her arms, kneeling, being restrained and spanked — all had taxed her body.

At the Den, he'd asked her about limits, and she'd truly believed she had few, if any. She was in charge of her thoughts, and nothing got to her.

But their scenes had confounded her.

Though she continually attempted to intellectualize the process of submission, the more she learned, the more there was to know.

Several more teens came down to the pool area, so she went back upstairs. As she showered, she took down the handheld showerhead and rinsed off.

At the Den, Master Alexander had been a spectacular lover. There'd been an intimacy about the way they interacted that she'd found lacking in previous relationships.

And now, away from distraction, she once again replayed the evening's events, kneeling, being in the posture collar, having her hands secured, having his hand blaze across her ass. In retrospect, none of it had been awful. He'd ensured her safety and he'd talked to her the entire time.

She'd only started to spiral when she was swept up in her own thoughts.

How different would the evening have been if she hadn't struggled against his orders or defied him?

Would Master Alexander have given her a shattering orgasm?

As she thought of him and his gorgeous face and amazing body, she moved the showerhead down her body, from her chest to her belly, then between her legs. She used one hand to spread her pussy.

Heaven help her. She craved his attention, his touch, gentle caresses, sex…

With a sigh, she continued to move the showerhead between her legs. Then she turned the dial so that the water pulsed, rather than sprayed, and she teased her clit with the warmth and the pressure.

The orgasm she'd wanted loomed out of reach, so she rose onto the balls of her feet and clenched her buttocks, striving for completion.

She needed pressure on her nipples, she realized. And with the way she was using the showerhead, there was no way to do that.

A minute or so later, she gave up in frustration. Until he'd introduced her to some nipple play, she'd been able to reach orgasm quickly.

In frustration, she shut off the water.

Nothing about today had gone the way she'd anticipated or hoped.

Once she'd dried off, she grabbed her purse and fished out the tube of arnica. The fact he'd given it to her showed he had been thinking of her, no matter what her mind had told her at the time.

Unsure what to do with that realization, she crossed to the bedroom to stand in front of the mirror, then she squirted cream onto her fingertip and dabbed it on the red mark.

Afterward, she debated what to do. Restless energy still filled her.

Instead of changing into her pajamas, she dressed in a pair of yoga pants and a T-shirt and buried herself in housework, trying to ignore the truth that was nagging at her — part of her wanted to continue her training.

In life, she'd learned that mastery came from practice. Why had she expected submission to be any different?

She might decide he was right, that the lifestyle didn't suit her and that an occasional scene satisfied her.

On the other hand, at the Den, there'd been transcendent moments when she'd experienced peace, when she'd stayed present instead of allowing her thoughts to gallop.

There was only one way she knew of to decide whether or not she wanted to continue on. By testing her commitment.

Despite the fact she was tired and a little overwrought, she set an alarm for twenty minutes.

She knelt, then continually moved between the positions he'd taught her, from kneeling up to standing, from kneeling to inspect.

The repetition quickly became uncomfortable. Her muscles started to fatigue, and she glanced at the timer to discover she was only halfway through.

Drawing on the same determination that had gotten her this far in life, she kept going.

With five minutes remaining, she realized how badly her body hurt, and she was thinking of all the other things she could be doing, like a load of laundry, paying some bills, making a grocery list, even getting some much-needed sleep.

But instead of quitting, she pictured him standing in front of her, arms folded, legs spread in a commanding way. Then she imagined him ordering her onto her back so he could lick her pussy.

She stumbled.

The man had the power to discombobulate her, even when he wasn't there. If she'd conjured that image while she had been in the shower, she absolutely would have been able to orgasm.

By the time the alarm rang, she was perspiring. She had to give credit to Brandy for her graceful movements. Making elegance appear effortless required a tremendous amount of work.

When Chelsea finally went to bed, she fell into a disturbed sleep, and she looked at the clock at least half a dozen times before dawn.

Finally, giving up, she tossed back the covers and practiced her moves before going to the office. Then, on her lunch break, she gathered up all her courage and telephoned Master Alexander.

He answered on the first ring. "Chelsea."

Her heart fluttered.

"How are you doing emotionally?"

His concern for her well-being made her soar. "Much better, Sir." And a good night's sleep would help restore her equilibrium the rest of the way. "I appreciate you asking."

"Anything specific you wish to discuss?"

"I wanted you to know you were right."

"Oh?"

His voice, so rough, so sexy and inviting, made her toes curl in her pumps. "Last night and this morning, I thought a lot about BDSM being a journey, questioning whether it's what I truly want, if I'm doing it for the right reasons. It's more emotional than I expected, and rigorous."

Another realization occurred, one at a much deeper level. He hadn't spoken, and instead, he gave her the freedom to sort through her thoughts. "I've always believed that success is about mind over matter. Meaning that if I'm committed and keep pushing forward, I can do anything."

"That can be a helpful mindset."

"In general, maybe. But last night's experience humbled me."

He was silent for so long that she stood and paced the small confines of the room. At some point, she'd be able to afford a bigger space, but until You're The Star reached the next level of success — signing a minor celebrity that they could make into an A-lister — the firm would have to make do.

"Is that necessarily a bad thing?"

As she considered his question, she swiped back a lock of hair that had fallen onto her forehead. "I hadn't thought of it that way."

"Perhaps you can reframe it as a breakthrough."

If she learned from it, perhaps.

"Become stronger, more resilient?"

"I'd like that."

"Have you reached a decision yet?"

"Yes." She straightened her shoulders. "I'd like to continue on. If you're agreeable, Sir?"

"Chelsea, there's nothing I'd like more."

His purr of approval slid through her, reinforcing that she'd made the right decision. Instantly she gave herself a mental shake. Master Alexander was a Dominant, her trainer, not someone she was dating.

Wanting to be close to him had been part of her problem last night. If she had learned anything, it was that she had to keep him at an emotional distance, constantly reminding herself this was a professional relationship and nothing more, no matter how much her body responded to his touch and the sensuality in his tone.

"For the next week, I'd like you to practice your paces and call me every day — at whatever time you choose — to discuss your experiences."

His statement caught her off guard, making her blink. *What?*

"Is that agreeable?"

"I'd thought" — *hoped* — "we'd continue as we were."

"Taking time to test your resolve and to communicate is the best use of our time."

She didn't like his decision, but what choice did she have?

"You'll be expected to go through your positions every day. Today for ten minutes."

Which was less than she'd done last night and again this morning.

"Each day you'll increase the time by five minutes until you reach half an hour."

"I agree, Sir."

"During our check-ins, I'll expect you to be forthcoming, hiding nothing."

As she already knew, that would be the most difficult thing of all.

"I'll be here for you. If you struggle, call or message me."

Did he have any idea how much the offer soothed her? "Thank you for that."

"Your safe word still applies."

Like an excellent Dom, he thought of everything.

"Be aware that I'll know if you don't follow through. It will be obvious."

At his comment, she bristled. "I keep my word, Sir."

"Just for my own personal pleasure and perhaps perversion, at some time during the week, expect that I will ask you to video chat with me while you're going through your exercises. At that point I'll have further instructions."

"Like what, Sir?"

"Always, girl, be prepared for the unexpected."

Her tummy lurched. *What are you planning?* Master Alexander Monahan was diabolical, keeping her guessing.

"Call me tomorrow, pet."

The intimacy in his voice would ensure her compliance. "Yes, Sir."

Outside her office window, traffic zipped past, and she barely noticed it.

Master Alexander consumed her.

And the fact she had to wait a week to see him again made her restless. Being with him, feeling the brush of his fingers on her skin was the stuff of dreams.

Somehow, she had to get through the next week. No matter what, she would endure, even when it was challenging.

Each morning, after getting out of bed, she went through the motions for half of the time he required. Then she did the same when she arrived home from work, no matter how long or tiring her day had been. And because her muscles ached, she headed for the hot tub before bed.

The first few times she followed his instructions, she had difficulty reining in her thoughts. Then it had become somewhat easier.

By Sunday, things were less challenging, mentally anyway.

When she called him late that afternoon, she reached his voicemail. Sighing from disappointment, she nonetheless forced a chipper note into her voice — act enthusiastic, and you'll *be* enthusiastic as she'd learned at one of her first sales training events — and left a pleasant message.

As she watched a television show, she checked the phone screen several times, even though it had been silent.

Finally, he returned her call just as she was heading to the pool deck.

She exhaled a few times to steady herself before answering. "Good evening, Sir." It amazed her how using the honorific instantly calmed her.

"I informed you previously that you needed to be prepared to video chat."

Her heart stopped. "Yes, Sir. However —"

"Are you at home? Alone?"

She exhaled. For a moment she considered fibbing, but she couldn't bring herself to utter the lie. No doubt he'd simply ask her to do so later, and perhaps at a less convenient time. "I am."

"Alone?"

"Also yes."

"In that case, was there anything about our agreement that was unclear to you?"

"No, Sir," she agreed miserably. But before he could speak again, she rushed on. "I just wanted you to know that I already practiced today."

"That's relevant how?"

From his point of view, perhaps it wasn't.

"I'm not aware of any reason a few more minutes would be detrimental. Are you?"

Glad that he couldn't see her responses, she tipped her head back in frustration. Her body was sore, and she was looking forward to soothing her muscles in hot water beneath an inky, starlit sky.

"I'm waiting for your answer."

"No, Sir. You're correct."

"In that case, I'd like to see you. Now."

She touched a button on her screen to turn on her camera.

Because she'd been in his home, she recognized that he was in his study, lazing back in his chair. He wore a crisp white shirt, with the top couple of buttons open.

At the sight of him, her mouth watered.

Even though it had only been a few days since she'd seen him, she'd forgotten how incredibly sexy he was.

"It's nice to see your face, Chelsea."

Since her tongue was suddenly twisted, she couldn't respond.

"Find a good place for your phone so that I can see all of your movements, whether you're on your back or standing."

She spent several minutes propping it at the right angle and distance until he said he was satisfied.

"You were heading for a swim?"

"I'm not that much of a glutton for punishment—I mean exercise—Sir. I was just on my way to the hot tub."

"In that case, we should make sure your muscles are really demanding to be soothed."

This time, because he could see her, she schooled her features.

"Remove your swimsuit and begin by kneeling, then standing. Do it fifteen times."

Her first few transitions were awkward before she took a breath and momentarily closed her eyes to steady her nerves.

"You're doing well."

If this seemed like an improvement, how terrible had she been that first night at his house?

When she continued, she was much more refined.

"Excellent. Your discipline is showing."

His words fed her.

"Keep going."

Concentrating on his pleasure rather than her discomfort, she did as he said.

"Good. You may stop."

She blinked. This was much sooner than she'd anticipated. She wasn't even breathing hard yet. "Really, Sir?"

"I'm satisfied with your progress." He leaned forward, his features filling her screen. "*Very* satisfied."

At this point, she might do anything for him.

"Now we'll move on to an inspection."

A what? "I'm confused. I have no idea how that would work."

"No need to worry. I'll provide you with adequate instruction."

She was afraid of that.

"Have you been keeping yourself properly groomed?"

Though she hadn't expected him to ask that, as part of her morning shower, she shaved. "Yes, I have."

"You're being an extraordinarily good girl. You wouldn't have been punished for not doing so as I didn't specifically require that you take care of that, but that you thought to makes me happy."

Chelsea basked in his approval.

"Grab your phone. I want you to kneel, knees wide, your camera between your legs. You're going to spread your labia and show me what a good job you did."

Trembling, she did as he said, and she had to move the camera several times until he was once more satisfied.

"Good, now lower your body a little."

"That's obscene, Sir."

"Don't make me repeat myself, girl. Otherwise you'll be spanking yourself while I enjoy listening to your whimpers and cries."

Panic filled her senses. "You wouldn't!"

He chuckled, a diabolical sound that terrified her more than a display of anger would have. "Try me."

Knowing he was serious, her face heating with embarrassment, she immediately followed his instructions.

"Your pussy doesn't appear to be wet."

"A little fear does that to me, Sir." And so did the uncomfortable position.

"Simply do the same things to yourself that I did to you at the Den. Run your finger everywhere. Pull back the hood of your clit and let me see it. And fuck yourself with your hand."

This may be one of the worst things she'd ever experienced.

Softly he spoke again. "Transcend your reactions and know you're pleasing me."

She exhaled a soft breath.

"Now get on with it."

Shaking, drawing on all her mental strength, she spread herself wide for the camera, for him.

"Clean shaven. Nice. You *have* been a good girl."

"Thank you, Sir." Still shaking, she exposed her clit.

"Very pretty. Stay as you are for a few more seconds."

The position, the exposure, the emotional discomfort, all piling up, she did as he said.

"That's it. Now lick your finger and play with it."

Knowing he was watching, approving, her own touch seemed to electrify her.

"I'm thinking you like this."

As she stroked, Chelsea rocked back and forth.

Shocking her, an orgasm started to build. *Nooo.* This couldn't possibly be happening. But it was.

"Now stop."

For a couple of seconds, she didn't react. How long had it been since that night at the Den when she'd had her last orgasm? She was on edge in a way she'd never been before.

"Stop immediately and spank your pussy." His voice was a whiplash. "Three times. And you'd better fucking do it as hard as I would."

Whimpering, she protested.

"Last chance, or I'll make it five."

Squeezing her eyes shut, she followed his terrible order, crying out from the pain and because the act left her shockingly more aroused.

"Fuck." His curse purred with pure male satisfaction. "Red is suddenly my favorite color. I should keep you like that at all times."

Her body jerking, she struggled for control.

"Now finger-fuck yourself, girl. Hard and deep. If you even get close to your clit, you'll get more punishment." His demands were constant, horrible.

"You're being beastly, Sir."

"So far, I've been a gentleman, and more generous than you deserve."

Though he might be right, his words didn't soothe her agitation.

"Since you're considerably smaller than I am, I want you using three fingers."

She complied, becoming more and more aroused. Her impending orgasm couldn't be denied. "Oh, Sir!" Spinning back to their time they'd had sex, Chelsea closed her eyes, imagining him inside her.

"Problem, girl?"

Unable to respond, she thrust her hips.

"You're not going to come, are you, Chelsea?"

The warning in his tone didn't penetrate her haze.

"Chelsea?"

She was almost there, so close, so desperate...

"Stop immediately."

His loud command penetrated her self-induced haze. "But..."

"Immediately," he repeated with force.

Ceasing her movements, she fought back her aggravation.

"Now pick up the phone and place your fingers in your mouth. Taste yourself and know how happy I am to know you're so needy."

"But... Sir, it's been so long since —"

"And it's going to be even longer. Your denial is delicious."

Once she had the device in hand, she sucked on her fingertips.

He picked up a glass of something — whiskey maybe — and took a sip.

His eyes were intense, his nod filled with triumph. "That's satisfactory."

Relieved, she dropped her hand to her side.

"Your orgasms belong to me."

Hardly able to comprehend his words, she blinked.

"To give, to withhold. Understand?"

"I..." When he quirked an eyebrow, she reluctantly relented. "Yes, Sir."

"That means you require permission before coming, and this is not a situation where it's better to ask forgiveness than permission."

"Is this part of my training, Sir?"

"No. It's whim, and I'm indulging myself. I like to think of you suffering, my pet."

Did his demands have no end?

"After this experiment, do you still wish to continue forward? Or do you prefer to choose the time and place of your climaxes and set your own schedule without interference?"

As she considered her answer, she looked into his eyes and had a jolting, overwhelming sense of connection.

Perhaps it wasn't a surprise.

No one else had ever pushed her to this extreme, with such high expectations, but offering much more in return. Because of the way he demolished her defenses, she experienced an intimacy with him unlike anything she'd shared with anyone else.

Without saying another word, he took a sip and waited.

"Yes, Sir."

"Those were the words I hoped to hear."

Did this mean he'd shorten the amount of time until she needed to wait before seeing him?

His next words dashed her hopes.

"In that case, two days from now, repeat this process. Record a video and send it to me."

Her mouth fell open.

"Any questions?"

"No, Sir." Did he stay up at night thinking up ways to keep her guessing?

"No orgasms. As always, call me tomorrow." He flashed a charming smile, as if trying to disguise his diabolical manner. "Enjoy the hot tub."

Her phone screen went blank.

Staring at it, she tipped her head to one side. He'd dropped all of that on her, then ended the call without saying goodbye?

How was she supposed to survive him and his sexy, need-inducing demands?

Chapter Six

"Would you like to come over tomorrow evening?"

Master Alexander's suggestion slid through Chelsea, igniting her senses and making her heart leap into her throat. Pressing the phone closer to her ear, she strode to her office window.

This was the moment she'd been anticipating, wanting, but afraid wouldn't happen.

When she'd called him the day after she'd left his house, he'd said they should spend a week apart. Since then, she'd done everything she was supposed to, including sending him the video. She honestly wasn't sure she'd done anything more difficult.

But his instructions clearly had a purpose, and the embarrassment she experienced now wasn't as profound as it had been the night they'd met.

"Chelsea?"

"Yes, Sir. I would love to see you." She probably shouldn't have admitted that, but her enthusiasm bubbled over.

"Does six o'clock work for you? Or is seven better?"

"Whatever is best for you, Sir."

"Six. We can spend some time together, then we'll have dinner."

Where she'd be expected to wear something revealing and no undergarments? "Is there anything specific I should wear?"

"Since I'll expect you to remove your clothing the moment the door closes behind you, it doesn't matter."

"But what about dinner?"

"I want you to be comfortable. Jeans are fine. We're not going anywhere fancy."

Really?

When she didn't respond right away, he asked, "Questions?"

"Only about what happens once I arrive. I presume you'll open the door and then I'll undress?" She started to pace, a habit she'd picked up since she'd started seeing him.

"Let yourself in, strip, then wait near the fireplace. I trust that you will be in the correct position at six o'clock precisely."

"Yes, Sir."

"Anything less than perfection will require chastisement."

She shuddered.

"Before you go, have you been masturbating?"

"You forbade it."

"Answer the question."

"I wanted to, but no. I didn't, Sir." She exhaled. "I hate the rule. Sometimes it's the only way I can get to sleep." And not being able to use the showerhead between her legs seemed like a constant punishment.

"You're going to continue to do as I say, though, aren't you, girl? Because you like being my good pet."

God help her. She squeezed her eyes shut. Every word he said was true.

"Now get on with your practice. And deal with the fact that I intend to push you further than you've ever been."

Her insides curled into a knot of dread…and sexual anticipation.

Then he hung up, once more ending the call on a cryptic note.

Damn you.

He tilted her world off its axis and expected her to go on as if nothing had happened?

Later that night, at home in bed, she couldn't get comfortable, and she was convinced he'd intended that for her.

Since he'd denied it, need crawled through her. Right now, she knew even the gentlest of touches against her clit would get her off. She could feel her pulse there, demanding. *Confounding man.*

She was aware of the ache in her pussy that a simple touch would vanquish. Her breasts felt full, and she desperately wanted to play with her nipples.

She thumped her pillow into a different shape, and that didn't help, either.

Finally, half an hour later, in abject frustration, she climbed out of bed and went through her paces again, while wearing her pajamas. If she took off her clothes, she would be tempted to touch herself.

The act of thinking of Master Alexander, of making him proud of her, helped calm her.

As always, sleep eluded her.

She turned on her side and shoved both hands beneath her head. She forced herself not to think about her upcoming time with Master Alexander, and instead, she counted sheep, something she hadn't done since she was a child.

The technique must have worked because the alarm dragged her to a groggy consciousness. She'd hit the snooze button often enough that she was running late for an appointment with a potential new client. The coffee maker took its sweet time, and she glared at it, as if that would hurry it along.

She was pouring the first cup when she remembered she still needed to practice her movements.

With a frustrated sigh, she glanced at the clock on the microwave. Since she'd done extra the day before, surely that put her ahead for today, right? She dragged a hand through her hair, wishing it worked that way. Either she intended to keep her word, or not. If she'd jumped out of bed when the alarm had first rung, she wouldn't be in a time crunch.

After taking a long drink of the life-sustaining caffeine, she knelt. It took a lot of mental effort to keep herself calm rather than panicking about the time.

Fortunately, her potential new client called to say he was behind schedule, and she arrived at her office half an hour ahead of him.

By the time she greeted him and showed him into the conference room, she was cool and competent, impressing him enough that he signed on the dotted line. And of course, she and her team would have to begin work immediately to promote his upcoming independent movie. Still, that didn't stop her and Jennifer—Chelsea's executive administrator—from grabbing hold of each other and screaming before doing a dance around the office.

At last! After years of hard work, scraping and scrimping, and paying off bills, her business was finally achieving the success she'd dreamed of.

The rest of the day passed in a blur, and they brought lunch in.

All too soon, four-thirty arrived. Even though they'd been swamped, thoughts of being with Master Alexander had intruded. She'd been relieved to stay busy all day, otherwise she wasn't sure how she'd have survived the nine hours.

She hurried home for a shower, and to shave properly before meeting him. The sensual tension that had been simmering through her body heated to a boil. She needed him — and relief.

As she drove to his house, she distracted herself with outrageously loud dance music.

She arrived with enough time to get inside and prepare herself for whatever was going to happen at six o'clock.

As per his instructions, she let herself in.

After securing the door behind her, she called out a greeting, but silence echoed back at her.

A little unnerved, she undressed then walked into the living room, drew a steadying breath, and lowered herself to the kneel up position near the fireplace.

She couldn't help but glance at the items he'd left on the side table — the dreaded collar, a box of surgical gloves, lube, several coiled lengths of restraints, and a curved metal hook. Something that might have been a tawse lay across the arm of the couch.

Rather than focusing on what might happen, she stared straight ahead, jumping at every sound.

Is Master Alexander even in the house?

Not that it mattered. She had her instructions, and no doubt this was a test.

Finally, heavy footsteps fell on the hardwood floor, and it took all her internal fortitude to remain where she was, waiting for him.

Long, interminable moments passed in silence.

But she breathed in the undeniable scent of him — determination, undercut with crisp mountain air — and that slammed her pulse into overdrive.

"Very good," he said.

Hot and heavy, his approval slid through her.

"Please present yourself for inspection."

Forcing herself to be mindful, she stood with her hands behind her neck, then brought her shoulder blades together. After parting her legs wide, she looked straight ahead.

"You have been working on that."

She wanted to please him. Why it should matter so much, she didn't know. "Thank you, Sir."

When he stepped in front of her, he took away her next breath.

He was dressed casually, in jeans, motorcycle boots, and a tight black T-shirt. Judging by the stubble on his jaw, he'd obviously missed his morning shave. That made him appear all the more dangerous.

But his next command came so fast that she had no time to savor his sexiness.

"Open your mouth."

Schooling herself, she followed his orders, but then he surprised her by saying, "Now close it."

He never did what she expected.

For a moment he was quiet.

"Thank you, Sir," she remembered to say, rushing the words together. She definitely didn't want to experience the dental dam again, and his mercy truly was something to be grateful for.

"You've shaved again."

"Yes, Sir." She wasn't sure whether he'd expected an answer or not.

"Present your breasts."

Though he hadn't asked that of her before, she'd seen Brandy do it at the Den. Chelsea lifted her breasts and drew them together, hoping she was doing it right.

"Perfect. Pinch your nipples."

Because she knew his expectations, she grasped herself harder than she liked. Even when the pain became uncomfortable — almost unbearably so — she continued to do as she was told.

"Now release them and part your pussy lips. Hold them back, as if they were butterfly wings."

Taking care not to touch her suddenly achy clit, she complied.

His inspection was gentle, much more awful than the terrible one he'd given her at the Den. This aroused her, driving her even madder than she already was.

"Such a good pet." He wet his thumbpad and brushed it across her clit.

Moaning, she jerked desperately. "Sir!"

He tutted. "Such lack of control."

Fuck. Already she was on the verge of an orgasm, and it was all his fault.

"Show me your ass."

Until now, this had been a wonderful inspection. Trying to rein in her galloping emotions, she lowered herself to all fours, then placed her forehead on the floor. Once she'd found her balance, she reached back to spread her ass cheeks.

What was he doing? *Watching? Thinking? Planning?*

Whatever it was, it stretched her nerves to their fracture point.

His footsteps bounced off the floor, and she forced herself to resist the temptation to turn her head and peek.

Then something wet and solid pressed against her anus.

"Open up, naughty girl."

This was awful. But when he started to enter her, she closed her eyes and bore down, anxious to make it easier on herself. He inserted something, probably his finger, and probed her, stretching her.

"Have you ever worn a plug?"

"No, Sir."

"And what you mean is, no Sir, not until now."

"No, Sir," she repeated. "I have not worn a plug *until now.*"

Suddenly, more pressure was back there.

"A second finger is going in. You can make it easy on yourself or not. The choice is yours."

Gulping, she clenched her hands.

"Slow, deep breaths will help."

Sure they will.

"Relax and let me in. Now I'm going to put a starter plug in your ass, though I'm tempted to go with something bigger."

She recognized the inherent threat and knew why he'd made it. "Thank you, Sir, for stretching me and for using a small one."

He chuckled.

"Nice save. But I will expect you to work up to something much, much larger. Being comfortable with it will make your life easier."

The reminder she was doing this for someone other than him caught her off guard, and she wasn't sure she relished his comments.

"Turn your head and look at this." He crouched next to her.

Their faces were mere inches apart, and for an instant, their connection sizzled with electricity. She blinked first.

He held up the red silicone plug. "This is going inside you on the first try without you carrying on. Are you clear?"

Though the widest part didn't appear much bigger around than the two fingers he'd just inserted inside of her, the toy had a base that would hold it in place.

"Do you remember your safe word?"

"Yes, Sir."

"Good. In that case, ask me to put it in place."

She'd convinced herself that he wasn't as beastly as she sometimes remembered, then he proved that wasn't true. "Please, Sir, will you put that...nasty thing in me?"

He smiled. "Lucky for you I'm not marking you down for lack of enthusiasm."

"Sorry, Sir," she said, trying not to smile as she drank in their momentary closeness. "Shall I try again?"

"Do."

"Please, I beg you, Sir. I want you to put that hot thing straight up my ass in a single move."

This time he laughed, but he also smacked her left butt cheek, hard. "If you insist," he responded.

He left her for a moment. The unmistakable sound of lube being squirted filled her ears.

"Spread your cheeks farther," he said.

Her Dom placed the unyielding tip against her opening. The thing had appeared flexible, so she hadn't been prepared for its unwelcome rigidity.

"Bear down...*now.*"

He pushed ahead, and Chelsea had to fight his momentum and her desire to escape in order to stay in position.

Through gritted teeth, she told him, "This is way more difficult than a finger, Sir. Damn it!"

"Almost there. You can do it."

As the widest part entered her, she whimpered. Then finally it slid all the way in. When the momentary discomfort had receded, she sighed.

"Very pretty."

Although she didn't argue, she doubted the red thing looked attractive at all.

He twisted it so that the hilt was seated between her buttocks.

She gave an unladylike grunt. "Not a fan of that," she said. "Sir."

"Too bad. Now kneel back. I want to speak with you."

Wildly she wondered if she'd already upset him. But damn, that had hurt more than she'd expected. Frustrated with herself for expressing displeasure, she moved into position and kept her gaze straight ahead.

"You may relax and look at me. Do you still wish to continue?"

Chelsea adjusted herself, trying to find a comfortable position with the plug inside her. The slick silicone made her feel full, and she was dealing with the intrusion without complaint because it pleased her Master. "Yes, Sir. I do want to continue. I'm just trying to think about how to deal with this butt plug."

"Quit thinking and allow it to be."

That was easy for him to say. He didn't have a long thing stuck up his rear channel.

"Lie on your back," he instructed. "You may use the rug."

She knew better than to argue.

The thing moved about as she awkwardly did as he said. Her movements were exaggerated as she tried not to move too much.

"Now, draw your knees to your chest and keep them there."

She closed her eyes, imagining the sight she made, with her pussy and the base of the plug revealed to him. She'd never been shy, even in bed, but this was an entirely new level of exposure. He'd expected a tremendous amount from her. And she hadn't been here half an hour.

"Stop the struggle."

In less than a minute, the position became uncomfortable. Air whispered from the nearby vent and cooled her hot pussy, and she closed her eyes, attempting to harness her wayward thoughts.

When she shifted a bit, he moved to the table and returned to show her his cane.

Her eyes widened.

"Like at the Den, you won't be struck by this, but I will use it to correct your position."

She closed her eyes. At home, alone, it was easy to rationalize submission, and she could convince herself it wasn't all that bad and that he never demanded more than she could give. But it became a different thing when she was being tested by his unyielding ways.

No matter what he said, she didn't want that rattan on her body, so she remained still.

"Good."

She held on to his approval. A simple word from him provided huge encouragement.

He left her there for so long that she stopped thinking about the plug and only about him. Her breathing evened out. At one time she would have sworn it was impossible to tolerate the plug. But it wasn't all that bad.

"How is that?"

"Fine, Sir."

"Would you like to continue your training?" he asked eventually.

"Yes. Yes, please, Sir."

"In that case, I'm going to fuck your ass with that plug, and you're going to encourage me to go faster and harder."

She wrapped her hands tighter around her legs.

"Aren't you, Chelsea?"

Her breath was shaky.

"It seems you need time to work through various aspects of submission, that you naturally want to rebel."

"I'd hate for that to be true, Sir."

He stood close, tapping the cane against his ankle. He loomed over her, large, broad and imposing. Being in this position, looking up at him reinforced their roles.

"Am I wrong?" he asked.

"No." She wanted to drag her hand through her hair or fold her arms across her chest, but he compelled her to remain open. "Are you sure you have the patience for this? For me?"

Tenderness softened his expression. "Yes. I do. I consider it all to be part of your training."

For the first time, she understood that this couldn't be easy for him, either. Why would he choose to tolerate a recalcitrant and stubborn woman when he could have his pick of already-perfect submissives?

In so many ways, he was an enigma. She'd learned a little about him through online searches, but she only knew those things that had put him in the press. It appeared he didn't participate in any social networking, and even though she was laying herself bare to him, she knew next to nothing about him.

"You're doing fine," he assured her. "We'll work together until you give up the struggle. I recognize that you're trying, that you're thinking. I've told you before, you will never disappoint me."

"But you tanned my hide last time, Sir."

"You will be punished for a bad attitude and for not following rules," he clarified. "But that doesn't mean I'm displeased with you, just an aspect of your behavior. Again, I'm going to fuck your ass. We can use the plug you already have, or we can use a larger one?"

"No. No, Sir. This one is fine. Thank you, again, Sir, for your kindness."

"You *are* learning. On all fours, if you please."

When she didn't move fast enough, he tapped her with the cane to encourage her.

"Your choice, you can remain as you are, or you can put your head on the floor and reach back to hold your buttocks apart."

That wasn't an easy decision. If she stayed as she was, it might be more difficult for him to get the plug in and out. On the other hand, if she moved, it would be easier to lose her balance. In the end, she asked, "Is it acceptable for me to...?" Some of their conversations mortified her. "Stick out my bottom a bit?"

"Your decision," he said. "Doms may not always offer you that choice. Be aware."

"Yes, Sir." She pushed out her rear in his direction, waiting with huge impatience.

"It's customary to thank a Dom when he grants you a favor."

Damn it all. He overwhelmed her so much that she forgot half the things she was learning. "Sorry, Sir," she apologized straightaway. "I appreciate your under-standing."

"As always, I'll reinforce the lesson later."

She froze. "Did that earn me a punishment?"

"Did you expect it wouldn't?" Behind her, he grasped the plug and pulled it out. "The more you relax, the easier this will be."

Chelsea barely had time to absorb the shock of being stretched then having it out before he shoved it in again.

Relentlessly he pounded her, and she was gasping and shaking, moving forward and back as he fucked her with it. A dull throb of anguish overwhelmed her, leaving her unable to think.

"How is it?" he asked.

"It's..." *Horrible. Awful. Hideous.*

Unbelievably, as he continued, as she moved with him instead of fighting to remain still, she started to become aroused. "Sir!"

"Yes?"

"I... Oh, my God, I think I might come."

All of a sudden, with the plug out, he stopped.

She swore beneath her breath.

Silence shrouded the living room, and the temperature seemed to drop.

"Thank you for telling me," he said. "Now we'll go on. This is the penalty for having to be reminded of your manners."

Unreleased need vibrated through her. With her teeth gritted, she nodded. "The lesson is hitting home, Sir."

"I'm glad you see that. Still, I'll be edging you for a bit."

What the hell is that? "Edging?"

"I'll bring you to the precipice again and again. But I won't let you come."

She pressed her lips together. There were many parts of this that she didn't like — or actively despised.

"Since your ass is stretched and so wide open, you'll tolerate a larger plug."

Instinctively, she tightened her buttocks.

"It's going in," he said, tone implacable. "How difficult do you want it to be?"

She heard him moving around the room, and not knowing what he was doing made her crazy.

"Would you like to see it?"

"No." She barely remembered to express her gratitude. "No, thank you, Sir." Knowing what was coming might make it worse.

"I'm doing this because you didn't remember to thank me earlier."

More than anything, she wanted to look at him, see his eyes, maybe gather some reassurance from the way he looked at her. "I thought you were going to spank me for that?"

"There are many ways to reinforce lessons," he said. "Corporal punishment is only one of several."

"I think I prefer that, Sir, to something else you might choose."

"As your Dom, I will make that decision."

This relationship was a juxtaposition. The things she liked most about him, that he was firm and unyielding, were also the things she hated the most.

"You were going to have to work your way up to a larger plug, regardless. This just accelerates my timeline."

"Yes, Sir," she said miserably. When would she learn to keep her mouth shut?

"Look at me, pet."

She turned her head. Thankfully, he had the plug behind his back.

"You are here for training. Of course you'll make mistakes, plenty of them. That's to be expected. We only have two weeks together, and that means moving forward every day in order to accomplish what you want."

Reluctantly, she nodded. "I understand, Sir." Then she added a second lie. "I'm ready."

"Good girl."

The diabolical Dom moved behind her, and she thrust out her rear again. He was going to do this whether she protested or not. She could stall or use a safe word, but eventually his will would prevail. So why not get on with it?

Although she hadn't heard him squirt lube on the plug, it was slick as he pressed it into her.

This was bigger — wretched — making her whimper. She should never have complained about the smaller one.

He had only managed to insert it part of the way when he pulled it back out. "You can do this, Chelsea."

"Do what, Sir? Be torn apart?"

"Bear down," he advised, shaking his head. He forced the thing in deeper.

"I... Fuck this!"

"Stop fighting me," he said.

"I'm trying to cooperate, Sir."

"In that case, relax your sphincter." He worked the thing in, then eased it out, going a little deeper and farther each time.

"I'm not sure I can manage this, Sir!"

"You can," he said, his tone both encouraging and soothing.

She was afraid his determination was no match for her inability to take the plug's girth. Feeling helpless, desperate for this to be over, she inched away from him, trying to escape.

"Stick out your ass, Chelsea." He reached forward to clamp her left shoulder and hold her in place.

She screamed when he stretched her ass even farther.

"That's it," he said. "It's going in. *Now.*"

With his hand on her shoulder, he forced her backward, and he shoved the plug deep.

Tears swam in her eyes as her safe word hovered on the tip of her tongue.

"You're there," he said.

Just like last time, it settled in, and her anus relaxed around the stem.

"That metal bling looks hot, Chelsea."

"Bling?"

"The base has blue jewels. They reminded me of your eyes."

He'd noticed that about her?

"I really am looking forward to fucking you up the ass. Maybe even tomorrow."

She gulped for air, trying to steady her trembling body. That had to be a joke.

Soothingly, he stroked his fingertips up and down her spine, and luxurious calm enveloped her. "That's nice, Sir."

"How does the plug feel?" he asked.

She hated to admit it, but now that it was in, it wasn't too bad. In fact, the full sensation, compounded by the fact he liked the way it looked, made her feel slightly sexy. How was that possible?

"Chelsea?"

"It's fine, Sir."

He squatted next to her.

"Thank you."

"You are very welcome." He moved one hand from her face and smoothed her hair.

No one seemed to know her as he did. Because he demanded honesty, refused to allow games, didn't let her get away with prevarication, held her accountable, pushed her through her feminine embarrassment, he'd seen aspects of her personality even she hadn't known existed. He'd even uncovered a bratty part she hadn't known of and wasn't proud of.

He responded to her needs, meeting them with a touch or soothing word, even without her needing to ask.

"The Dom who ends up with you will be one lucky man."

For a single, mad moment, she wished that man were him.

Chapter Seven

"You may kneel back."

With those words, Master Alexander re-established his authority.

When he released her, Chelsea shook her head to clear it. For a moment she'd slipped, believing in their intimacy and forgetting he was her trainer. Nothing more.

She forced herself to gracefully move into the position he required.

"Nice," he said, nodding. "Ready for dinner?"

"Uhm…" Was he serious? "With the plug in place?"

His grin was quick and wholly evil. "That's why I put it there."

"I have to sit on it?"

"Might help your posture." He lifted one shoulder in a shrug.

This couldn't be happening. But it was.

While she dressed, he waited patiently, then asked, "Comfortable enough?"

"Not at all, Sir."

"In that case, we're ready to leave."

After helping her into his luxurious SUV, he backed out of the driveway and glanced in her direction. "Pizza okay?"

He couldn't have shocked her more. "I didn't take you for someone who liked pizza," she observed.

"We all have secrets." He turned onto a main street. "The difference is, I plan to uncover all of yours."

He'd already discovered a few even she didn't know existed.

"Since it's an Italian restaurant, they also have excellent lasagna, antipasto, manicotti."

"Carbs are my favorite foods."

Inside the cozy building, he was warmly greeted. "Alex!"

The woman rounded the counter to kiss his cheek.

"Daniela, please meet Chelsea."

Immediately, Chelsea was swept into the woman's welcoming arms.

"Daniela and her husband own the restaurant. They are originally from Brooklyn."

"Seriously?" Chelsea asked, delighted. "Does that mean you make New York style pizza?"

"It does." The woman grinned.

"This is why I'm here once a week," Master Alexander confirmed.

"How soon can we order?" Chelsea teased.

Even though there was a waiting line, Daniela showed them to a private alcove. Knowing the owner clearly had privileges.

"Something to drink?" she asked.

"Your choice." Master Alexander met her gaze.

Chelsea knew his rules about drinking and sceneing. Though a glass of chianti appealed to her, she was interested in what he had planned. "How about a soda?" Something sweet and syrupy, a rare indulgence, just like the dinner.

"Pellegrino for me."

As Chelsea attempted to get comfortable on the plug, Daniela returned with the beverages and a basket filled with warm, yeasty garlic knots.

"This place must be what heaven is like," Chelsea exclaimed, placing one of the small treats onto a plate.

"I'm glad you're happy." Daniela smiled then looked at Alexander. "Much better than your ex-wife."

Without another word, she bustled away.

Her curiosity sky-high, Chelsea offered the plate to her trainer.

"You remembered." He nodded, and his voice held a note expressing his pleasure. "I know it may not come naturally to you, Chelsea, but you are learning fast."

He offered the plate back to her.

"Sir?" She drew her eyebrows together.

"It matters that you thought to do it. Enjoy." He helped himself to one of the rolls.

Her first bite was amazing, pure buttery goodness, everything she could hope for. "This is wonderful."

"I'm glad you're happy."

"You can't seriously come here often." She slid a glance over his lean, sexy body.

"Followed by a workout the next morning."

"I bet." She slid her plate to one side after only two small bites.

"Eat up." His grin was wolfish. "You're going to need your stamina."

Eating — thinking — when he spoke like that was nearly impossible.

After she'd finished her piece of bread, she considered him. "The woman Daniela mentioned was Liz, right?"

He took a sip of his water, and she wondered if he intended to answer.

"You've been digging around in my past a lot."

"Doesn't mean I need to return the favor. Wiggle your butt."

Dratted Dominant.

Under his watchful eye, she ground herself on the plug. Then he smiled.

"Your discomfort is wonderful. I enjoy it very much."

"That makes one of us, Sir."

He grinned. "And yes, Liz came here with me, once. But she behaved badly."

"Oh?"

"You may stop moving but sit up straight."

Intrigued, she didn't consider arguing. "You mentioned she was a masochist and that she ended the relationship?"

"That's correct."

"Why? I mean, if you're a Dom and she's a masochist... I don't understand."

"My punishments were not enough for her, and the challenges she presented to me — to us — kept escalating." With a shrug, he shoved his empty plate to the side. "When it became clear I couldn't meet her needs, she found someone who would. Someone much more extreme. A sadist." He raised his brows. "Someone who delights in inflicting pain. That person is not me."

When he was silent for a long time, clearly finished with his story, she spoke. "It had to hurt."

"It was a long time ago."

"Wounds take time to heal."

"They do. Indeed."

"Then it means even more that you are willing to work with me. But I'm curious about something."

"Hmm?"

"Is that one of the reasons you're so tough on me?"

"No. That's part of training."

The arrival of their pepperoni pizza stopped their conversation.

This time, when she offered him the first slice, he accepted. His nod of thanks made her warm inside. Maybe this service thing wasn't all bad.

The sight of the warm, gooey cheese made her mouth water. After dousing her piece with crushed hot peppers, she sank her teeth in. "Oh my God." She sat back. "That's it. I'm packing my stuff and moving so I can be closer to this place."

"You wouldn't be sorry. Everything on the menu is amazing. Sit up straight."

He was merciless.

After she swore she couldn't eat another bite, Daniela packed their leftovers in a box, then placed a white bag on top of it. "Tiramisu for you and your lovely lady."

"That's too kind," Chelsea protested.

Master Alexander reached for his wallet, but Daniela waved him off. "Seeing you finally happy is worth it." With a wave, she left them.

"You are well liked here." Another new side to him. She saw him as a badass while he showed other people different parts of his personality, intriguing her more.

"Shall we?"

Outside, the air was mild, a picture-perfect Colorado summer evening. "As we were getting out of the SUV, I noticed a park. Would you mind if we took a short walk?"

He cocked an eyebrow.

"I could use the exercise."

"Not a bad idea."

They placed the leftovers in the car, then followed the sidewalk to a path leading into the green space.

Side by side, they walked in companionable silence, and she was so relaxed she was almost able to forget about the plug, barely noticing it shifting around inside her.

Without discussion, they stopped on a bridge that crossed a gently flowing creek.

Motion caught her eye, and she looked up to see a shooting star. "Make a wish!" At that moment, she closed her eyes to make one of her own... *To experience true love.*

The thought startled her. She hadn't been expecting that. Success, happiness, money? Those were the things she wanted.

When she opened her eyes, Master Alexander was studying her.

"Looks serious," he observed. "Care to share?"

"It's secret. If I tell you, it won't come true."

"Fanciful."

"Probably. But harmless, right?" She shrugged. "Did you make one?"

"If I told you, it won't come true."

"Touché, Sir. Well done."

They continued on for a few more minutes, before walking back to his SUV.

"You know," she said when they were on the road, "I would still like to earn Monahan Capital's business."

"We shouldn't complicate this any further."

Complicate? She turned to look at him, but his gaze was focused out the windshield.

When he'd first talked about Liz, he mentioned how much the ending of the relationship bothered him — partly because their lives had been so entwined.

Before she could ask for clarification, he pulled into the driveway and shut off the engine.

Once inside, he locked the door. "Take off your clothes and return to the living room while I put away the leftovers."

The easy camaraderie they'd shared earlier was instantly a thing of the past.

As she lowered herself to her knees to wait, she realized she shouldn't allow herself to forget that she was always in training.

He returned to stand over her. "Before we go any further, shall we discuss your training schedule? We have only a short time together and several things to cover. Of course, we will spend some time on anal."

She wrinkled her nose. "I was afraid of that, Sir."

"As well as holding your tongue." He smiled.

Good luck with that.

"We'll also work on being bound and restrained, service, and how to take a spanking properly. We've had some time apart. Is there anything you'd like to add to your limits list?"

"No, there isn't."

"Your Dom will expect you to be excellent at sucking cock, so you'll spend time practicing that, as well."

Her nerves shattered. "Can I ask a question about that?"

"Of course."

"We had sex at the Den…"

"Would you prefer we didn't fuck?"

"No." She chose her words. "I know you don't want things to be confused, but I would like you to fuck me."

"That's no hardship," he assured her.

"I also find it difficult when I'm naked and you're dressed."

"It's a good reminder of our positions. Be assured, it's quite intentional. And besides, I rather enjoy looking at your body."

"I understand, Sir." *Even if I don't like it.*

"Is there anything specific you'd like to learn or spend time on?"

She was silent for a moment as she considered what she wanted to say. He expected her to reveal things that made her uncomfortable—that was part of the whole submission thing. She was accustomed to playing coy games with men, to teasing, to saying what they wanted to hear. But he'd proven he wouldn't settle for that.

"Chelsea?"

The knowledge that they would part after two weeks gave her confidence. It didn't matter what she said, since they wouldn't have a relationship going forward. The honesty demanded of a D/s arrangement left her a bit breathless. "I want to be able to endure whatever my Dom wants with confidence."

"As long as it's not on your limits list," he amended. "Or something where you need to use your safe word. This isn't about heroics." Even as he said that, he moved across the room to pick up the hated collar. "I'd like to see how well you're doing on your postures."

Nothing like an immediate test of what she'd said. "Of course, Sir."

"Anything to say before I fasten you into it?"

Right now, she understood why his firm had been such a big success in business, despite the Bartholomew deal, and why many of the firm's big clients had stayed with them. With the way he focused so intently, he had a way of making people feel listened to and heard. He didn't multitask. He gave his full attention. "I think I said this before, I felt humiliated." She gnawed on her bottom lip. "Unimportant."

His touch gentle, he took her chin and tilted her head back. "Let me make this clear," he said. "I no longer train subs. So the fact you're here says you matter, that I find something remarkable about you. I respect you, Chelsea, and your commitment. I keep my distance on purpose to ensure your safety and to remember our boundaries."

After his experience with his former wife, maybe she didn't blame him.

Quietly, he continued on, in the same serious vein. "You may struggle with your feelings, and it's my job to help you manage your emotional state, as well as my own. BDSM is a serious business and needs to be treated as such. Make no mistake, Chelsea. There is nothing, *nothing*, impersonal about this to me."

Hearing those words released some of her angst.

"Any questions?"

"No, Sir."

"Please, Chelsea, use your safe word or ask me to go slow if you need to. We can talk about anything at any time."

"Thank you, Sir. I'm better now." Submission was uncharted territory. Playing at parties was nothing like being with Master Alexander.

"When you're ready, stand and turn your back to me."

Conscious of the way he watched her so intently, she stood. Since he hadn't given instructions on what to do with her hands, she clenched them by her sides.

"Constricting any of your muscles will increase your mental discomfort. Uncurl your hands, Chelsea."

He truly didn't miss anything.

"I'm going to tighten the collar more than last time, to keep your chin a bit more rigid."

Part of her wished he wouldn't tell her his intentions. She gulped as he fastened it, and even Master Alexander's breaths were sharper than before.

When he was finished, he said, "Face me."

Slowly, she pivoted.

"Good." He took a step back to look at her. He adjusted her collar slightly and moved hair back from her forehead. "Come with me," he said.

He picked up the ever-present cane.

Curious, she followed him up the stairs and gripped the banister lightly to retain her equilibrium. She was more aware of her body than she'd ever been. With every step the plug jostled inside her. And the collar prevented her from looking around. She moved slowly, exaggeratedly, in a way that left her feeling utterly feminine.

He led the way into his bedroom. "Over there," he said, pointing and stepping aside.

A cheval mirror was angled in the corner. "Sir?"

"I want you to see what I do," he said.

Feeling somewhere between awkward and ridiculous, she moved toward the mirror. The room was reflected behind her, and she saw him drop the cane on the darkly masculine bedspread. "I don't understand, Sir."

He stood behind her and placed his hands on her shoulders.

Instead of looking at herself, she stared at his reflection. For the first time, she noticed a slight jagged scar above his right eyebrow.

"Look at how symmetrical your body appears with your head so straight and your shoulders back. See how open you appear. It's that juxtaposition. You look more confident, which also makes you more appealing as a submissive."

She looked at her reflection and scowled. All she noticed was her flaws—the extra weight around her hips and the swell of her belly. "The mirror and I are not best friends, Sir."

Since he didn't let go, she had no choice but to continue to stare, even though she hated to. Generally, she hurried through styling her hair, which consisted of scrunching the short, wet strands with a dollop of mousse. Then she slathered foundation on her face, applied a coat of mascara and walked away.

"I want you to see yourself through my eyes," he prompted. "Look at your beauty."

Instead, her gaze went to his reflection.

"Be proud of yourself. Now arch your back slightly so your chest sticks out farther."

She did.

"Do you notice the difference?"

Looking at herself, she wrinkled her nose. "Maybe? Some."

He frowned. "Don't move." Then he took off her collar. "Stand the way you usually do."

She shook out her arms, drew her feet closer together, and allowed her shoulders to roll forward. Her chin lowered a bit, too.

"Now look again."

"I think I finally understand." The contrast shocked her. Standing up straight did add a confident air.

Without being instructed, she moved around, lifting her head, drawing her shoulder blades together, spreading her legs for balance. The plug continued to remind her of its presence, but she no longer found it annoying.

"Your confidence in your submission makes you even more beautiful, Chelsea."

"But..." She tried to express her inner struggle. "I'm always confident."

"This is next level. You're naked, exposed, and you're standing there proudly. God, it's sexy. And you can express gratitude for the compliment."

She couldn't believe she'd forgotten. "Thank you, Sir."

Once more, she tilted her chin as he secured the collar and checked the fit. This time, she admitted it changed the way she stood.

"Because of your aversion to looking at yourself, I will put you through your paces in front of the mirror. Watch yourself and correct any flaws."

"Yes, Sir."

"Kneel up."

He stood to the side of her, cane held loosely in his right hand. She concentrated on each movement.

Watching her movements helped her to notice that she was leaning slightly to the left. Frowning with determination, she brought herself back to center.

"That's it," he approved.

In the glass, she met his gaze. He was impossibly handsome, and so different from men she had ever been attracted to before. So why did her heart quicken when she looked at Master Alexander?

"Inspect."

Since he didn't touch her, she knew he was just checking her positioning.

"Legs farther apart." With the cane, he tapped the inside of her right ankle. "Much better. Kneel up."

He made her go through every move no less than a dozen times. With each movement, the plug shifted.

"We have the matter of the unfinished practice from the first night you were here—when you defied me. Do you recall?"

Her mouth opened slightly. *As if I'd ever forget.* The evening had started wonderfully and ended up being one that made her question everything. "I thought we were even on that."

"Oh? Why would you expect that?"

Standing here, facing him, remembering that night, her heart pounded.

"If you refuse to do something and walk away without safe wording or using your slow word, you expect transgressions to be pardoned and never mentioned again?"

"Sir..." Being unable to use her hands challenged her muscles in unique and uncomfortable ways. "You did spank me," she reminded him desperately.

"True. But even after that, you still refused to do what was required."

His version of BDSM was much more rigid than hers. In her world, a spanking should even the score. Yet, knowing about Liz and how she'd been a masochist, she understood his viewpoint better.

"I'll give you two options. Three dozen movements now…"

At the end of the day, when she was already tired and stuffed full of a metal plug?

"Or six dozen at a later date of my choosing."

Her breath whooshed out. Was that his version of an actual choice?

"What's it to be?"

She squeezed her eyes shut, hoping to hide her frustration. "I'll do them now."

"Smart. Very smart. Get on with it when you're ready. The longer you delay, the worse it will seem."

That was probably the truth.

Aware of his scrutiny, she once more lowered herself to the floor.

"And look in the mirror."

The second part of his order was the most difficult.

Lesson learned. If she'd safe worded or simply performed her movements that night, she'd have spared herself a spanking and him adding additional requirements to his original order.

Because she was already fatigued, her motions were less elegant than even minutes before, and she moved slower, which meant it took more time than usual to get through her paces.

By the time she'd finished, her body was dotted with perspiration, and her muscles demanded a long soak in Epsom salts.

"Well done."

That one little statement vanquished all her agony.

"Now stand with your hands folded loosely at your back." When she did, he asked, "Do you recall how you insisted you didn't want the cane to be used on your pussy?"

She shuddered. "Uhm…" She couldn't get enough air into her lungs. "You said you might punish my pussy with it."

"Tonight I'm going to show you it can be pleasurable."

The sight of him holding the cane filled her vision.

"I'm going to have you move through the positions again, but this time your wrists will be attached to the collar."

Did he say and do things in order to keep her guessing? She was expecting him to use the rattan on her, but instead he'd decided to cuff her. Suddenly that seemed like the lesser of two evils.

"Anything you say, Sir."

"*Very* well done." He leaned the cane against the mirror where she couldn't forget about it. Clearly he had a sadistic streak.

He walked into his closet and returned with cuffs. Within seconds, he had her wrists attached to the D-rings on her collar.

"Keep your eyes on your reflection as you kneel back."

She was concentrating on him, and on what she was doing, so intently that his strict bondage didn't upset her.

"Fabulous," he said, when he'd had her stop in the inspect pose. "You were wobbly a couple of times, but since you couldn't use your hands for balance, you did better than I expected. Your practice is paying off. Soon you'll have full mastery."

Soaring, she grinned. "Thank you, Sir."

"Do you have a full-length mirror at home?"

"I do."

"Good. From here on, do your exercises in front of it."

Which meant making friends with the mirror, or at least not seeing it as an enemy. He didn't ask for much.

He moved around her to pick up the cane then stood next to the mirror.

Wave after wave of nervousness crashed into her.

"There's not as much room in here as I'd like. We'll go to the play room."

Walking behind him, she was very much aware of her submission. She tried to drop her head, but the collar prevented it.

He moved aside the chair so that they had a large, open space.

"Stand in the middle of the floor, face me, and spread your feet as far as you can."

All of a sudden, her legs were leaden, and she had to force herself to move.

"If you have the right attitude, you may enjoy it. Do you need to discuss anything?"

"Do I have to be wearing the collar?"

"I prefer it, yes. I want to keep your hands out of the way."

"So I can't protect myself?"

"You won't need to. I promise you."

When he used that tone of voice—part purr, all Dominant assertiveness—she'd follow him anywhere, do anything for him.

"Any further questions?"

"No. No, Sir," she amended.

He flicked his wrist a few times, and the rattan whistled as it cut through the air. She curled her toes into the floor. "Sir, I don't think I've ever been more terrified in my life."

"Would you like an orgasm this evening?"

"Not from that thing." She scowled at the cane.

"Ye of little faith," he mocked.

Doubtful, apprehensive, she exhaled. "But yes, I would like an orgasm, Sir."

"In that case, open your mouth."

Without argument, she complied.

"Suck my fingers," he said, voice sandpapery and sensual.

A moment later, he moved his hand between her legs, sliding his slickened fingers across her pussy until she helplessly jerked against his hand, crying out.

"Oh, Sir." She wanted to wrap her arms around him and thrust her hips.

"Not so quick. You *are* needy, aren't you?"

The effects of his orgasm denial collided inside her, ratcheting up her tension. Her legs trembled as she wordlessly sought more. He continued to play with her until she was on her toes, within moments of coming.

Then once more, he stopped.

"Sir! You're an absolute nightmare," she protested, slamming her heels back to the floor.

"You'll earn it."

"I thought I already had, Sir."

"I'll decide that, girl." He stepped back and picked up the cane. "Let's see how desperate you are."

Fear licked at the edges of arousal.

Lightly, he brought the rattan between her legs to tap her clit.

"How's that?"

"Not as bad as I feared," she admitted.

"A little harder?"

"I'm not sure about that, Sir."

"We'll try it, shall we? Remember to say slow or use your safe word if you freak out or can't endure it." With those reassuring words, he stepped back a couple of inches and increased the pressure of his skillful strokes.

As he continued, Chelsea cried out. Not from pain, but because she liked it. The fact she was restrained and helpless added to the delirium. "Sir, I'm really turned on," she admitted, surprising herself. "I need to come. Please? Please, may I?"

He didn't answer, and she jerked and whimpered from her arousal.

"Sir? Master Alexander? I can't take any more. I swear. Please!"

Instead of allowing her to get off, he frustratingly moved the cane away, leaving her heaving, nerve endings singed.

She drank in several deep breaths.

"Do you have yourself under control?" he asked softly, about fifteen seconds later.

She met his gaze, but wished she could look down. Until he had introduced her to the posture collar, she'd had no idea how often she would glance at the floor to hide her emotions. "Yes, Sir."

"Good. You're doing very well. I'm proud of you. But there's more." He placed the length between her labia. "Slide your clit against the cane," he instructed.

She had to bend her knees a bit to get enough pressure against the rattan. "This seemed easier in theory."

"I meant it as a challenge. Now move as if you're fucking the implement."

His dirty talk made her tummy turn somersaults.

The wood was thin, and her damp pussy slid effortlessly along the waxed length. Despite her initial embarrassment, she ground herself against it, becoming wetter and wetter with each stroke. The sensations of the plug shifting inside of her and the way it dragged against the rattan overwhelmed her.

Her breathing rate increased as physical desire trampled rational thinking.

Master Alexander slipped an arm around her, drawing her closer, lending her more of his strength.

"That's it," he encouraged.

The raspy sound of his voice against her ear drove her on. She'd never been with a man this primal, and he unleashed a wild, wanton part of her.

A climax unlike any other built inside her. "Sir, may I?" Her entire body shook from the exertion and denial.

"Have you earned it?"

Her response was instinctive and honest. "That's for you to decide, Sir." Since he hadn't told her to stop, she continued to frantically grind herself against the cane.

He forced the wood against her even harder. Her craving became desperation, and she clenched her buttocks, frantic to fight off the orgasm. "I beg you, Sir! Please, *please*."

"One more time."

"Please, Sir," she begged him. "Please."

"That's a good pet. You may come for me."

His permission unshackled her, leaving her jerking and sobbing. The slickness of her pussy and the unyielding force of the cane became one, then gathered force. His voice encouraged her, his motions drove her.

"Come now," he ordered. "Right now."

As the long-denied climax crashed into her, Chelsea screamed.

Her body shook, from the intensity as much as the relief.

She'd been wholly unprepared for an experience like this one.

At some point, while she sobbed, the rattan clattered against the floor, and she was swept into his embrace as he whispered soft, reassuring words in her ear.

When she finally became aware of the world around them, she was in his lap and seated in the chair, curled up against him. In her entire life, she'd never felt safer, more secure. Or wanted.

"You pleased me."

She met the glittering passion in his eyes.

"There's more for you. If you dare."

Chapter Eight

"Let me get you out of this collar," he said.

Chelsea looked at him through dazed eyes. Again and again, he shattered her, leaving her changed, so different from the woman she'd been even a month ago.

Remembering herself, she thanked him for the orgasm.

"Your trust in me earned you the privilege."

She wanted to remain where she was, as close to him as possible.

But his next instruction meant she had to leave his reassuring embrace. "Lean forward."

In mere moments, he'd freed her wrists.

"Remember, move slow. Rotate your shoulders. Give yourself a few moments to adjust."

"Thank you."

When she'd complied, he drew her back against his chest, digging one hand into her short hair and holding her tight until her breathing returned to normal.

The orgasm he'd given her was shattering, but she yearned for a deeper connection with him. Did she have the courage to ask? "Sir?"

"Hmm?"

"You mentioned giving head as part of my training."

He adjusted her on his lap and tipped back her chin. "I think you've endured enough for one evening. We can do that tomorrow."

"I…"

He frowned as he looked at her. "Tell me what you want, Chelsea."

"You'll think I'm ungrateful."

His lips quirked in a quick smile. "Allow me to be the judge of that."

The smile had transformed him, subtracting years and seriousness from his face. She caught a glimpse of the man he'd been before the perils of life had battered him. For a moment he'd looked carefree and a lot less stern. "I want sex," she admitted, then quickly she ran the rest of her words together. "But I do realize you just brought me off, and I should be thankful for that instead of asking for more."

"On the contrary, open communication is the key to a BDSM relationship. I try to anticipate your needs and meet them, but I'm not a mind reader. And of course, the Dominant is free to accept or deny your request."

"Makes sense."

"If I were to agree, I'd expect you to leave the plug in."

She sighed. *Really?* "Is that even possible, Sir?"

"The fit will be tight. You'll either like it or hate it." In a lower tone, he added, "As for me, I will enjoy the tightness very much."

Placing her palm on his chest, she pushed back from him. "So it's not an option to remove the plug first?"

"Those are my terms. Accept them or not."

She exhaled. The blasted thing was getting uncomfortable, and having his cock inside her would no doubt make it worse.

But if that was his cost, she'd pay it. "I'm willing to try, Sir."

He nodded. "Please crawl to my bedroom."

Her mouth fell open. "Do you mean that?"

"I'm not repeating my command, Chelsea."

Silence stretched and tension ratcheted up.

He was always in control, even when he was giving her what she asked for.

Without saying anything, or encouraging her, cajoling her, he waited, his heart thudding rhythmically beneath her hand.

Fighting back a sudden—familiar—mutinous sensation, she slipped off his lap to lower herself humiliatingly to the floor.

"And since you have a similar reaction to this as you did to the posture collar, you'll be adding this to your practice time."

"Sir…" *Damn you.* Once again, she would prefer to be spanked than to repeat actions that she hated.

But truthfully, was there a better learning experience? *Especially* if she hated it?

"After you," he said.

Her hips swayed as she led the way down the hallway, and the plug had to be clearly visible sticking out of her ass. Mortification threatened to consume her.

"Keep your head up," he told her. "Unless you need assistance from your posture collar?"

Dread knotting in her tummy, she instantly complied.

"So sexy. Any Dominant will be delighted to see you doing this."

Though he said it with all seriousness, she didn't feel sexy, and her instinct was to rebel against his orders.

"Get out of your head."

How did he read her so well when he couldn't even see her?

Once she reached his bedroom, she stopped.

"Kneel up." He turned back the comforter and top sheet before ordering her onto the bed. "Lie on your back, across the mattress," he added. "And put your hands above your head."

Wondering about his instructions, she complied without question.

She savored the sight of him undressing, and he took little care with his clothes. He tossed his shoes toward the closet, and his socks followed. After unbuttoning his shirt, he hung it from the closet door.

Once more, his honed biceps reminded her of his power.

His gaze was focused on her as he unbuckled his belt and pulled the leather through the loops. For a wild, wicked moment she wondered what it would feel like if he used it on her.

"Curious, are you?"

"How…?"

"Your eyes are wide, but not with fear." He dropped his trousers, and his magnificent cock was already hard. She wasn't sure she'd ever seen a man who was so broad, with such well-defined muscles.

She parted her legs and expected him to enter her. Instead, he knelt over her.

"Suck my dick, sub."

Oh, Lord. He loomed above her and filled her vision with his ball sac and erect cock.

Feelings of helplessness slammed into her.

Because he had leverage, he could have choked her, but he initially only shoved his cockhead inside her mouth.

"Take a little more," he said.

She started to move her hands so she had some control, but he ensnared her wrists.

Chelsea squeezed her eyes shut as she licked and sucked, trying not to focus on how big he was and how totally he filled her.

"Good girl." He groaned.

That was all she needed to redouble her efforts to please him. He jerked his hips, going deeper down her throat, exercising his dominion over her.

By the time he pulled out, she was gasping and choking, owned, no longer able to think.

"That will do. For now."

At first, she'd done okay, but toward the end, physical sensation had swamped her. And the gruffness in his voice told her he'd been as into it as she was.

Master Alexander moved off the bed, and she pressed her hand to her mouth to savor his taste.

As he grabbed a condom from the top drawer of the nightstand and put it on, she became hotter and hotter for him.

Cock jutting, he grabbed hold of her and drew her toward him, making her gasp.

He knelt and wrapped his arms around her thighs to bring her closer to his face. "Only fair," he said, teasing her clit, then swirled the throbbing bundle of nerves with his tongue.

"Sir!" She arched her back.

"You're slick for me, Chelsea," he said approvingly. "Inviting."

Desperate. "It's because you're so sexy, Sir."

"My rules still apply. No coming without permission."

"Oh, Sir! I'm not sure I can wait."

"Soon. But not yet." He played with the base of the plug, tapping on it and pulling it out a little before releasing it.

He inserted a finger inside her, then a second as he continued to eat her out. She grabbed hold of the sheet, digging in her fingers as she fought to be a good sub.

When she was thrashing her head back and forth, he finally stopped and stood.

"Sir, fuck me."

"Scoot back."

He helped her toward the middle of the bed, before moving between her legs to press the tip of his cock to her entrance.

Even that much stretched her, and she clenched his forearms.

As he stroked in and out, the plug filled her insides, making the fit impossibly tight. "This is too much, Sir."

"Try for me," he said as he went in deeper.

Never having experienced anything this maddening, she whimpered his name.

"Wrap your legs around my waist."

Which would give him more power and leverage.

"Do it, girl." He pulled back slightly so she could lift her hips.

With his support, she was able to do as he asked. Then, when she was helplessly spread, he surged into her, burying his cock all the way.

She screamed against the intrusion.

"Chelsea?"

"I'm…" The room swam. Were there words? "So tight, Sir."

"Would you like me to stop?"

The fit was impossible, incredible. Looking at him, she admitted her darkest desires. "No. I'd like you to fuck me."

"Put your hands above your head as I instructed earlier."

"Sorry, Sir." When she'd put them where they were supposed to be, he pinned her to the mattress, his grip firm and seductive.

"That's it."

"Do me, Sir."

"My pleasure, girl."

This moment, with him poised over her, staring into her eyes, was everything she'd wanted.

He slid into her again, and she was overwhelmed by the depths he went to.

"Oh yeah," he said on a groan. Then he pulled out an inch or two before reentering her.

She was swimming in sensation. "I want more." When he waited, she added a soft plea.

Face contorted with dark desire, he fucked her, slowly at first, then building the response in her. She thrashed her head as he stroked her insides with his power. "*Yes.*"

Harder, and harder, he rode her. "You are tight. Such a hot little submissive. *Fuck.*"

Pure feminine pleasure bloomed, heating her with a feverish intensity. Master Alexander was so restrained, and clearly the sex was affecting him, too.

"You may come." The words emerged on a guttural groan. "Anytime."

This. She needed it so badly.

Closing her eyes, she gave herself over to his unholy domination.

He pistoned his hips, making her delirious.

"Sir… Master Alexander…" She didn't know what she was asking. The only thing she knew was that she couldn't survive much more.

Finally, a climax overtook her, but not in a way it ever had before. This started in her soul and unfurled itself in sustained waves of pleasure.

The orgasm approaching, she squeezed his cock, and he moaned.

"So damn hot," he growled, lifting his body. "Look at me."

She did, and he captured gaze, refusing to let it go.

"I want to see you come." He jerked his hips, creating shallow motions in her.

How did he know so much more about her than she recognized herself.

"Scream for me." He pressed a thumbpad to her clit, rocketing her to the heights of delirium.

And then, overwhelmed, she did scream.

"Yeah."

Once the waves receded, he forced a second orgasm from her. Where fantasy ended and reality began, she had no idea.

"Chelsea…"

Her breaths were shallow and ragged. She wasn't sure how much more she could take. "Come in me, Sir."

His eyebrows furrowed, he gritted his teeth as he relentlessly pounded her.

He was unbelievably hard inside her, stretching her even farther. "Sir!"

"Fuck!" Shuddering, he froze, and his pulse throbbed as he ejaculated.

Master Alexander possessed her body, and maybe a part of her heart.

Then he collapsed on her, making it impossible for her to draw a full breath. But she didn't protest. This was a completion she'd sought her entire life.

Overcome, she wrestled her arms from his grip and threaded the fingers of one hand into his hair. She ran her other hand down his back.

Under his tutelage, she was evolving. She had never been the nurturing type, but he brought out an ultrafeminine side of her.

After a few moments, he shifted their positions so that she was on her side, and he was behind her, his arm across her as he held her against his chest.

"Don't fight me."

"As if I could, Sir." Surprising herself, she wasn't even tempted, which might lead to future heartache that she couldn't afford.

He placed a hand right above her pelvic bone and inched her backward so that her rear was curved against him. She was aware of the plug still, and his half-hard cock.

She might have drifted off to sleep, because her body was cool when he released her and moved from the bed.

"I'll be right back."

When he returned, he pressed a warm cloth between her legs.

"Mmm. I like that, Sir. Thank you."

"If you're sore, I can't fuck you again."

"So you're doing this for selfish reasons?"

"Of course."

"I see." Chelsea knew better. He didn't have to fetch a towel at all, and he could have handed it to her.

His courtesy was delicious, and she saw how a Dominant might appreciate being taken care of, also.

"I can take out the plug here, or I can do it in the bathroom."

Nothing like reality to shatter her inner peace. "I could do it myself."

"You could," he said agreeably. "But I'm going to. Decide where you'd like it done, or I'll make the choice for you."

This might be the worst thing he'd forced her to face.

"It's no different from me fucking you with it."

"I know." She shook her head. "It just seems more personal than what we did earlier, Sir."

"Let go of your need to control this."

She curled into a tighter ball.

"Now the choice is mine." He scooped her from the bed.

Gasping, she wrapped her arm around her neck so he wouldn't drop her. "Sir!"

He strode into the en suite bathroom and continued to hold her for far longer than necessary.

Tension grew, and she stopped breathing, wondering if he might kiss her.

But he didn't.

Instead, he cleared his throat, severing the insanity of the moment.

"Get on all fours, forehead on the floor," he said, sliding her down his body and holding her waist until she found her balance. "You may use the rug."

She frantically glanced at one of the shower benches. "How about that?" She pointed. And they could turn the water on.

"I'll take away the option of the rug if you prevaricate any further."

"This is miserable."

"You'll survive."

So much for sympathy.

He kicked the rug aside. When would she learn not to test him?

"The floor, now. Or I'll fuck you with it again before taking it out."

Waging war with her own hesitation, she followed his command.

"Reach back and spread your ass cheeks."

For long minutes, maybe three or four, he left her there, obviously reinforcing his order.

Her knees grew tired, and her muscles ached.

"Ask me to take it out."

This would have been over a long time ago if she'd behaved. Afraid of him dreaming up something even more diabolical, she quickly asked, "Please, Sir, will you remove the plug from my ass?"

"Since you asked so nicely, I'd be happy to."

She stiffened her fingers as he pulled out the metal piece.

It landed in the sink with a clatter.

"That wasn't so bad, was it?" he asked.

Her ass burned for a moment, then the pain faded instantly. Where the plug had felt invasive, she now felt vaguely empty.

"Your tiny hole is nicely stretched. I'm looking forward to the opportunity to fuck you up there. Please stand."

She did and she met his gaze.

"You've done well this evening."

"Thank you, Sir."

"You're more than welcome to stay this evening. I'd welcome it."

After everything she'd experienced, she needed some alone time to process the events and her reactions. "I'm planning to leave, Sir."

"How about we shower first?" He reached inside to turn on the faucet.

Another first.

Once he'd checked the water temperature, he extended a hand in invitation.

As she stood under the spray, tension drained from her body.

Moments later, after cleaning the plug and washing his hands, he joined her, and she stepped to one side, even though there was more than enough room for both of them.

He pumped a generous amount of soap into his cupped palm. "Enjoy this." He washed her breasts, her abdomen, her belly, even her legs.

"I thought I was supposed to do this for you, Sir."

"At times," he agreed. "But caring for a sub's needs is part of being a good Dominant, especially after a day like today."

She could get accustomed to being pampered like this.

"Turn around."

Her considerate Dom soaped her shoulder blades and her back before moving lower, between her buttocks, making her tense. "Sir, this is really personal."

"Yes, pet. It is."

Apparently unconcerned by her protests, he continued, washing, then taking down one of the showerheads to rinse her completely. "You'll get the hang of submission eventually."

Will I?

As he continued his ministrations, she was tempted to accept his invitation and stay the night, curled up next to him in bed. But she knew herself too well. If she gave in, she might begin to care for him. He'd reminded her numerous times that he was her trainer, and when she returned to him, she'd vowed to keep their relationship professional.

Boundaries, as he'd noted, were important.

He used the warm spray to clean her pussy, and when he was satisfied, he allowed her to step out while he finished his shower.

As she dried off, she watched him, admiring the hard, masculine angles of his body.

Chelsea was glad she'd gone to the Den, and thrilled he'd agreed to be her two-week Dom. In this moment, she might be the luckiest submissive on the planet.

"Uhm, Sir, I think I'll go downstairs, if that's okay?" What was the protocol at the end of an evening like this?

"I'll be right behind you."

By the time he'd joined her, she was dressed.

He was wearing loose-fitting athletic pants and a fresh T-shirt. No matter what he chose, he was breathtakingly hot.

"There's a party a week from Saturday night at the Den," he said as she picked up her purse. "I understand Evan C will be in attendance."

Excitement and anticipation thrummed through her at his words. She'd sent the confounded rocker several emails and even an unsolicited proposal for his career PR. She'd received nothing back except an automatic response saying that he appreciated her writing to him and, due to the large volume of correspondence he received, he regretted he was unable to send a personal reply. Which was exactly why he needed to hire her. He didn't realize how many more sales he could generate if he had a strategic social media plan and a way to capture names of his superfans and bring them into an established, exciting community.

Seeing him at the Den was the opportunity she'd been working toward. She might not be the world's most fabulous submissive yet, but she had made significant improvements since she'd seen him last.

And she still had some time left with Master Alexander to perfect her skills.

"Would you like to go?" he asked.

Her heart quickened. "Are you offering to take me, Sir?"

"If you'd like a companion. Otherwise, you can go alone. I'm sure Master Damien will add you to the party list. It's a chance for you to show what you've learned. It's your call. But if you'd like, I'd be honored to accompany you. What do you say?"

Chapter Nine

Alex folded his arms and looked down at the naked Chelsea. For the sixth day in a row, she was at his home.

As always, she'd let herself in, followed his instructions, and waited, kneeling next to the fireplace.

Every time she visited, her behavior was more and more perfect. She'd told him she'd joined some online communities where she was getting feedback from other submissives, and her dedication showed.

Once in a while, she still set her chin in a stubborn line, but those occasions were becoming rarer. Though he occasionally fastened her into a posture collar, there was no longer as much need. She'd become comfortable in it, and her own body.

As much as her efforts to become a better sub pleased him, they also annoyed the hell out of him.

Everything she did was for Evan C's benefit. In the community, he was recognized as an asshole of magnificent proportions, his confidence only eclipsed by his arrogance.

The man didn't deserve someone as wonderful as Chelsea. Unfortunately, she was blinded by both ambition and infatuation.

Each passing moment meant he was closer to losing her forever.

That shouldn't matter. But it fucking did.

This evening, she was naked, except for a pair of stockings and heels she referred to as 'stupid high.' In his opinion, that meant they were *almost* tall enough.

Finally, he moved to stand in front of her and spoke. "Present your breasts, sub."

"Yes, Sir." With no hesitation, still looking at the floor, she lifted her breasts and drew them together.

If he had a sub, he'd want her to be just like Chelsea. Honest, determined. Caring. "Ask me to clamp your nipples." This was the first time he'd asked that of her, and he wondered how she would respond.

"Please, Sir, clamp my nipples as hard as you want."

Her response was even better than he'd expected. *Well done.*

Bending, he pinched the rosy tips, making her wince. When he tugged hard, she moaned but didn't protest.

"Thank you, Sir," she said when he released her and she could draw a full breath.

"These are Japanese clovers," he told her, reaching for the set on the mantel. A sturdy chain ran between the silver metal clamps, and he draped it over his index finger.

Crouching in front of her, he dangled them in front of her face so they filled her vision. "I've selected a fairly vicious pair."

Her spine stiffened.

"If you learn with these, others will be very easy to tolerate."

"Anything you say, Sir."

So perfect. "Ready?"

"If you think I am."

He squeezed her left nipple hard, then closed a clamp over it.

"*Jesus*, Sir!"

"I take it that hurts."

"Holy shit." Gasping, she glared.

"If it's unbearable, use your safe word." He stroked her cheek, and she turned her head, seeking comfort in an instinctive, submissive move. "There's no heroics in toughing out something you can't manage. A safe word isn't shameful — it's a powerful tool, and you've already shown you don't use it every day."

Slowly she nodded.

"No true Dominant expects you to go through something physically or emotionally hurtful to you." He paused. "Understand?"

"Thank you, Sir. Yes."

"But if you're being stubborn, you need to figure out how to change your attitude and compartmentalize the pain."

She breathed in. Despite her obvious discomfort and the obvious fact that she didn't like this, Chelsea continued to hold her breasts for his torture. She was not just learning the art of submission, she was excelling at it. "Good girl."

At his words, she exhaled a shaky breath.

More than any other woman he'd been with, she responded the most favorably to his approval. A few simple words from him worked magic.

How different she was from Liz. Chelsea did get off on spankings, but she didn't obsess about them, which made it a pleasure to give them to her. "In preparation for the second, pinch your other nipple."

"Sir is an absolute..." She trailed off.

"Good thing you didn't finish that sentence," he said into the silence, suppressing a grin. "Though you've given me reason enough to correct you, and I'll enjoy doing so."

She stuck out her lower lip.

At her antics, he actually laughed. "And you'll receive extra for that feeble attempt to manipulate me."

"I..." She sighed. "I apologize."

"Please don't. It's been some time since you felt my wrath. I'm looking forward to unleashing it. Now do as you were told." He looked at her and waited for her reaction. Though she blinked several times, she said nothing, so he gave the chain a fast yank.

She screamed.

"I'll repeat myself one last time. Pinch your nipple. Hold it for five seconds."

Once she'd complied, he released the clamp. Even though her breaths were ragged, she continued to cup her breasts. "At times, you really are a well-behaved submissive."

"Thank you, Sir."

"You may let go of your breasts."

She remembered to express her gratitude again.

"The reason these are my favorites is that when you tug on them, they tighten, rather than coming off." To show her what he meant, he stood and then gathered the chain. "Stand." He exerted pressure on her nipples as she climbed to her feet in a shaky move. He did love the sight of her in stilettos. Once she'd found her footing, he tugged again, urging her onto her tiptoes. "I should have clamped you a long time ago. It works great as a leash."

"Sir! *Fuck!*"

"Over here." He led her toward the couch.

She had no choice but to follow, but she didn't question him.

"Kneel up." He released the chain, and the sudden change in tension made her wince again.

When she had settled into position, he said, "Remove my belt."

"Are you…?"

"Going to punish you? Yes."

Her lower lip trembled, but he knew this time it was from fear, rather than an attempt to sway him.

She unfastened his buckle, then slid the leather through the loops. "You're staying dressed, Sir?"

"You told me that it reinforces your subservience. So yes. I want you to be aware of your station."

"Of course." She doubled the leather over and held it.

"Offer it to me."

As she extended her hands, she looked downward.

"That was very nice. But if you're hoping to get me to go easier on you, it won't work." He accepted her offering.

Shuddering, she returned to the kneel up position. He took a seat. "Over my lap, girl." To hurry her along, he grabbed the chain.

"Yes, Sir."

"Was that hostility in your tone?"

"No, Sir."

She draped herself across his lap. He jostled her around slightly. "If you need to grab hold of my ankles for support, you may. But you may not try to evade what you have coming to you."

"I understand."

"I'm going to give you eight strokes."

"Thank you, Sir."

Such a delicious mixture of defiance and obedience. He rubbed her skin to get the blood flowing. If she were his, he would enjoy seeing marks that lasted, but no doubt she wanted to look good for Master Evan C. "How do your nipple clamps feel?"

"Fine, Sir."

"I could put weights on the chain if you need a bit more pressure."

"I think they're sufficiently evil as they are, Sir."

He grinned. She sounded so prim and proper. "Are you ready for your spanking, Chelsea?"

"Yes, Sir. And before you get started, I do promise to watch my mouth more in future."

"Good plan," he approved, swinging the belt hard, catching her across both butt cheeks at the same time.

She yelped, but she said, "Thank you, Sir."

After the second, she lifted her head slightly but thanked him again.

For her training, he'd been concentrating on the small details of submission—tone of voice, pretty motions, anal penetration, bondage, and posture. This was her first time with the belt, and she took it well.

He traced her spine—mainly because he enjoyed touching her—before he laid the leather to her again.

Though Chelsea arched in response to the bite of the pain, she didn't protest.

For the fourth stroke, he applied more pressure.

She sighed deeply, but otherwise, she remained quiet. In such a short time, she'd come a long way.

"Move forward a bit," he told her. "Palms flat on the floor. The backs of your thighs deserve some attention. Don't you agree?"

When she hesitated, he dropped his left knee a bit to tip her off-balance.

He finished the punishment, belting her several times in rapid succession.

She hadn't protested even once, and when he tossed the strap aside, she said, "That was hot, Sir. Thank you."

Vixen. "It was meant as punishment, not pleasure."

"It absolutely hurt," she said.

Was she trying to reassure him? His lips quirked. He'd intended to teach her a lesson, but if she'd liked it as well, he could live with that. "Present, lying down on the floor."

She moved quicker than he thought she might. Oh, yes, she was pleasing.

He bent to rub a finger up the inside of her pussy lips. With a frown, he asked, "Did you shave this morning?"

"Err…" She hesitated. "I had to work early this morning, and knowing I needed to have time for my paces, I took my bath last night and did my grooming then."

"Take a little more care next time."

Her thighs quivered. "Sorry, Sir."

He slapped her exposed pussy hard.

She cried out.

"That's a gentle reminder." One to drive his lesson home, rather than a turn-on.

"I won't be so remiss next time, Sir."

He believed her. He wouldn't be surprised if she started keeping a razor at the office. "How do those clamps feel now?"

"They're starting to burn, Sir."

"Shall I distract you?"

"Please."

He stroked the place between her legs where he'd just spanked her, and she shifted beneath his hand, arching toward him with a soft mewl of pleasure.

"Oh my…"

"Yes?"

"Sir, that's…"

"Go on."

"The pain in my nipples is making me more aroused than I could imagine."

"Not so bad now, Chelsea?"

"It's exquisite, Sir. With my ass throbbing, too, it's… Oh, God. I can't believe this. I want to come!"

With each moment, she became slicker. Shamelessly, she pushed her pelvis against his hand, seeking fulfillment. "Should I let you get off?" She'd been punished, and she'd deserved it, but the musky, heady scent of feminine arousal filled his senses. The bigger question was, could he possibly deny her anything?

"Please, Sir. Please," she begged. "Will you please give me an orgasm, even if I haven't earned it?"

The idea of her pussy weeping with desperation, and her suffering in the anguish of denial fucking fed him, and he moved his hand away. "That's enough for now."

Digging her feet into the floor, she tried to lift her body higher, seeking completion. "But—"

"I said enough."

His trainee whimpered, pitiful in her misery.

"But I'll give you the pleasure of sucking my dick as a way to thank me for putting up with such an ill-mannered trainee."

She didn't respond, and he didn't expect her to.

Alex helped her from the floor, and she slowly stood and pulled her shoulders back. Then he stood to unfasten his trousers and lower the zipper. The material fell around his ankles.

"I never get tired of seeing your dick, Sir."

"Flattery is useless." Which was a lie. He liked her genuine approval.

"So thick and gorgeous." She lowered herself to her knees. "May I touch you?"

When he gave his assent, she stroked his cock, making it even harder.

Spanking her, holding her, hearing her moans, had made him greedy for her.

Through her long eyelashes, she looked up at him, and he'd swear it was one of the most seductive things he'd ever seen. Then she cradled his balls and ran her thumb over the slit in his cock to transfer the first drop of pre-ejaculate onto her tongue, making a show of sucking her thumb.

Wouldn't take much more of that to make him come.

Determined to remain in charge, he captured the chain that ran between her nipples. "Let's make this more interesting, shall we?" He looped the chain of her clamps over his cock.

"Oh God. That's outrageous, Sir."

"Now pleasure me, and don't touch yourself."

Chelsea set to work giving him head, keeping her mouth open wide to take as much of him as his thrusts demanded. She sucked him, licking his cockhead. He dug his hands into the short waves of her hair, cradling her head, holding her prisoner.

He rocked his hips until he found the rhythm he wanted, then he tightened his grip so he could go in deeper. "You're doing well."

She made slight gagging sounds, something she'd need to work on correcting, but she continued to service him. Of course, with the way he was holding her and the way the chain dragged on her nipples, she had little choice.

"When I come, you'll swallow every drop."

She nodded as much as possible and made a sound that he took for agreement.

Gritting his teeth, he tipped back his head and closed his eyes, loving the feeling of having his dick down her throat. Absently, he wondered why he'd been so adamant about not playing with subs. Being with a woman who was so desperate to please was the stuff of dreams.

Her enthusiasm increased as his cock thickened. Need boiled from deep in his balls. "Every drop," he repeated before he could no longer speak.

He groaned as hot ribbons of release pulsed into her mouth.

Dutifully, she worked to take his load, swallowing, licking.

He immobilized her head until she sucked him dry.

When she was done, she exhaled a deep, shaky breath. Her attempt to kneel back was prevented by the chain.

"I may do that to you every time you give me head."

"It was something, Sir." As she met his gaze, she licked the remnants of his climax from her lips. "I like sucking your dick, Sir," she said. "Thank you."

"You did well. And your manners are appreciated." He studied her. "How wet is your pussy?"

"Not very," she admitted.

"You're no longer on the verge of coming?"

She shook her head, then stilled as the chain moved.

As his cock became semierect, he dropped her chain, causing her to wince.

"You may get dressed."

"Sir?" She blinked, looking up at him.

"That's enough for tonight."

"But..." A tiny frown formed between her eyebrows. "The clamps?"

"I'll change them out for something not as painful."

"You never do what I expect."

"I lay awake at night dreaming up ways to torment you."

She flashed him a half-smile. "I actually believe that."

"You know you don't have to leave." He brushed back a lock of hair from her forehead. That she never stayed or accepted much aftercare bothered him.

"Thanks for the invitation. Tomorrow's another long day. I'm working on a proposal for a reluctant client, and I'm putting a lot of work into it."

"Are you?"

"I need to get You're The Star to the next level."

How well he understood her drive and dedication. "Come with me." He walked back to the fireplace. "Remain standing while I do this. Hands behind your neck."

When she was in position, he released her right nipple.

"Fuck." Her knees buckled. "Holy... Fuck, fuck, *fuck*."

Instantly he sucked the tip, laving it with tongue, taking away the hurt.

"I've never..." She blinked rapidly. "That was something."

"Ready for the next one?" Without waiting for an answer, he removed the left one and once again laved away the hurt while she grabbed hold of him for support. Even though she'd sucked him off less than half an hour ago, his cock responded to the sound of her distress.

"Is the world spinning backward? It is, isn't it?"

"Hated it?"

"No." After a moment, she added, "That pain was shocking, but short-lived."

He reached onto the mantel for a pair of his lightest clamps — tweezers, with tiny jewels on the end. "Because you're tender, you may feel these more than you ordinarily would." At least that was his hope.

After adjusting them both to the correct pressure, he studied them. Very different from the others, more decorative than anything.

"Is this what submission with you is like?"

"How's that?"

"Always something new. A full-time thing? We talked about that the first night, how each relationship is different. Or is this just part of your training process?"

"I'm a Dominant," he said simply. "It's not part of who I am, it *is* who I am. I don't turn it off and on."

"I see."

"That's something for you to consider if you stay in the community." He added the if because he preferred not to think of her on her knees, mascara wrecked, sucking any man's dick but his.

Disturbed by his thoughts, he pulled up his pants, zipping and buttoning them as she made her way to the doorway to wiggle into her panties and skirt.

Then he walked to the entrance and folded his arms as she shrugged into her blouse.

Her movements were slight in deference to the clamps, and she left off her bra entirely.

"Call me when you get home for permission to remove the clamps."

"Yes, Sir."

She gathered her belongings, removed her keys from inside her purse, then stuffed her bra in the bottom.

"I'll walk you to your car."

Outside, he followed her, loving the way the shoes made her hips gently move from side to side... He'd be a fool not to have her wear them regularly.

He held the door while she slipped inside the compartment. Being sure no one could see them, he reached inside her shirt to give the chain one last tug.

Around a gasp, she asked, "Do you show any mercy?"

"Would you like to sleep in them?" The threat was empty. He'd never demand that.

"Thank you for your generosity in letting me remove them when I get home, Sir."

"I'm happy to give you a bare-assed spanking right here in front of the neighbors. Mr. Jones across the street will enjoy the view."

She gasped. "You wouldn't!"

"I'll have you over that hood with your skirt around your waist and your panties pulled down so fast you won't remember your name."

Sinking deeper into her seat, she regarded him. "I actually think you might."

"I most certainly would." To reinforce his point, he raised an eyebrow. "Drive safe." With that, he sealed her inside the vehicle.

She accelerated away. Even though she looked in the rearview mirror a couple of times, she didn't wave. Then she turned the corner and vanished.

Alex realized why he didn't play with subs more often. He had discerning tastes. He wanted someone like Chelsea.

Like Chelsea?

Fuck that.

He wanted *her.*

Less than half an hour later, while he was sitting behind the desk in his study, a half-finished whiskey nearby, she called him.

"I'm home, Sir. Thank you for an instructive evening."

She truly was learning the art of submission. Words that had once been forced now flowed naturally. "How do your nipples feel?"

"Sore. Distracting me because they cause constant arousal."

"Picturing you in them does the same to me."

"Does it?"

"The next time you're here, be wearing them and see for yourself."

"I'll do that, Sir."

"Put your phone on speaker while you remove your shirt." Rustling in the background indicated she was following his directions.

"Whew. Every little motion hurts, Sir."

"Good. Good. You'll remember this experience."

"Honestly, Sir? There's not a single moment with you that I'll ever forget."

He clenched his hand. "Remove the right clamp."

"I'm doing that now, Sir." Then she gasped. "Damn it! This is as bad as earlier."

This time, he wasn't there to take away the ache. "Now the other one."

"Damn. I wish there was a way to get this off without it hurting."

"That would defeat my purpose."

"You want me to suffer," she said.

"Oh, yes, my sweet pet." *For me.* "Quit stalling."

She whimpered.

Silence crackled, followed by her loud hiss.

Incessantly, his cock pressed against his pants, demanding a second release.

"Damn. That's just... I'm not sure I have words."

"Too bad I didn't put one on your clit."

Her response was instant. "Thank you for your kindness."

"Your manners are not always on point, girl."

"I'll be honest, Sir. It's hard to remember when I hurt so bad. It's as if I experience life through a haze."

"When you're instructed to do something, you may want to think it all the way through. Break it down in your mind before starting. For example, tell yourself you'll remove the clamp and immediately express your gratitude. Think how much your Dom wants to hear those words. There are many things he or she could be doing other than listening to your complaints."

"You're right, Sir. I beg your pardon."

"You're going to be tempted to masturbate tonight," he said. "Your breasts and nipples will be sensitive, and with the way I played with your lovely pussy earlier, you'll want to come. But I forbid it."

He remained silent until she miserably answered, "I understand, Sir."

"As a reminder, when you arrive tomorrow, I want you wearing the clamps." He pictured her gritting her teeth to hold back a disrespectful response. He was pushing her limits now, and he knew it.

"Anything else, Sir?"

"That will be all, Chelsea."

"I was wondering…"

"Go on."

"If it's not too much to ask, can we spend some extra time together tomorrow?"

The day before their outing to the Den.

"I know you're busy, but I was hoping you could maybe tie me to the Saint Andrew's cross and, well, you know, use some different implements on me. More than what I've already experienced."

"You know what you're asking?"

"Master Evan C likes to tie up his subs and whip them."

Alex nodded. She was right about that. If she wanted a taste, he'd happily give it to her. "Does mid-afternoon work for you? I'd like to take you out to dinner to give you a little more exposure to being in public."

"I'll rearrange my schedule. Three o'clock all right with you, Sir?"

"It is."

"I appreciate you accommodating me."

It was no hardship. "Before you go to bed, look at your rear in the mirror. If there are any red marks, put arnica on them. Oh, and there is one more thing for tonight. Sleep in the nude." He didn't give her time to respond before ending the conversation.

After dropping his phone on the desk, he picked up his glass.

He wished it wasn't Evan C that had prompted her to ask for new experiences.

The prick didn't realize how fortunate he was.

Honoring her request for tomorrow's session, he headed back upstairs to prepare the play room. He moved the Saint Andrew's cross into the middle of the floor, placed the chair nearby, then he opened his storage unit to select two floggers. The first would warm her nicely. The second would satisfy her desire to experience something like she could expect from Evan C.

Alex looked forward to using both.

Even though he'd forbidden Chelsea to touch herself, he climbed beneath the hot shower spray and jacked off to the image of her on her knees, the clamp's chain hooked over his thick cock as she sucked him deep into her mouth.

As he came, he tipped back his head, consumed by one blazing realization.

Chelsea was his.

And he intended to have her.

Chapter Ten

"What is this?" Scowling, Alex glanced at Gavin.

"Have a look yourself." His younger brother hedged with a shrug. "Worth considering."

Alex picked up the glossy blue presentation folder from the middle of the conference room table.

As typical, on Friday after lunch, they met with some of their managers to discuss what had happened in the days prior. The team also strategized about where they were going and set expectations for the upcoming weeks. Mostly the time together ensured he had no blind spots so that nothing slipped through the cracks, like it had in the past. The company — and their clients — deserved it, even though it was a big-time commitment.

He snapped his back teeth together when he saw the front of the glossy packet was embossed with their logo…and that of You're The Star. Chelsea's company.

Persistent didn't begin to cover the extent of her determination.

Despite himself, he flipped open the cover.

Inside were numerous full-color documents, all containing various ideas for PR events. Naturally, handled by her — for a nice fee.

What was surprising, but shouldn't have been, was the amount of detail she'd included. Timelines, possible venues, suggestions for catering, charities to consider helping, resources required, commitments needed from him, Gavin, and the team. She'd done her research well, with no feedback from him. "Where the hell did you get this?" He studied his brother.

"Arrived by courier yesterday afternoon, addressed to the office manager. She gave it to me since you were working from home."

So Chelsea had paid the expense to have it hand delivered. Impressive. "You know who put this together, don't you?"

"Yeah. Your trainee."

Alex flipped the proposal closed and tapped his finger with finality, then slid the packet back to the middle of the table. "That would mean mixing business with pleasure." He dropped into his chair at the head of the table. "It's a bad combination, and you know it."

"Is it? I think you're letting your relationship — or whatever the hell you two have — cloud your judgment. She's right that we could use the positive PR. We've had a couple of conversations about our current company. That's been on the agenda more than once. They collect payment every month, but what do we get in return?" Gavin allowed his question to hang in the air.

After picking up his water bottle, Gavin added, "When's the last time you saw anything this comprehensive?"

"Firms do anything to win business." Which they knew all too well. "Retaining it is another matter."

"It's time to consider making changes. The company we're using is great at crisis management. That's their specialty, and they've earned their money. But we need to keep our name out there, and doing things that give us a good name is crucial. We need to terminate our contract with them and move on."

Though he agreed in principle, he couldn't work with Chelsea. "This isn't the right option."

"One of the reasons we have meetings is to look at places where we need to be more thoughtful." Gavin twisted the lid on his drink, then leveled a hard look at Alex. "You're not being objective."

Fuck that. Even if it was true. "And you're proposing a risk that we shouldn't take."

The first of their management team arrived, then, as if sensing the tension between the brothers, headed straight for the cookies and power drinks.

"Consider it," Gavin suggested.

Alex didn't respond.

An hour and a half later, working on projections in his home office, the unresolved conversation still rankled.

At two minutes before three o'clock, a car engine shut off.

Alex glanced up from his computer screen and turned to look out the window of his study. Unsurprisingly, Chelsea was right on time.

Beautiful and sassy, with sunshine playing off the highlights in her hair, she emerged from her vehicle. After grabbing her purse, she closed the door, then, at the bottom of the driveway, she paused to smooth the front of her skirt and square her shoulders.

As always, she took his breath away. Pleasing him, she'd worn heels. Maybe because he'd told her he intended to take her to dinner. Or perhaps she'd had an important day at work. It couldn't be because she knew how much they appealed to him.

Fuck it.

If he were a smarter man, he'd have stopped training her before now.

Instead, he was becoming addicted to her.

Relinquishing her to another was going to be one of the most difficult things he'd ever done.

Turning away from the window, Alex rubbed the back of his neck.

Why the hell hadn't he stayed true to his vow not to train submissives — especially ones he was attracted to?

Maybe twenty seconds later, she knocked on his front door. Even though he'd said it wasn't necessary, she did so, regardless.

Slight sounds floated toward him as she entered, then a soft *snick* informed him she'd closed and locked the front door behind her.

The staccato beat of her heels on hardwood followed. Presumably she was making her way into the living room. Then there was silence.

More so than usual, he'd looked forward to her arrival.

He enjoyed her company, and he liked knowing she was preparing for him, stripping off her clothes and folding them in a perfect pile.

Not liking the way he hungered for her — as if he were her Dom instead of a trainer — he fought back his gnawing impulse to hurry to her and instead, he took his time closing his files and tidying his desk.

But that didn't vanquish thoughts of her.

Damn, he loved compelling her surrender, forcing her to give up the control she liked to exert. And the way she responded to him in bed... A transformation came over her when she ceased her struggle. In bed, she was unrestrained. He'd never been with a woman so responsive and so vocal about it.

Each time he'd inserted a plug up her tight ass, she'd protested, but when he fucked her with it in, she screamed out her pleasure. When they had sex, her hot pussy enveloped his cock, and more than once over the last few days, she'd squeezed him so hard, she'd made him ejaculate sooner than he planned. His little pet wasn't the only one drowning in physical need.

But it was more than that. Chelsea was passionate — relentless — in all her pursuits. She'd sent numerous emails reinforcing her suggestion that Monahan Capital host a charity function. Of course, she'd recommended her firm handle the event. Each solicitation contained a new suggestion or reason, so he knew she was always thinking about his business. She was nothing if not persistent. Taking no for an answer didn't seem to be in her vocabulary, which pretty well meant he and Evan C were both done for.

Satisfied that he'd kept her waiting long enough, he pushed back from his desk.

Downstairs, he found her in the kneeling up position, with the dainty tweezer clamps biting into her nipples. "You're doing well," he told her.

After tomorrow, there wouldn't be any reason to continue her training. She was comfortable with anal, her movements were pleasing, and for the most part, she followed direction without argument. Though they hadn't spent a lot of time on service aspects, she didn't seem to object like she had in the beginning. And...she sucked cock like a goddess. "Afternoon, sub." He stopped behind her. "Have you climaxed since you left here last night?"

Though her breathing became more noticeable, she didn't turn. "You forbade it, Sir."

Clever. "Answer the question, Chelsea."

"That was my answer," she asserted.

He walked around to stand in front of the fireplace so he could look at her. And maybe he shouldn't have. Her pouty lips were painted a sensual red, so damn sexy it was like waving a flag in front of a bull.

"I do not go behind your back, Sir, no matter how tempted I am. I wanted to please you. So, no. I did not come."

Her answer delighted him, ridiculously so. He ached to grab her shoulders, yank her to her feet, devour her with a kiss, then fuck her until she acknowledged she belonged to him.

Where the fuck did that idea come from? Was he losing what little remained of his restraint? "Crawl upstairs to the play room." His voice was gruffer than it needed to be, because once more, he needed to remind himself she wasn't his — would never be his.

With elegance that proved she'd continued to hone her skills even when they were apart, Chelsea lowered herself to all fours. She managed to navigate each step without protest.

When they reached the landing, she continued.

"Very nice," he said as he followed her down the hallway.

"Thank you, Sir."

She didn't ask him to remove the clamps, and with the way her body swayed, she had to be a little uncomfortable.

In the play room, she paused.

"Keep going. I want you on the cross, facing away from me."

When she reached the sturdy base, she stood and spread her arms and legs wide, into the shape of an X.

Focusing on her as a trainee and not the woman he wanted, Alex secured her limbs then captured her chin. "How are the clamps?"

"Bearable, Sir. They're better than the clovers."

"Would you like me to remove them?"

Her answer was quick and honest. "If it pleases you, Sir."

Those words... Could she be any more perfect? "If I were giving you an erotic flogging, I might request you leave them on as they would heighten your arousal in the event I let you come. For now, I'm all right with you concentrating on the flogging. So I will leave the choice to you."

"In that case, Sir, I'd appreciate it if you got rid of the little beasts."

"Chelsea, Chelsea, Chelsea." He grinned.

"Sir is awesome. Amazingly generous." Radiantly, she smiled at him.

He doubted she meant to be manipulative, but he liked the sight of her smile so much he'd allow her to get away with almost anything.

Refocusing, he captured her right breast in his palm and squeezed the flesh before releasing the clamp.

She sucked in a shallow breath. This time, he didn't soothe the hurt.

Her body trembled, and when he released her, she sighed. "Thank you, Sir."

"Ready for the next one?"

"Please."

He squeezed her other breast and plucked the clamp from the tip. Then he gave in to temptation, licking and teasing the nipple until her breathing returned to normal.

"Sir, I know you don't want me getting aroused, but…uhm, I am."

Studying her, wide-eyed, pouty lips slightly parted, he slid two fingers between her legs. "You *are* damp."

"I…" She moved her hips toward him, as much as her rigid restraints would allow.

He continued to rub her, back and forth, across her clit.

"Sir, may I come?" She strained against her bonds.

"Having your nipples clamped made you this wet?"

"Oh, Sir. Yes. No."

He slid a finger inside her, pulled out again.

"Yes, it was from the clamps. But it was also because of last night's spanking with your belt. And the way you smacked my pussy. I hardly slept last night because I wanted to have sex with you. I woke up thinking about you."

Alex hadn't just thought of her — he'd been obsessed with her.

"The truth is, it's you, Sir. You turn me on. Everything about you, about this…" As she struggled, digging her toes into the floor, her eyes filled with tears. "I'm begging you. Please, please stop. If you keep doing that, I'm going to be helpless."

"In other words, you don't want to earn a punishment?"

"That's not it." Frantically, she shook her head. "I don't want to displease you."

To him, there were no sweeter words. "Come for me, Chelsea." *For me.* Hand-fucking her, he bent his head to suck on the nipple he'd previously ignored.

Everything about her filled his senses, and he drank her in as she writhed and screamed.

He inserted a third finger, spreading her wide, teasing her nipple with his tongue, and pressing his thumb against her clit.

"Oh God…" She thrashed around helplessly, crying his name.

"Give it to me."

Finally, her pussy constricted, and she shattered.

He released her nipple but kept his hand in place while he placed a gentle kiss on the side of her neck. "I love the way you come for me. Shameless little pet."

As he removed his hand, she sobbed words of gratitude.

"You deserved it, and your responses are so delightful."

After drawing several breaths, she lifted her head slightly. "I've never been like this with anyone else. It's…what you do to me. And I wanted to tell you how much I enjoyed sucking your cock last night. I don't know how to say this…"

"Take your time."

"You make me happy to be a woman, Sir. Thank you for this experience. You opened a whole new world for me, and I'll never be the same." She blinked furiously. "And I'll never forget you."

For a moment, he froze, unsure how to respond. With the singular exception of Liz, women had been interchangeable. But Chelsea's honest, raw expressions touched a place inside him that no other woman ever had.

Evan C is one lucky sonofabitch.

And Alex had a miserable, lonely future in front of him.

"Thank you for everything, Sir."

"Believe me when I say the pleasure is mine."

She swallowed deeply. "That means the world to me."

"Do you still want to continue with a flogging?"

"I do. Being on this structure is mind-blowing. I wasn't sure how I'd like it since I hated the posture collar. At first, I mean."

He nodded.

"But I think I'm finally starting to understand what you meant from the start. I am freer to explore my own reactions when I'm restrained. I can fight, but I can't get away. With the wrong person, it could be scary. With you it's not."

"There's still more," he said.

"I think I'm ready, Sir."

He left her for a moment and returned with one of the floggers he'd selected in advance. "You'll notice this one has fairly thick strands. It will make a thuddy kind of impact. As far as floggers go, it's considered quite innocuous. Do keep in mind, how it's wielded makes all the difference."

"You showed me that when you used the cane on me, Sir."

"Precisely. Where I land the spank, the force behind my wrist, where I stand, all of it factors into your corresponding pain." He shook out the leather.

She looked at it with an expression of curiosity rather than fear.

"If I wanted to flog you for half the night until you went into subspace, I'd choose this one." And maybe he should. He'd had no idea she would respond so favorably to pain. "After I've warmed up your skin, I'll switch to a different one." He exchanged the floggers and returned to her. "This is one of several I use for punishment, or for a very experienced sub who enjoys impact play. I want to be clear that you're neither being punished, nor do I consider you anything other than a novice." He flicked his wrist, and the sound was that of a distant waterfall. He'd forgotten how much he liked holding this type of whip. "I am introducing you to its feel. If you'll notice, the strands are thinner, so it results in a powerful sting. Are you willing to try it?"

She hadn't looked away from the leather strands.

Chelsea licked her upper lip before responding. "I think so, Sir."

"You can always use your safe word."

"In that case, can we get on with it, Sir?"

"You do like to tempt fate."

"The longer I think about it, the more my dread will pile up."

"In that case, perhaps I'll tease you a little longer."

She closed her eyes and sighed. "I should have known."

He circled her, trying to increase her tension.

"Uhm, Sir… Can I ask about something?"

As a way to cope with his intentional stress? "Yes, sub?"

"Did you get my proposal yesterday?"

Stunned, he stopped walking. *You want to talk about business?*

Before he could answer, she went on. "I was thinking the Den would be an excellent place to take some photos. You know, maybe we could go early and catch the sunset as a backdrop. The firepit is also a good option. And maybe a hat like you wore that first night. We can try some each way, different looks, capture something that would be good for your image. The idea is to make you look more relatable, rather than the boring, same old, same old corporate headshots."

Impressive spiel. "Did you rehearse that?"

Rather than responding, she breathlessly continued. "You could wear business casual like you are now, and then maybe, change into some leather pants. I mean, they'd be super sexy on you."

The hell? She'd presented her ideas and then ended on a compliment to hopefully disarm him. All while being naked, secured to the cross. He'd thought she'd stop at nothing to win at business. Turned out, he'd underestimated her.

"I will choose my attire, girl. And yours."

"That's awesome. Because I never know what to wear."

"As I've mentioned, and I'm final, Monahan Capital has its own PR firm. And I'm not running for political office. I don't need to look anything other than professional." In fact, he did that on purpose to rebuild trust and credibility.

"Seeing you as a whole person can only enhance your image."

Jesus. Did she ever stop? "Would you like to wear a dental dam?"

"Shutting up, Sir."

"Good choice. In that case, we'll get on with it." Bringing himself back to the present, he crossed the room and placed the flogger with the first.

Then, as he took each step back to her, he was enchanted by whatever spell she held over him. He shook his head, reminding himself to concentrate on the fact he was her trainer. For the last night ever.

When he reached her, he trailed his touch over her body. "Release some of the tension out of your muscles." He pressed his body against hers to uncurl her fists. The proximity hardened his cock, rocketing arousal through him.

Her breath caught. She felt his erection as surely as he did.

"Splaying your fingers will keep your muscles more supple."

"Oh, Sir," she said on a moan. "Do me?"

He couldn't. Not any longer.

Resolved, he moved away to select the gentler flogger.

"I know I have to deserve your cock, Sir. I'll do whatever I need to in order to earn the privilege."

Temptress. If she only knew how close he was to dropping his pants and fucking her hard...

He took a few moments to mentally center himself. No way could he flog her until he was more in control of his reactions.

At least a minute passed before he was comfortable taking a few practice swipes with the flogger.

She flinched even though he wasn't near her.

Finally satisfied, he returned to her. Her body looked so beautiful, so perfect, so ready to be reddened. He ran the handle down her spine, then between her buttocks. She stayed still like a well-behaved sub.

"Would you like to proceed?" A saner part of him preferred that she use her safe word.

"Yes, Sir."

"I'm going to use this all over your back and buttocks, even your shoulders. I'll warn you before I do anything more than that."

"Thank you, Sir."

He used light pressure as he allowed the leather tongues to caress her naked body. She moaned with each lick, and he smelled the sharp musk of her arousal. He'd advise any Dom who claimed her to do this to her regularly. "Ready for the next level?"

"Yes, Sir."

He changed his angle and took a step back so he could get a fuller swing.

"*Oh*! Wow, Sir," she said. She pulled as far away from the cross as possible in a silent offering.

Greedily, he accepted, flogging her bared body. Her skin turned a beautiful pink. Perspiration covered her. Her submission made her even more beautiful. "Are you doing okay, Chelsea?"

When she didn't answer, he repeated the question. She wasn't heading for subspace already, was she? He flicked his wrist with more pressure, and this time he elicited a moan from her.

"Please," she said.

"Please?"

"Continue, Sir."

He switched to the other flogger, and her first few moans exuded bliss. Then she fell silent. Her body went slack against the bonds. Beneath the steady rain of blows, the color of her skin changed from pink to light red, and her little sighs urged him on. Realizing she was mumbling, that she was flying in subspace, he tossed the flogger aside and knelt to release her ankles.

"You've pleased me immensely," he told her as he stroked her skin. "I'm going to take care of you."

"More, *please*."

"Another time." But that wouldn't happen, even if he wanted it as well.

After unfastening her wrists, he scooped her into his arms and carried her to his suite.

That she snuggled against him rather than protesting told him she wasn't in her usual frame of mind.

Somehow, he managed to pull back the duvet and place her on the mattress. He covered her and she burrowed into the pillow. "Please, Sir? Hold me?" She shivered a little.

How could he resist?

Alex bent to remove his boots, then kicked them to the side before crawling in next to her.

"Please fuck me," she said when he pulled her against him.

"Chelsea…"

She turned to face him and placed a palm against his cheek. "I want you inside me."

"You're not thinking straight. Give it a few minutes."

"I know this for a fact, Sir."

He snagged her wrist. She had no idea how goddamn difficult this was for him. "Chelsea, I'm warning you…"

She pulled her hand away and trailed it down his chest, then lower to squeeze his cock. Despite the fact he was still wearing jeans, he hardened beneath her determined touch. She tightened her grip and moved her hand up and down with a firm stroke. The vixen used her free hand to unbuckle his belt. By the time he stopped her, she'd loosened the waist and started to pull down the zipper.

"I know what I'm doing," she reasserted. "And I want your cock."

The primal need to own her driving him, he grabbed a condom from the nightstand. He pressed the packet into her palm and said, "Open it."

While she did, he stood to remove his clothes.

"Let me put it on for you?" she asked.

"I should make you use your mouth."

"If that's what Sir wishes."

With her red lipstick? His dick pulsed in response. *Fuck yes.*

He stood at the side of the bed, cock jutting out. Her touch wasn't skilled, and that made it all the more arousing. "Roll the condom," he coached. "Don't pull it."

"Oh." Her face flushed, and that delighted him.

She didn't manage to get it all the way down with her mouth, but he'd never forget the sight of her choking on his length, eyes watering as she valiantly fought to be a dutiful pet.

"Spread your legs, girl." Instead of holding her down, he took her in a single thrust. She was already slick with arousal. "You *were* ready."

"With you, I'm insatiable, Sir."

While he fucked her, he lifted his upper body so he could play with her clit.

Within seconds, without permission, she climaxed in a sensual gush that temporarily soothed his inner beast. She'd come. For him.

He dug his hands into her hair.

Because it would blur the lines, he had a rule not to kiss the women he trained. But the sight of her, her perfection, blasted away his determination. He held her and gently brushed his lips across hers.

Her eyes widened, and she looked at him. For a moment, it seemed she didn't breathe.

And then, needing to give more, receive more, he took her again, claiming her as if they were making love.

She responded to his demand like she did everything else. With passionate abandon. She met him thrust for thrust and she shocked him by capturing the tip of his tongue between her teeth for a moment before letting go and becoming the aggressor. This was a side of her he'd never experienced, and it aroused him.

"Incredible," she murmured after he ended the kiss. "That was..." She licked her upper lip. "Can I be on top, Sir?"

"Excuse me?"

"It must be the jeans. You gave me all these cowboy ideas, and I want to ride you."

He grinned and considered her question. There was no danger of her forgetting their respective roles, so he put his hand beneath her buttocks and reversed their positions. "Straddle me then, girl. And remember, you need permission before you climax. I might excuse you one time. Might. But never twice."

"After that kiss, Sir, that may not be possible."

He pinched her.

"I mean, yes, of course, Sir."

"That's what I thought you meant."

She rose onto her knees. She grasped his demanding cock, then she sank down on him. He gritted his teeth to prevent himself from coming too soon.

He held her to help guide her motions.

"Oh, yes," she said. "That's... I love the angle, Sir."

He so enjoyed the sight of her breasts jostling. She was a beautiful sight, and he visually feasted on her as he filled her tight warmth.

"I think I'm going to come. Sir, may I?"

He let go of her and captured her nipples. "Do it," he said, squeezing hard.

"Master Alexander!" She came, her internal muscles clamping down on him, hard.

Within a moment, he ejaculated. He pulled her tight against his chest as his balls drained. He held her for at least a minute as their breathing returned to normal.

She propped one elbow on the mattress near his head and she cradled his face between her palms in a tender move. "I like the way you fuck me, Sir. Thank you."

"We'll make a halfway decent sub out of you yet." *Another damn lie.* She was perfect right now. "You have ten minutes before we leave for dinner. Be ready, waiting near the door, dressed and kneeling."

She stayed where she was, as if she had all the time in the world.

"There are ways to punish you if you're not ready on time," he warned. "Ways you won't enjoy."

He clamped his hands on her waist, lifted her, then eased her to one side. "Go."

With a grin, she scampered toward the bathroom.

The red marks were already fading from her skin. It didn't appear he'd left any that would be visible at tomorrow night's party. That realization didn't please him.

He decided to shower in the guest bathroom, and when he headed downstairs to grab his keys, he found her exactly where she was supposed to be, kneeling up. "Well done."

"I am such a very good sub, Sir. Just pointing it out in case you forgot."

Humble, too. Even though she was right, he kept that to himself. "Stand up, lift your skirt, turn your back to me, then grab your ankles and ask me to slap you for being so saucy."

She stood with the grace he demanded, despite the heels. And she flipped up the skirt, exposing her naked rear. No underwear. God save him. She performed an exquisite pivot then spread her legs so far apart that she revealed her pussy to him. She took her time and exaggerated her motions as she reached for her ankles.

"Stay there," he said.

He went into the guest powder room and grabbed a condom. *Minx wants to play with fire...?* He rejoined her and teased her pussy with his fingers. "Freshly shaven?"

"Yes, Sir. I took the liberty of using yours while I showered."

So damn hot.

Without any warning, he slapped her between the legs, hard. "I believe I instructed you to ask me to spank you."

"Please spank me, Sir, for being so saucy."

More than willing to oblige, he did so.

She froze, then a moment later, she pushed her bottom back toward him. "Again," she demanded. "Please, Sir. Again."

She was impossible to resist. Three more times, he gave her what she begged for before dropping his jeans. Looking at her damn pussy, he vigorously fisted his cock then rolled on a condom before gripping her hips and dragging her backward to meet his thrust, impaling her, making sure she'd never forget him.

She cried out from obvious shock. "Wow, Sir!"

He fucked her hard, holding her securely but penetrating deep, making it impossible for her to breathe.

On and on he went, trying to exorcise her from his mind, trying to satisfy her every womanly demand.

"Oh, Sir, I want to come."

"You will have to wait." He thrust into her, grunting, coming hard, and riding her until he drained out every drop of semen.

Then he pulled out and flipped her skirt back into place before helping her to stand.

"That..." As she faced him, she pressed a hand against her mouth.

The way she'd sucked his cock had wrecked her lipstick, and the sight satisfied him.

"Sir?"

"Always more than one way to punish a mouthy sub." But that wasn't what it was about. It was about the frustration of losing her.

He removed the condom and extended it toward her. "Be a good sub and dispose of this and the wrapper."

"My pleasure, Sir."

Her response made him blink. She bent to scoop the wrapper from the floor, then she took the filled latex from him. Without a single word of protest or wrinkling her nose, she went into the small bathroom.

He had finished securing his pants when she sashayed into the room, smiling happily. With a frown, he tipped his head to the side. "What are you up to?"

"I want to come, Sir. I figure behaving will help me earn it." She flashed her rear as she grabbed her purse. "Besides, I like it when you lose control and fuck me all wild-like."

"After you." Until her, he'd been deliberate in how and where he fucked. No one goaded him. But she was getting to him.

And that meant only one thing.

He absolutely needed to turn her over to someone else.

How the hell would he be all right with a realization he despised?

Chapter Eleven

Tension knotted Chelsea's stomach, and she picked at her dinner despite the fact the food was fabulous. He'd chosen an upscale seafood restaurant in the foothills with spectacular views of Denver and the plains in the distance. Even though they were together in a wonderful place, her mind drifted away.

When she'd started this journey, the idea of letting someone else tell her what to do and make decisions for her had rankled. The suggestion that she should serve him in any way had annoyed her. But over the last couple of weeks, things had changed.

She recognized the myriad ways he served her, from wonderful dinners—no parsley in sight—to holding her gently, from opening doors to bathing her in the shower. She'd come to understand that submission wasn't a one-way street. And the more he required from her, the more he also gave. He made her feel cared for and appreciated—something no other man had ever done for her.

And what she shared with Master Alexander was even deeper than that. There was a thrill and sexual fulfillment that she'd never experienced before.

And part of her never wanted it to end.

"Not hungry?" he asked.

"Sorry. I was playing with my food, Sir." She laid her fork on top of her plate. She was looking forward to tomorrow night at the Den and finally sceneing with Master Evan C. But she was going to miss seeing Master Alexander. She realized that she was starting to care for him, deeply. Falling for a trainer was stupidity, she knew, but she hadn't seen it coming.

"Is everything okay?"

No. "Fine. Thank you." It had been even an hour ago, but now, she was closer to leaving him than she'd been before.

"Would you like to finish your meal? Or would you like to leave?"

She folded her hands together in her lap. "I don't want to rush you, Sir."

He looked at her, his gaze focused on her. He frowned slightly before nodding. "I'd rather get home, as well."

Home. Which meant his place. Not theirs.

He signaled for the check and paid the bill.

"Thank you for dinner, Sir," she said, when he pulled back her chair.

"You have the loveliest manners," he said. "This time I want you to walk in front of me."

It seemed he gave a different order every time they were together. That was part of his plan, she supposed. With a new Dom, she wouldn't know what to expect, and so he prepared her for everything, which made him excellent at what he did.

They waited at the valet stand, and when one of the men opened the door for her, Master Alexander said, "I'll see to the lady."

The valet nodded and accepted his tip. Master Alexander handed her into the SUV and waited while she buckled her seatbelt before closing the door.

"You seem quiet," he observed after he'd eased into traffic.

"Just trying to concentrate," she said, fabricated.

He shot her a sideways glance.

"I don't want to be a disappointment," she added, hoping that would dissuade him from further questions.

"You won't be." He took her hand and drew it to his lips.

Oh hell. That was it.

Earlier, he'd kissed her.

Though she'd continued on as if nothing had changed, everything had.

And now that she'd had a few minutes to reflect, she realized it.

Being spanked, fucked, even tended to was one thing. His passion that created an emotional connection was another.

Her heart had melted as she'd looked into his eyes.

The sex they'd had afterward, with her on top, had been different, magnificent.

"Would you like to continue to play this evening?" He slid a sideways glance her way. "Or would you like to call it a night?"

And never scene with you again? That would be the smartest way to spare herself any further anguish. But maybe she was a glutton for punishment. Greedily, she wanted as many experiences as possible to remember him by. "If you're agreeable, Sir, I'd like to stay a little longer."

"I was hoping that would be your answer."

They both remained silent until they neared his house.

"When we arrive, leave your clothes inside the door and then go up to my bedroom. When I get there, I want to find you leaning over the bed, your ass cheeks spread apart."

Her mouth dried. "Yes, Sir." Obviously he intended to do more anal training, and she didn't object. Now that she'd become more accustomed to it, she sometimes enjoyed it. When he fucked her with the butt plug in place, the fit was so tight, so overwhelming that the sensations made her nerve endings sing.

He pulled the vehicle into the garage, and she preceded him into the house. As soon as the door closed behind him, she kicked off her heels and started to unbutton her blouse.

She expected him to walk straight past her, but he paused. He dug a hand into her hair and tipped her head to one side.

He sank his teeth into the tender flesh near her shoulder. Her knees bent, and before she could lose her balance, he caught her.

"Better not keep me waiting, sub." He walked away.

Chelsea finished stripping.

In the distance, a door closed, and she assumed he'd entered his home office. Not knowing how much time she had, she hurried upstairs to prepare for his arrival.

The beast kept her waiting.

She fought to harness her racing thoughts and to keep her ass cheeks spread. She listened intently for any sound that would indicate his imminent arrival.

Just because she heard nothing, it didn't mean he wasn't standing there, watching her, waiting for her to make a mistake.

This time, he wasn't being stealthy.

His masculine footfalls resounded in the hallway, then outside the door. For a moment she forgot to breathe. But he continued on. Exhaling, she started to relax, but then realized he might return soon.

He kept her waiting for a few minutes more before joining her.

"Perfect," he said.

Her heart stuttered. His growl of approval made the wait worthwhile.

"You know I'm going to take you up the ass tonight, sub."

Her breath threatened to strangle her. She couldn't have spoken now if he'd paid her.

"Since I'm feeling generous, I'll start you with a small plug."

Small mercies. "That's kind, Sir." Out of her peripheral vision, she saw him place a few items on the nightstand.

He rubbed her bare buttocks. "You only have a couple of small marks, and they'll be gone by tomorrow," he told her.

Before she was ready, he placed the cool, wet tip of the small plug against her. "Keep your cheeks spread." He pushed in a little. "Open up. Bear down." In a single move, he slid it all the way in.

Because she'd had some practice, she barely noticed its insertion, and it took no time to accommodate the silicone toy.

"You're getting better at that," he told her. "Now a larger size."

She still found it a bit humiliating for him to remove a plug, but protesting wouldn't change anything.

A little at a time, he worked a bigger one in, easing forward then back, going deeper with each thrust.

She groaned when the biggest part stretched her apart.

"Keep that asshole exposed for me," he warned. "Unless you want to wear clovers while I do this?"

Instinctively she tightened her body and forced her buttocks farther apart.

"I didn't think so, even though I like the idea of you helplessly grinding your breasts against the mattress. Can you imagine how bad your nipples would hurt?"

Since they still stung from the last time she'd worn them, she didn't want to consider the amount of pain they'd cause.

Once he had it seated, he fucked her a couple of times with it. Keeping her stretched?

"Now you're going to take one that's larger than either of those."

She whimpered. His words frightened her enough that she almost moved her hands.

"It's your choice. Do you want it or not? It will help prepare you, or I can simply put my dick up there now."

Master Alexander was much thicker than either of those. Being stretched wider was a mercy. "Another one is fine, Sir."

Though he eased the current one from her, the respite was temporary. Almost instantly something much larger demanded entrance. "Damn, Sir!"

"Relax your muscles," he encouraged.

She curled her toes against the unyielding floor. "I can't do this!"

He slapped her ass hard.

The distraction allowed him to sink the nasty thing farther in.

"You have a safe word. Use it or quit carrying on."

"This one is different," she complained after expelling a breath. And she hated it.

"It's made from tempered glass," he said. "Unbreakable. It's considerably less forgiving than the others we've used until now."

She shuddered. Having his cock up there had to feel better than this.

He reached beneath her to play with her clit. Always this man knew how to touch her. As need built in her, he spun the glass piece in slow circles, working it deeper a little at a time.

She cried out as he continued the assault on her rear.

Despite all her good intentions, she moved her hands and tried to stand. He pushed her back down and forced the glass in even deeper.

She panted, drenched with sweat, tears swimming in her eyes as the pain engulfed her.

He shoved on the base, sinking it all the way home. "Good girl."

"*Fuck off,*" she muttered under her breath.

In an instant, he flipped her over so that she was on her back looking up at him.

"Were you being disrespectful, girl?"

She shook her head, but then she looked away and closed her eyes.

"Chelsea?"

Digging for courage, she faced him again. "You're right, Sir. I was. I'm sorry. It hurts so much, and your words struck me as condescending." She bit her lower lip, afraid of his reaction. Even in a vanilla relationship, speaking to a partner in that way was disrespectful and unacceptable. "I was out of line. I accept whatever punishment you deem necessary."

He loomed over her, fully dressed, arms folded implacably. "Do you or do you not have a safe word?"

She wanted to look away. "Yes, I do, Sir."

"Do you remember what it is?"

"Parsley, Sir."

"And do you or do you not have a way to request a pause if you can't deal with something?"

With a bravery that she wasn't feeling, she continued to meet his gaze. "Yes, Sir."

"A good sub communicates with her Master."

That wasn't what he was to her. He'd been clear about that from the night they'd met. He was a temporary Dom. Nothing more. So why did she feel so terrible?

"Talking, expressing your feelings...that's the only way for the relationship to develop trust. Otherwise you have something meaningless where you could get hurt. That's not what I want for you. Is that what you want?"

"No, it's not, Sir."

"Your disrespect can't go unnoted," he observed. "Get on all fours and fuck yourself with the plug."

Desperately, she searched his features. A pulse ticked in his temple, and his eyes held no mercy.

"Do it, girl."

"Can we negotiate this?"

"Absolutely not. Safe word. Or if you want to stay and finish the scene, fuck your ass."

The world shifted beneath her. This might be his most dreadful request yet.

"Talk to me, girl." His use of the word was obviously intentional to reinforce their roles.

"I will do what you said, but I'm embarrassed as hell. I don't want to do it. I'd rather you did it or spank me."

"That's why I've chosen this. I've learned a thing or two about you. I like flogging and belting you, but you get off on it. Keeping physical chastisement in the erotic realm is what works best with you."

She'd never felt so exposed. He didn't just see her physically — he understood her deepest emotions.

"But when you're a brat, the most effective thing is something you hate. It's the only way to reinforce a lesson. Is that clear?"

Closing her eyes, she admitted the truth. "Yes."

"Then pull the plug out and reinsert it twenty times. If it needs more lube at any point, just let me know."

He continued to stand over her as she clambered into position. Keeping her gaze down so she didn't have to see him, she reached back and grasped the slippery glass hilt. In order to extract it, she had to curl her entire hand around the base and bear down.

As she repeatedly inserted the thing, she silently counted, wishing she were anyplace but here.

"Faster," he instructed.

It took all her willpower not to fire back, to say something else that would get her in trouble. She'd thought she was becoming a better sub. This showed her how much further she had to go.

When she was about a dozen strokes in, he said, "Stop and give me the plug."

Once she had, he squirted more of the thick lubricant onto the glass before returning it to her.

"Continue."

Each stroke became easier, but it was every bit as uncomfortable. When she finished, she forced out a relieved breath and looked up at him.

"Another five," he said.

"Another—" She clamped her mouth shut.

He raised his eyebrows and silently regarded her.

"Yes, Sir." *Curse you.* He absolutely understood how to reinforce a message.

Vowing to finish as quickly as possible, she repeated her motions, although a little slower. Her body was becoming fatigued from the awkward position, and her rear burned.

"That will suffice," he said.

His words were a balm to her soul. "Thank you, Sir."

"The last five could have been avoided if you'd remembered your manners after the first twenty."

Will I ever learn?

"We'll leave the plug in for another few minutes."

She could barely breathe with the way it filled her.

Master Alexander crossed to the bathroom, ran water, and was wiping his hands on a towel when he returned. Then he crouched in front of her. "Always make the choice to make things easy on yourself."

More than anything he'd ever said, those words sank in. "I... Yes. Thank you." It wasn't always about respect, then, but also about making decisions about what was best for her.

"It's better when you're being cherished rather than punished, I expect?"

"It is, Sir." Lesson finally comprehended, now that it was too late.

"Undress me," he said.

Moving with the plug in was difficult. Having his dick up there surely couldn't be any worse than this.

After removing his shoes, socks, and belt, she lowered his zipper. His already-hardening cock protruded toward her.

She quickly removed his pants, then she awkwardly stood — trying not to shift the plug — to unbutton his shirt.

"Condom is on the nightstand."

He could have easily reached it.

"Crawl," he said.

Will this nightmare ever end?

Aware of the hilt of the plug sticking out, she did as he demanded, and once she'd fetched the packet, she offered it to him.

Shaking his head, he said, "Put it on me then lube my dick. I recommend using a generous amount. Then remove your plug and place it on the nightstand."

Imagining she was on a beach in the Bahamas drinking rum, she did as he said. Pretending to be elsewhere was the only way to survive what was coming.

"Bend over the bed."

Fear made it feel as if the room temperature dropped several degrees.

"Your ass is stretched so wide," he said when she'd displayed herself, parting her butt cheeks without being told. "You look so fuckable, girl. I'm going to do you hard."

His cockhead sought entrance, and she wasn't sure she'd ever endured anything worse than this.

He took hold of her left shoulder, drove himself a little deeper, and slid his other arm beneath her midriff.

"Push out," he told her.

Even though it hurt, she didn't object. She wanted his flesh, rather than the cold and impersonal piece of molded glass. Suddenly she craved his possession. *"Yes."*

He continued to ease in and pull back. Within seconds, she discovered that having him inside her wasn't as bad as she imagined. It was different. A plug snuggled in, but a cock kept her spread.

"My sexy girl," he murmured.

The sound of his pleasure made her heart skip. "More, Sir."

"Are you sure you're ready?"

"Yes. I want all of it, Sir."

Holding her tighter, he jerked his hips, burying himself up to his balls in her ass.

She released her hands when his thrusting forced her deeper into the mattress. She sobbed, and the sound was muffled by the bedcovers.

"Chelsea?"

"Oh my God! This is so good." Her reaction surprised her. She'd never been more complete. His rigidity in her most private part filled her, awed her. Sensually, she was drowning. "I want to come, Sir."

"Do. Anytime. As many times as you want."

He lifted her upper body slightly off the mattress. That changed his angle slightly, allowing him to penetrate even deeper. As if electricity singed her skin, she was aflame Chelsea lifted onto her toes and arched her back. "Sir!"

She trembled as an orgasm overtook her. "Zow. That was amazing, Sir," she managed, her chest heaving.

"Damn, girl. That was so powerful I may never let you go."

"Don't." Nothing but this moment existed for her.

He continued to fuck her hard, and a second orgasm teased her as he surged, his cock thickening in that way it did right before he ejaculated.

Obviously still considering her, he moved one hand to unerringly find her clit. He stroked and teased, tipping her over the edge one more time.

He collapsed on top of her. If this was what submission was about, she wanted more. This kind of union had not existed with anyone else.

She was barely aware of the world around her as he withdrew his spent cock and went into the bathroom. She somehow managed to crawl up onto the bed and turn onto her side.

Moments later he pressed something warm and damp against her rear.

"Shh," he told her.

She didn't protest as he cleaned her with a washcloth. The water soothed her burning skin. A few moments later, the bed sagged beneath his weight. He eased her against him and held her tight. She stiffened.

"I'm not open to negotiation, Chelsea. Freaking relax."

He smoothed her hair as he tucked her under his chin. Despite the fact her overnight bag was still in her car, she'd refused to spend a night with him. That spoke to an intimacy she didn't want with him. But now, here she was, in his house, his bed, his arms. And she wanted to stay. She gave herself permission to stay where she was for five minutes. That couldn't hurt anything. *Right?*

When she woke, it was the middle of the night.

She started to get out of the bed only to have him pull her tight. She knew he wasn't awake, so his grip was instinctive and domineering, but she didn't want to struggle and risk a confrontation.

Before she'd sorted through all of her thoughts, his warmth and strength offered her peace, just enough to pretend, for a moment, that things were going to be okay.

Even though deep down, she knew her entire world was about to change.

Chapter Twelve

The scent of coffee helped Chelsea swim through the layers of sleep, back to the first edges of consciousness.

Disoriented, she blinked. When her eyes focused, she saw Master Alexander sitting on the edge of the bed, looking at her with a warm smile and holding two cups.

She'd stayed with him the entire night, though she hadn't been anticipating that.

"Morning."

"Hi." Struggling to find her equilibrium, she propped herself on her elbows and acted as if everything were normal when it was anything but. "Are both of those for me?"

"They could be. But I was hoping you'd share."

"If I'm feeling generous." She scooted to a sitting position, dragging the sheet with her, and rested her shoulders against the headboard. After accepting a cup, she inhaled deeply. "Thank you." The first sip — all creamy and tasting of sweet vanilla — was heaven.

"Perfect, Sir. If you spoil me like this, I might never leave."

"What makes you think I was hoping you would?"

Oh Jesus. Her heart stopped. He couldn't have said that. Couldn't have meant it.

Their gazes locked.

"Sir..." She looked away first. She had a goal. And she needed to focus on it.

As if he'd been kidding—and maybe he had—Master Alexander cleared his throat and went on. "I'd like to leave for the Den by five o'clock," he said. "Do you mind meeting here since I'm closer?"

"That's a good idea. Uhm..." Then, desperate to restore some normalcy between them, she peered at him over the rim of the cup. "I know I mentioned it last night, but the mountains are a perfect place for a photo shoot."

"As I've told you, I have a PR company." Finality rang from his statement.

So this really did mean that their time together was almost over. "Is there any way to convince you to reconsider?"

He stood. "Would you like to shower here?"

His abruptness sent her emotions reeling. Suddenly uncomfortable, she brought her drink closer to her mouth. "That's a nice offer. But I've got a lot to get done, so I think I'll get going."

"Understood."

In less than five minutes, her beverage almost untouched, she was dressed, with her purse slung over her shoulder.

He walked her to her car then paused once she was behind the steering wheel.

Neither of them spoke, and his eyebrows were knitted into a serious line, as if he had something to say.

Words failed her.

And she was afraid that if she said goodbye, she might cry.

"Five o'clock."

"Yes, Sir." She gave him a brave nod.

After closing the door, he rapped on the hood and walked away.

Concentrating on what she was doing, she pulled onto the road and didn't relax her shoulders until she stopped at a traffic signal. *What happened back there?*

Was the distance between them because she'd asked again about the photo shoot?

Or something else?

For a moment, when he'd suggested that he didn't want her to leave, she'd wanted to believe he was serious, and immediately she'd dismissed the idea. After all, he'd changed the subject right away.

Being in her apartment didn't settle her, nor did the hour-long soak in the bathtub.

Weeks ago, when she'd approached Master Alexander, she'd been so confident, and her plan had all seemed so easy. He'd train her. She'd land Master Evan C as a client and Dom. Another success in her business and her life.

Yet here she was, having fallen for her trainer. They'd scened for the last time, made love for the final time.

And the rest of the day loomed in front of her — long and lonely.

Determinedly, she dressed, cranked up some music, tossed a load of laundry in the washing machine, and tidied the already-neat surroundings.

All that done, she settled behind her computer. There was always some business-related task to handle. Today she thanked goodness for that fact.

She checked her emails and she was delighted to find one from Master Evan C. *Finally.* He said he was interested in talking to her more about her proposal, and said he'd be at the Den this evening, and maybe they could connect there.

She pumped her fist in the air and swiveled her chair in circles.

But when silence echoed back mockingly, she frowned. The small victory rang hollow with no one to share it with.

There was another message from her admin. Jennifer suggested that, since Monahan Capital hadn't responded to their proposal, perhaps they should consider contacting his brother.

Chelsea tapped her fingers on the desktop.

No doubt Master Alexander wouldn't approve of that tactic.

Master Alexander?

She stopped herself.

He was no longer her trainer, so the honorific no longer applied.

And that also meant she could pursue Monahan Capital's business like she did with any other company.

Still, going behind his back—and no doubt he'd see it that way—was risky. She might not take a chance, except for the fact You're The Star could generate his firm some amazing publicity. Even if he didn't want it, he deserved it.

What the hell.

She had nothing to lose and everything to gain.

After telling Jennifer to go for it, Chelsea changed into her swimsuit. Luckily there were no teenage boys at the pool, and she had the area all to herself.

Despite the fact she wanted to think about business, random images of Master Alexander flashed through her mind in a rapid-fire slideshow. She pictured him in jeans. Wearing slacks. Naked. Setting his jaw and dragging her over his lap. Showing her a flogger. Affixing her to the cross. Doubling over his belt.

She leaned her head back and closed her eyes. And the truth smacked her. The reason she'd hesitated before letting Jennifer run with her idea was that she didn't want the relationship with Master Alexander to completely end.

Where does that leave me?

Anxiety churning in her anew, she opened her eyes and sat up. She needed action so that she could drown out the clamor in her head.

Once she was back in her apartment, she showered, then put some gel in her hair and squeezed the locks with her fingers. But now that it was time to get ready, courage deserted her.

The idea of stripping to play with Master Evan C — having her dreams come true — should have made her giddy with anticipation, but it didn't.

Instead, she felt hollow inside.

Still, her course was set, and she was due at Master Alexander's house soon.

She dressed in a lacy black bra with a matching thong. She added a skirt, a tight-fitting top, and a pair of ridiculously high heels.

She swiped on some mascara and applied a layer of foundation before grabbing her purse and heading for her car.

At his house, she knocked as was her custom, but he shocked her by opening the door rather than waiting for her to let herself in. The sight of him made her mouth water.

As she'd suggested—hoped for—he wore leather pants and a tight T-shirt that he'd tucked into his waistband. His hair was raked back from his square forehead, emphasizing his piercing green eyes. He hadn't shaved, and that left an intentional scruffy look that made him look even more masculine. Her knees weakened.

"Shall we?" he asked.

The earth shifted beneath her stilettos. She was slightly early, but he hadn't invited her in.

The difference from last night to today was almost too much to take, even though she should have expected it.

He placed his fingers lightly at the small of her back as he led her outside to his waiting vehicle.

"You look nice," he told her as if they were going out to a simple get-together, as if this were just two friends hanging out. *Except for the leather pants.* The leather pants said this wasn't an ordinary date.

Until they'd passed through the town of Winter Park, the conversation was mainly idle chitchat.

"About tonight?"

She turned slightly to look at him. "Yes?" Since it had become so natural, not calling him Sir required fierce concentration.

"Does Evan C know you're coming?"

"He does. I've been in contact with him with a few business proposals."

"Is your approach simply to wear people down?"

"Sometimes it works." She shrugged. "But it's an indicator of how much I personally believe in a business. I mean, I don't send one to every company in the entire metro Denver area."

Alexander didn't respond.

"And I'm taking a huge risk. I put tremendous resources into my proposals. I know companies have taken them to their existing PR firms to execute."

Momentarily he took his gaze off the road to glance at her. "Does that bother you?"

"It's a risk of my approach, isn't it?" She grinned. "But no one can deliver on those ideas like I do because they were mine, and I see how they fit into a bigger plan. They're a cog."

"Whereas you're the wheel."

"Exactly." *Sir.* "Back to your question about Evan C. He said he's looking forward to talking with me."

"I also assume you want to play with him."

Was he gripping the steering wheel tighter than usual? "If it works out that way." The words seemed to catch in her throat.

"I'll give you the privacy you need."

Did that also mean he was going to play with some submissives? The idea made her grit her teeth, even though she told herself her possessive feelings were ridiculous. Until this moment, she'd never experienced jealousy, but there it was, raw and awful.

All too soon, they arrived at the Den.

Opting to leave her purse behind, she exhaled, then pasted on a smile at the valet who opened the door for her.

Then Master Alexander met her in front of the hood and offered his elbow as she negotiated the uneven terrain. Spiky heels and the Rockies were not a good mix.

The sun was making its trek toward the Western horizon, and the summer air was as wonderful as could be.

Once they were inside, he said, "I'm with you, but not as a trainer. Stay as close as you wish, or not."

What would it be like to be here as his submissive? "I appreciate that."

Master Damien greeted them personally and asked Chelsea if she recalled the Den's safe word.

"Halt, Sir."

He nodded. "Enjoy your time with us, Ms. Barton."

"Thank you, Sir."

"Much better behaved than last time," he observed to Master Alexander.

She didn't wince, and that alone showed her how far she'd come from her previous visit.

"Shall we go downstairs?" Alexander offered when Master Damien excused himself.

Am I ready for this? "Yes. I could use something to drink."

"Alcohol and sceneing don't mix."

"I know." Even if she could use a drink. "A soda will do."

She followed him down the stairs, and while he fetched them each a drink, she kept a lookout for Master Evan C.

She saw him in the corner, chatting with a sub who was wearing a purple wristband, indicating she'd been hired by the Den.

He looked so different from any other Top here. Most were in black. He wore white. A bright red scarf was wrapped around his neck. He belonged on stage, rather than at a BDSM party.

Master Alexander returned with her sugary soda and a water for himself.

"You'll do fine," he told her, raising his bottle in a salute to her. "You've learned a lot. You should be proud of yourself."

"I'm nervous as hell, Sir." Here, all the usual BDSM honorifics seemed not just natural, but appropriate.

"Why?"

She sipped through her straw. "Probably just the idea of playing with someone new." *Or the fact I don't want to leave your side.*

"It's a good experience. Concentrate on pleasing your Dom. No matter who he is."

When Master Evan C's submissive left, Chelsea squared her shoulders.

Master Alexander regarded her but said nothing.

On impulse she kissed his cheek. "Thank you for everything."

"Remember I'm here. Standing by."

She moved away, placed her drink on a tray, then looked over her shoulder to make sure he meant it.

When she approached, Master Evan C frowned a bit, evidently having no idea who she was or forgetting they'd agreed to meet. "Chelsea Barton," she said, offering her hand.

"The PR chick. You mentioned you got some training?"

"I did."

"Your manners suck."

She blinked. "I beg your pardon?"

"You don't know how to address a Dom?"

That stung. "Of course, I do, Sir."

"You want to go to a private room?"

This was the moment she'd been waiting for. So why wasn't she excited? "That would be fine. I'd also like to discuss my PR's proposal."

"Yeah. Later. Down the hall."

Bristling at his reaction, she nonetheless followed him.

Once more, she looked around for Master Alexander. He was there, waiting, watching. Though she was grateful for his support, guilt stabbed her as she continued on.

"You with me or with him?" Master Evan C asked.

"With you, Sir. Of course." She followed Master Evan C down the hallway. The walk reminded her of the first night with Master Alexander. The same set of nerves that had assailed her then gnawed her stomach now.

"Get your clothes off and get your ass on the cross."

"Uhm...are we going to talk about a safe word?"

"You one of them pussy girls? I thought you wanted to do business with me."

She looked at him. His eyes were wide, unblinking, calculating.

"I'm not into being abused, Sir, not for anything or anyone."

"Heard talk about you last time, that you scream so much you need a gag."

She shuddered.

"Get your clothes off, bitch."

Chelsea debated what to do. Master Alexander had never spoken to her with this tone or inflection. Evan C was insulting. Before she could speak again, he grabbed her shirt, tugged it over her head and brutally squeezed her right breast.

The sudden assault of pain left her scarcely able to breathe. She grabbed him around the wrist. "Sir, that fucking hurts."

"What? Your tit's delicate?" He laughed.

"Please." She dug her fingernails into his skin. Then she called on all of the training, reminders, prompting that Master Alexander had given her. *"Halt."*

"The actual fuck, bitch? I thought you'd been getting some training."

"Yeah. I have." He still hadn't released her, and it was pissing her off. "Enough to know that I don't want a Dom like you. Let go of me."

"You've been fucking stalking me, begging for this."

She shook her head. "You're mistaken. I think you have talent. But that doesn't mean I'll put up with your brutality to get a contract. Fuck that." The more he hurt her, the deeper she dug in her fingernails. "Last warning. Halt."

"Cock tease."

She refused to allow his words to goad her. What Master Alexander had said all along was true. Submission was a gift you gave, not something that could be demanded. There was a big difference between submission and a little kink, and an even greater distinction between submission and masochism. Master Evan C was more a sadist than anything, she assumed. And she had no interest in that.

When he didn't let her go, another realization blindsided her. She'd allowed her career hunger to drive feelings in her personal life. You're The Star would benefit from having Evan C on their client list. She'd fallen in love with the idea of a partnership with him. Her ambition had blinded her. "Take your goddamn hand off me before I scream the place down."

Instantly he released her. The pain of the blood rushing back into her breast stole her next breath. Fueled by gritty determination, she snatched up her shirt and pulled it over her head before meeting his eyes. "You have some natural talent. You'll do well if you don't allow your reckless behavior to fuck it up."

"You giving me career advice?"

"Someone needs to. I'll send a bill."

"You're a tough chick." He wrapped his scarf tighter around his neck then strode away.

She exhaled and pressed her hands to her face, pretending her world hadn't shattered in the last sixty minutes. Everything she'd thought she wanted, hungered for, focused on, no longer mattered.

After she'd stopped shaking, she squared her shoulders and walked back toward the main dungeon.

As she neared Master Alexander, she overheard Master Evan C say, "You did a shitty job of training her."

She kept her head high, as if she were wearing a posture collar. She'd done nothing wrong, and she wasn't in the least ashamed.

"If she refused to scene with you, I'd say I did an excellent job."

Chelsea almost cheered. *My hero.*

"And I'll tell you this, little prick, be grateful you didn't harm her, because I would have fucking killed you."

In shock, she blinked up at Master Alexander.

Flipping his scarf, Evan C walked, or rather stalked, toward the bar and Brandy.

Master Alexander draped an arm around her shoulder and pulled her closer. "What the hell happened?"

"I figured out I want nothing to do with him." She smiled. "If it's all right with you, Sir, I would like to go home."

He nodded. Purposefully, he moved her toward the stairs, thanked Master Damien for his hospitality, then headed outside, where he turned over his claim check to the valet.

She shook her head. To think that at one time she'd thought Master Alexander was a tough Dominant. He treated her more like a princess than a submissive. She wished every man behaved so courteously.

When the vehicle arrived, he helped her inside then reached across her to fasten her safety belt before closing her inside.

As he pulled away, she stared at the darkened landscape, saying nothing.

After the last few weeks, how did she go back to her regular life?

She needed time alone. Lots of it.

Master Alexander waited until they had summited Berthoud Pass before looking at her. "Do you want to talk about it?"

"There's nothing really to say. He has a different opinion of submission than I do." She looked over at the man who had taught her so much. Since the moon was hidden by clouds, his face was in shadows. That didn't matter, though. She knew every plane and angle intimately.

"Are you hurt?"

She straightened her shoulders. "Not at all." In fact, she had more strength and courage than she'd ever had—gifts she'd received from her two-week journey into submission. "I've never been better, Sir."

He took his gaze from the road long enough to cast a quick glance in her direction. "Seriously?"

"I owe you a lot, Sir. I wouldn't have handled Master Evan C as well as I did without everything I've learned from you. I used the club safe word. He didn't immediately honor it, so I told him I'd scream the fucking place down. And I would have done it." She touched his thigh. "Thank you."

"I've never been prouder of you." For a moment, he closed his hand around hers.

When he pulled it away, she put on her brave face and pretended her heart wasn't breaking. Facing down Evan C had been easy for one reason.

She was in love with Master Alexander.

The truth destroyed her.

Chapter Thirteen

"What the hell are you doing here?" Bleary eyed, Alex looked up from the computer in his home office, where he'd spent every moment from the second he woke up this morning—if he was here, even doing nothing—he could pretend he was working. His brother stood on the threshold, an unwelcome intrusion. "Don't you believe in knocking? Ringing the bell? Texting before you show up uninvited?"

"I did all three," Gavin replied with an easy shrug. "When you didn't answer, I let myself in."

Though Alex scowled threateningly, Gavin strode across the floor to grab the alcohol decanter and remove it from the room. "We're not fucking doing this again."

Christ. Damn nag.

Last weekend, Gavin had shown up, demanding to know what the hell was wrong with Alex.

Since taking Chelsea to meet Evan C, Alex had been short-tempered. He was unfocused at meetings, and

Gavin had pointed out that their employees were avoiding him.

And Gavin wasn't having it.

Over a twelve-pack of beer, he'd spilled everything about Chelsea's training, and his own complicated reactions to her — including the fact he'd never wanted to let her go.

They'd both passed out on the backyard patio furniture, and before leaving the next morning, Gavin had warned Alex to get his shit together.

Since he hadn't, today was obviously Gavin's second attempt at an intervention that Alex didn't want or need. All he wanted was to be left the hell alone. Was that too much to ask?

Less than a minute later, Gavin was back, and he dropped into a chair on the far side of the desk.

"Part of the reason we do our weekly meetings at Monahan Capital is to look for potential pitfalls, and I'm telling you, you've got one."

He might be halfway through a bottle of cheap whiskey, but that made no sense. "And?"

"Maybe if" — Gavin paused — "we had been paying more attention, we would have noticed details about the Bartholomew deal."

Alex winced. What his brother meant to say was if *Alex* had been paying attention — instead of spending his time at the bottom of a bottle when his marriage fell apart — the outcome might have been different.

In salute, he raised his glass toward his brother.

"Even though you didn't ask, I'll enlighten you. I appreciate the way you put guardrails around the business and around your life, but answer me this. How are your choices making things better?"

"You're talking about Chelsea." His one obsession, no matter how he tried to drown her out of his system.

"I am."

Alex answered honestly. "Better to be kicked in the balls now than later, right?"

"Not a metaphor I would have used. But if it fits..." Gavin leaned back, at ease, obviously not planning to go anywhere. "Are you intending to remain single the rest of your life? Never date? Never get married?"

He scowled.

"Never have kids?"

The fuck?

"That's the only possible outcome from the way you're behaving."

"Don't you have somewhere else you need to be?"

"Nah."

"That was me politely telling you to leave."

Instead, Gavin stretched out his legs. "Look... Maybe there were warning signs with Liz. Red flags that you didn't see or didn't want to see."

There was more truth to that statement than Alex wanted to admit.

"Or maybe the truth is that Liz had some culpability. Did she manipulate you? Hide who she was?"

"Possible."

"Maybe her needs changed, evolved, and that's something no one predicted. Something no one *could* have predicted."

Which was another damn reason to stay the hell away from Chelsea. She needed the space to evolve and grow as she experimented with submission.

"You want to tell me how Chelsea is the same?" Gavin had a point. Chelsea was dreadful at hiding her emotions and reactions, even when she tried. "It doesn't matter, does it? Our agreement ended. End of discussion."

"And because you're as stubborn as you are blind…" Gavin let the words hang between them. "Did you ever mention the possibility of continuing to see her?"

"I hinted at it."

"*Hinted*? For shit's sake. You know damn well that every relationship—especially a BDSM one—needs forthright discussion."

He winced.

"Do you know how she's feeling today? What she's thinking? What she wants?"

Alex squeezed his eyes shut against the onslaught of a sudden headache.

"Do you care?" Gavin asked quietly.

Yeah, I do. Obsessively.

"Or are you so deep in your own black hole that no one else exists?"

He willed his brother to shut the hell up.

"What happened that night at the Den couldn't have been easy on Chelsea. I'm thinking a good trainer would have the consideration to check up on her."

Because it was accurate, the criticism burned as much as the cheap whiskey he was drinking. He should have gone with the more expensive Bonds choice.

"We're going to do business with You're The Star." Gavin dropped Chelsea's presentation folder on the desk.

Where the hell had that come from?

"I signed a contract with Jennifer yesterday."

"You did what?"

"Something we should have done a couple of weeks ago and would have if you weren't such a stubborn fucker."

Before that barb landed fully, Alex's addled mind registered something odd about what his brother said. Frowning, he asked, "Jennifer? You mean Chelsea?"

"No." Gavin shook his head. "She's Chelsea's executive administrator. If you'd engage at work, you'd know that."

"Ah." Which meant his bastard sibling hadn't seen Chelsea? "So you don't know how she's doing?"

"Chelsea?"

Hating how much he hungered for even a crumb of information about her, he leaned forward.

"From what Jennifer said, she's not herself. But you didn't hear that."

His heart grabbed hold of the information and tucked it inside.

The fact she'd continued to try to land his business even though they hadn't seen each other for a few weeks meant... *What? Nothing?*

"I came here for one reason."

"Get it over with." *And leave me in peace.*

"If you want to implode your personal life, go right ahead. That's your choice. But Monahan Capital belongs to both of us, and I won't let you stand in the way of growth over some fucked-up thing going on in your head."

His headache grew worse.

"Chelsea's proposal is solid, and it's worth the time and money required." Gavin stood and smacked both palms on the desktop.

Alex needed ibuprofen.

"Get some sleep. Eat some food. Take a shower. Go work out. If you want Chelsea, take a goddamn risk. Maybe she tells you to fuck off—couldn't blame her. But would you be worse off than you are right now?

And maybe she's waiting for you to make a move. In your dynamic, you've been the Top, setting the tone. One final piece of advice? Pull your head out of your ass." With that, Gavin strode from the room.

Moments later, the front door banged shut.

Wallowing in his abyss of misery, made worse by the blinding thunder between his temples, Alex lifted his glass once again.

No matter how much he had to drink, he couldn't vanquish the memories of their trip to the Den.

He'd accompanied her because it was the right thing to do, not because he'd wanted to.

Each mile that his tires had gobbled up had strained against his hold on civility. Watching her with Evan C, heading down the hallway to a private room had blasted possessive fire through his veins.

Repeatedly he'd reminded himself that she wasn't his.

Not that his brain received the message.

Needing to burn off some energy, he'd paced the dungeon, staring down the hallway until Gregorio had approached and said the Den often fielded requests from subs who were looking for trainers.

Alex had flat-out refused.

"You're not back in the business?"

Never fucking again.

Letting go of Chelsea had been gut-wrenching, which meant he wasn't cut out for it any longer.

He slammed down his glass.

Something had to change. Some damn thing. Before he lost what little remained of his mind.

* * * *

Chelsea clutched her clipboard to her chest and looked around the large room one last time.

She, Jennifer, and their team had spent six intense weeks doing the preparation work, and the big day had finally arrived.

In keeping with the Western theme, red-and-white checkered cloths covered rectangular tables. Bright yellow sunflowers dropped their fat faces over skinny vases.

Two bars were being stocked with good beer and fine wine.

A popular band was tuning up on the stage, and Jennifer was in last-minute discussions with the lead singer about the timing of announcements. Tables filled with silent auction items lined the walls. And the scent of the barbecue beef and pork wafted over the mountain valley.

For a month, they'd sent press releases to all the Denver outlets and to the news media in all the nearby towns, and they'd spent a day in the area about two weeks ago talking to local merchants and pinning up flyers.

Since Gavin had awarded her company the firm's PR contract, she had updated Monahan Capital's website and social sites. In addition, she'd harnessed the power of her own mailing lists and shamelessly peppered every social media account, and had friends, family, and colleagues to do the same. She'd blasted the band's fans, the catering company's client list, the charity's donors, along with the lodge's employees, and past guests. For good measure, she'd contacted some celebrity spokespeople, and all of her parents' friends. The last, her mother hadn't been too happy with. *Add one more thing to the list.*

Despite their annoyance, her mom and dad were both planning to attend — hoping to get their names and photos in the society columns.

Whatever worked.

At this point, Chelsea had ensured pretty much everyone in North America had heard of the event.

The weather had even cooperated, so they could also utilize the outdoor space. If things went as well as she and Jennifer hoped, they would need all the room they could get.

A table, manned by several temporary workers, was in the foyer. They'd been trained to sell raffle tickets as well as encourage high bidding on the auction items.

Everyone had dressed according to her specifications. She and Jen each wore denim skirts, white blouses, and they'd added red bandannas around their necks.

She'd tried to think through everything. Truthfully, her company had never worked harder on any project.

Nerves stretched to breaking point, Chelsea checked her watch. Thirty minutes until the doors opened. Things were ahead of schedule, thank God. And they should be.

For weeks, she'd barely slept.

And it was more than just the event bothering her — it was the fact she was going to see Master Alexander — *Alexander* — she mentally corrected herself.

Would she ever be able to think of him without seeing him in that commanding role?

More, would she ever get over him?

Jennifer walked toward her. "Seems we have everything under control."

"You've done an amazing job."

"It was teamwork," Jen replied.

"You're the one who got the deal over the finish line." After the night at the Den and saying goodbye to Alexander for good, Chelsea had been uncharacteristically detached from You're The Star and the pursuit of her goals.

Jen had stepped into the void, and she deserved that recognition. "It's time for you to get a raise." Chelsea also planned to add a nice fat bonus to her admin's next paycheck. "And sometime next week, when we've both had some rest, I want to talk to you about becoming my partner in the business."

Jen's mouth opened. "For real?"

"You're indispensable, the only person I've ever known who works as hard on the company as I do. Recently, you've worked your ass off and you've been far more focused than I have." She gave a wry smile. "You're my rock." At this point, Jen was also a friend and confidante, in addition to being the world's greatest executive admin.

Grinning, Jen hugged Chelsea. "I'm honored you'd consider it."

"We'll work out the details next week. Either over margaritas or coffee and dessert."

"And maybe champagne after?"

"A nice bottle. We both deserve it."

Then, because they were so close, Jen studied Chelsea closely. "How are you really doing?"

"I'm looking forward to the event, but…"

"It's going to be hard emotionally?" Jen guessed.

"Yes." Time and distance hadn't diminished Chelsea's love for Alexander.

How could she be happy when a piece of her heart was missing?

Keeping memories of him at bay had become a full-time job. Though she kept herself busy at work, writing proposals, juggling commitments, and had started going to yoga classes, he'd continually sneaked into her thoughts. Every night, he showed up in her dreams, wearing a wicked smile, beckoning her, and she'd abruptly wake up, only to find him gone.

"I'll be close by. I promise to keep an eye on you."

Chelsea nodded. "You'll be too busy." And hopefully the same was true for her and she wouldn't notice him at all.

As if.

"I just want to make sure — one more time — that the check-in staff understands how to upsell raffle tickets."

"I'll make a final pass through the space."

Chelsea had mentally rehearsed how she was going to act if — *when* — she came face-to-face with Alexander. She'd be wearing her brightest smile, exuding confidence as she offered her hand and wished him lots of success. Her demeanor would be professional, and she'd give a quick excuse, then move off and see to some pressing demand.

At the end of the evening, she'd leave Jennifer to deal with the Monahan brothers while she saw to the other guests.

She'd thought everything through.

"Haven't we talked about your posture?"

The sound of Alexander's sensual voice slid down her back, and she froze, fear all but holding her immobilized. How could she have missed his arrival?

"Face me, please."

It took several seconds to regain control of her faculties. What stunned her most was her instinctive reaction. His tone and expectation of obedience made her bend her knees before she caught herself.

Despite her mental practice, it never occurred to her to refuse to do as he asked.

As she turned, she straightened her shoulders.

And then... *Oh, God.* How was it possible that he was even more handsome than she remembered? His dark hair was styled back from his forehead, exposing its firm angularity. He wore tight-fitting blue jeans, cowboy boots, and a denim shirt. He'd skipped a tie and, instead, had left the top button of his shirt undone.

She couldn't find her voice, couldn't think at all.

"Evening, Chelsea."

His smile unwound all of her determination.

"You look beautiful."

How could she keep up her guard? "Hello, Alexander."

"Master Alexander," he corrected. "Or Sir will do."

She blinked, unprepared for his words. He wasn't her Dom or Trainer, and they weren't at a lifestyle event.

Trying to wrap herself in a protective coat of armor, she didn't respond, and instead said, "I hope the event is everything Monahan Capital deserves." *Everything you deserve.*

"I've received daily updates on your progress and God knows I think you contacted every person I've ever known. I've heard from friends I had in kindergarten."

She gripped her clipboard tighter. "Hopefully we've contacted hundreds more you've never heard of."

"You've done well," he told her. "And you're going to get what you deserve as a reward."

"Ah..."

"I think we could start with a spanking."

"What?" Her mouth dried and her skin heated. Even now, responding to him was all too easy, and she yearned to feel his hand on her bare buttocks.

"Do you need me to repeat that?"

She searched his features. His tone was neutral, and one brow was cocked, but more questioningly than anything. "I heard you." *Sir.* "But I'm choosing not to answer."

"It's time we talked."

"If this is about us working with Gavin behind your back —"

"That, and a lot more."

"I think you'll find we meet your expectations."

"There's no doubt of that."

"Then?" She blinked. He destroyed her focus entirely, and her breaths were becoming shorter and closer together.

"I saw the way you reacted to the sound of my voice. You wanted to kneel."

"No." She shook her head.

"Another three spanks for every lie you tell, sub."

Aware of time ticking, and voices growing louder from the lobby area, she brought her chin up. This was not the time or place for this. But she doubted he'd agree. "You want the truth? Fine. I'll give it to you straight up. Yes. That was my intuitive reaction to the sound of your voice." Hating the sudden lump in her throat, she swallowed frantically. His presence, the raw, masculine scent of him made her dizzy. "I've realized a lot of things."

Folding his arms across his chest, he waited without speaking, as if inviting her to go on.

None of this was going the way she'd practiced. "I no longer fight against the idea of submission. You were right initially. I did think BDSM was about feathers and playful swats on the ass, maybe a few scarves for bondage. To me now, it's so much more. It's a mindset and caring enough about someone else that their needs become paramount."

"Have you been playing with anyone else?" he demanded.

"What?" She exhaled. Why would it matter if she had. "Our agreement ended, which makes it none of your business."

Fury flashed in his eyes.

And because she cared—even though she didn't want to—she answered him. "I haven't been with anyone else." Hadn't even considered it. "I do like kink. As you suggested, it's different from subjugating your own will. My submission needs to be earned by the right man. And the right man is someone I love." She set her chin. "Someone who loves me in return and wants forever."

"Is that all?"

He cupped her shoulders.

When she tried to pull away, he tightened his grip. She'd all but confessed her love, and he responded with that?

"You're not the only stubborn one," he confessed. "I told myself I didn't want another submissive after Liz. But I learned a thing or two, especially after I saw you with Evan C. Liz would have surrendered to him, no matter how brutal he was, and she would have enjoyed it. Seeing you at the Den, your strength, resolution, determination, it all taught me something. You stood up for yourself."

His grip turned more reassuring. She struggled to hold herself back instead of leaning into him.

"Of course you should only offer your submission to a man you love, and a man who loves you in return. And I'm asking, humbly, for your submission."

Suddenly the room spun.

To steady her, he captured her upper arms.

Their first guests spilled into the room.

"*Alex!*" a woman called from across the room.

"This isn't the right time or place. We'll continue this conversation later," he promised, leaning forward to capture her lips.

In the distance, a camera flashed.

"You're mine."

With those mind-numbing words, he released her.

At that moment, Jennifer joined them. "Sorry to interrupt, Chelsea, but the mayor is here."

She watched him walk away and she clutched the clipboard close as if it were a lifeline on a storm-tossed sea.

Then she couldn't think at all.

"Are you okay?"

Chelsea shook her head to clear it. Then she remembered that Jen had promised to look out for her. "I appreciate your rescuing me." *Before I said, or did, something stupid.*

"Actually, the mayor *is* here. And you should probably meet her and glad-hand."

"I'll do that."

Jen glanced in the direction that Alexander had walked. "He's a seriously good-looking man. Just like his brother."

"He is." *Devastatingly.*

"I see your conundrum. If I'd slept with him, I wouldn't want to let him go either." She shrugged. "Anyway, I need to get back to the lobby in case any fires need to be put out."

"I'll say hello to the mayor." The woman's schedule was tight, and she wouldn't be in attendance for long.

As she made her way across the room, Chelsea scanned the surroundings. She'd opened the bars early so that alcohol would flow before dinner, encouraging people to bid higher on the silent auction items. Judging by the lines in front of some of the displayed items, the strategy seemed to be working.

So far, at least, everything was going according to plan.

Except for her unnerving experience with Alexander.

Soon, she was caught up in the event, thanking the mayor for her time, mingling with people she remembered from her childhood.

When the waiting line grew, she found the catering company and asked them to start serving glasses of champagne to the people in the lobby.

That idea was such a hit that she made a mental note to approach all future events in that way.

Master Damien showed up, with Gregorio at his side. As always, the Den's owner looked dapper and debonair as he sipped a glass of wine. Gregorio drank from a mug of draft beer and surveyed the room, giving off an air of danger and making her shiver. At the Den, he was in his element. But here, he didn't quite fit in.

A few minutes later, another man joined them, and she made her way over to say hello. She shook hands with Damien and Gregorio, then Gregorio introduced her to the stranger, Master Michael.

While other attendees were in suits, he'd opted for a black leather blazer, jeans, and boots.

He could have walked off the cover of a Western magazine. And if he'd never been on one, maybe he should be.

"Pleasure to meet you, ma'am." He tipped his felt cowboy hat in her direction.

That's when she saw it, the layer of wariness grooved next to his eyes.

"Everything is all set at the Den for the private weekend escape for you and Master Alexander." Master Damien, dragging her attention from the newcomer, a Dom, she assumed. Here without a submissive.

Wait. What had he just said? "I'm sorry, Sir." She gave him her full attention. "Did you mention a private event, Sir?"

Gregorio grinned, and the act only made him look more ferocious. His earring glittered in the light. "Good thing you're wearing boots, boss. You just stepped in it."

Master Damien took a sip from his wine. "Perhaps I misspoke. Seems you may want to have a conversation with Alex."

"I believe I will, Sir." *Sooner, rather than later.*

Trying not to betray her thundering heart, she excused herself, but she was waylaid with a half dozen questions. More guests than their wildest estimates had suggested arrived, and so there were decisions needed about extra food and more beverages.

These were her favorite kinds of problems.

Chelsea walked through all the individual spaces, looking for Alexander, and was in the lobby when her parents walked in.

In case anyone was watching, her mother swept her into a distant, awkward embrace. "Darling!"

Her father nodded but didn't offer a hug. "Decent turnout."

"Thank you." Delighted by the compliment, she smiled. Finally, she'd done something to earn their respect.

"If you had a husband, you could be here as an attendee, rather than the help," her mother observed, obviously having no idea how hurtful or insulting her words were. "I hope you enjoy your evening."

A server passed through with a tray of bubbly, and she snagged two glasses for her parents. Then she gave them a falsely sunny smile. "I'd love to visit, but I need to see the caterers."

"Of course, darling. Wouldn't want to keep you from your tasks."

Gritting her teeth, she resumed her search for Alexander and was in the main ballroom when the band's lead singer interrupted the festivities to say that one of Monahan Capital's owners had an announcement.

Across the room, she glanced at Jen, who shrugged as if to say this surprised her, as well.

Alexander took the stage—commanded it, really.

He thanked everyone for coming, commended You're The Star on their excellent work, then he called up a girl who'd been helped by the children's charity the evening was benefiting. He crouched next to the beautiful child, who had long, dark hair and big, luminous brown eyes.

Chelsea wasn't sure she would have had the courage to call the girl on stage, but Alexander did, and it had clearly been prearranged. He placed his arm around her shoulder as he held the microphone for her.

She spoke in a halting tone, telling her story and expressing her gratitude. She was as articulate as she was gorgeous. And people's eyes began to fill with tears. As she finished, Chelsea applauded, and she knew the evening would be a huge success, due in part to Alexander's strategic move.

The band struck up a ballad, and he found her.

"That was smart." But there was still the matter of their private event at the Den.

"Dance with me?"

Because it was a request more than a demand, he undid her.

Taking her hand, he led her to the patio where the first stars had started to appear.

As he wrapped her in the familiar comfort of his arms, resolve melted away.

The self-protective part of her wondered what she was doing. He'd broken her heart once. Wasn't that enough to last a lifetime? "Alexander..."

"*Master* Alexander."

"But you're not my —"

"Later," he interrupted. "Let's have this moment." He feathered his hands into her hair and drew her against him.

Without protest, so desperate for a moment of solace, she rested her head on his chest.

Too, too soon, the song ended, replaced by something much more up-tempo, and she reluctantly eased herself back from him.

"I need to work. We have to announce some of the raffle winners so people stay engaged."

"I'm not finished with you." It was delivered with part warning, part promise.

"I have something to discuss with you as well."

When he nodded, she made her escape.

As the evening progressed and dinner was served, she noticed both Monahan brothers were constantly on the move, congratulating winners, shaking hands, encouraging donations.

At the end of an evening like this, adrenaline generally receded and exhaustion washed over her. At this event, she was gaining energy. It was as if the pent-up hurt of the past six weeks had gathered enough steam to push her to the top of a fourteen-thousand-foot summit.

Finally, the event wound to a close. Attendees claimed their silent auction winnings, the band began to load their instruments into a waiting truck, and the catering company packed up.

After the last goodbyes had been said, Alexander appeared at her side. "Jennifer said you rode with her."

She nodded.

"I made your excuses. You'll be going home with me."

"I..."

"Your mouth looks attractive when it's gaping open like that. Makes me want to put a gag in it. Or my cock."

She shut her mouth.

"I've always particularly enjoyed your intelligence," he said. He took hold of her elbow and guided her toward the door. "Say goodnight to Gavin and Jennifer," he instructed her. But he gave her no time to say a word.

Instead, she glanced over her shoulder and waved.

Jennifer smiled. Gavin nodded approvingly.

At Chelsea's insistence, Alexander paused long enough to gather her belongings from the kitchen and then led her to the parking lot where the valet already had his vehicle waiting.

Not surprising her, he saw that she was safely seated and buckled tight before sliding into the driver's seat.

Master Alexander flipped a switch to turn on her seat heater. Always *thoughtful.*

The drive home was filled with discussion about the event, which she appreciated, and she gave him the approximate amount they'd raised and noted the things she'd heard from others, including the fact that her favorite online magazine, *Scandalicious*, had been in attendance and would be running a story in the coming days, filled with lots of photos.

"You impressed me." He looked at her. "As expected."

A ripple of pride ran through her.

"Mind if we go straight home?"

Shocked, she wiggled around so she could study him. "What do you mean by that? Your house?"

"Ours."

Her heart roared, drowning out her thoughts. He couldn't mean that. She didn't dare allow herself to believe that he did. "Look, Alexander —"

"We'll have plenty of time to talk."

She should insist on heading to her apartment, that way she would be on familiar ground, but the set of his jaw was implacable. "It's going to be a waste of time."

"Let's see about that."

When they entered his home, her breath vanished. "What is this?"

The great room was filled with balloons in all shapes and sizes, some hanging from the ceiling, others attached to walls, the mantel, and dozens covered the floor.

"Come with me."

He guided her toward the fireplace.

Now that she was closer, she noticed even more balloons on the couch and chairs.

A huge bouquet of red roses sat on the hearth, and a bottle of champagne chilled in an ice bucket.

"This is something."

In front of the fireplace he took both of her hands. "I heard what you said earlier, that your submission must be earned by a man you love, one who loves you in return and wants forever."

Self-protectively, she wrapped her arms around herself.

"I've realized a lot since we've been apart. The truth is, Chelsea, I love you, and I don't want to live without you."

"You..." She hugged herself tighter. *Is this real?*

"Everything you want, so do I. Love. Forever. Marriage. Children."

"Oh, Alexander."

"As Gavin pointed out, the biggest part of success in a relationship—any relationship—is excellent communication. From that standpoint, I let you down."

Studying him, she tipped her head to the side.

"I didn't want you to end up with Evan, but if that brought you happiness, I would have..." He dragged a hand through his hair. "That's a lie. I'm not sure I'm capable of standing by and watching you with any other man."

Alexander lowered himself to one knee, in the same place where he always had her kneel for him.

"Chelsea Barton, will you do me the honor of becoming my wife?"

He reached for her hand as he looked up at her.

So many thoughts tumbled through her mind. This was everything she wanted. She'd spent nights dreaming of this moment, yet she'd never believed it would become a reality. "Where does dominance and submission fit into that?"

"Wherever we decide it does."

"You once told me you can't imagine a relationship without it."

"Is that what you want?"

She shook her head. "No. But I don't know that I want to live it all the time."

"As I said, everything is a negotiation."

"I agree."

"In that case, Chelsea, will you marry me?"

She met his gaze, in his captivating eyes, she saw love, and maybe a touch of apprehension. Was he afraid she'd refuse?

Words lodged in her throat, and tears blinded her vision.

"Put me out of my misery? Kneeling here is fucking uncomfortable."

"Tell me about it, Sir." She couldn't help but smile. "And yes. Yes, yes! Yes. I'll marry you, Sir." God the honorific was so natural, and saying it was a welcome relief.

"You've made me the happiest man on earth." He reached into his pocket and pulled out a stunning engagement ring. The brilliant diamond was shaped like a heart.

"Oh, Sir. It's breathtaking."

He slipped it onto her finger, and the fit was perfect.

Flabbergasted, she shook her head. "How did you know?"

"I might have had a little assistance from Jennifer."

She blinked. "My executive admin?"

"Chelsea, I'll go to any lengths to figure out how to make you happy. And I selected the ring shape on purpose so that you will always remember that I've given you my heart. I know. There are things that we need to discuss. I'll let you set the wedding date, and you can take as long as you need as long as you know you're mine."

He got to his feet and pulled her against him. Leaning into him, she wound her hands around his neck.

"*Mine.*"

"Yes, Sir."

Master Alexander kissed her deeply, as if he would never let her go. And she realized that was his intent.

"I want to get started on our future, make love to you, and also have a scene so that we can embrace all aspects of who we are and this beautiful dynamic we share."

Her insides turned molten. "Take me, Sir."

"In that case, present yourself to me, *my sub.*"

His possessive inflection sent response galloping through her. This was her homecoming.

Her fingers shaking, the diamond winking in the overhead light, she stripped.

He inspected her, but more gently than he ever had before, cupping her breasts and squeezing with the most stimulating touch. He tweaked her nipples to full arousal. His touch was a full-on sensual assault. "Thank you, Sir."

"I love it when you use your manners."

He traced a fingertip across her lips, and dutifully she opened her mouth. In a promise of what was to come, he slipped inside.

Then he continued his lazy exploration, moving lower to investigate the insides of her pussy lips. "Beautiful. Smooth and silky."

She was wet for him, ready.

With his masterful touch, he teased her clit, making her jerk in helpless response.

"Were you hoping I might do this tonight?"

Since he wanted truth from her, she saw no point in lying. "Not consciously. But honestly, I haven't stopped thinking of you, hoping against hope that something like this would happen."

He rubbed her clit harder, then he inserted a finger inside her. "We're perfect for each other, Chelsea."

Before she could respond, he resumed his Dom mode and dropped his hand, leaving her frustratingly on the edge.

He moved to the mantel and picked up two lengths of rope, allowing them to dangle from his hands. "In keeping with the evening's theme, I'm going to use rope to bind you while I give you your first spanking as my future wife."

She shifted, trying to keep away the orgasm that threatened.

"Give me your wrists."

When they were secure, he bent to tie her ankles. The rope abraded her skin, adding a whole new sensation. Wryly, she thought they should have had a satin and lace theme for the evening.

With great intent, he pulled off his belt. "Cowhide leather for your skin," he said. "Of course." He doubled over the leather and snapped it in front of her face. Then he snared her chin with his thumb and forefinger.

"You want this?"

She sought reassurance in the depths of his drownable eyes. "Yes, Sir."

"Then ask for it."

"Please, Sir. Spank me for the first time as *your* submissive."

Before she'd finished speaking, he'd scooped her up and carried her to the couch, where he knocked aside balloons before sitting and positioning her helplessly across his lap. She desperately wriggled around, trying to find a position that wouldn't end with her being dumped on the hardwood flooring.

Beneath her, she felt the protective power of his muscles.

For long minutes, he rubbed her skin.

"Thank you, Sir. I've missed this." She all but purred.

"So have I."

This new level of honesty made her heart swell.

Slowly, Master Alexander increased the speed of his strokes, making them deeper, until her breasts jiggled.

"Are you ready?"

"More than, Sir."

He laid the leather to her deliciously, making her moan, drawing out her pleasure. Even though they'd played together repeatedly, she'd never experienced anything like this. "Mmm…"

"You like this?"

"Yes, Sir."

Her limbs loosened from the pleasure unfurling in her.

"Call me Master."

She exhaled, remembering that night at the Den when he told her she shouldn't use that word because he was a Dom, but not her Dominant. "Sir?"

Instead of responding, he continued to spank her sore buttocks.

"Master," she whispered.

"Fuck." He delivered the remaining spanks, then flipped her over and cradled her in the comfort of his arms. "I'll never tire of hearing you say that."

"I won't get tired of saying it." The tears she'd been holding back now spilled. As if a dam had burst, she couldn't stop. "I love you. You, Sir."

He released her bonds and gently brushed away a teardrop.

"Please, Sir, I need you inside me."

During the time they'd been apart, she'd ached for him. Since she knew that he was the man she loved, she hadn't even considered anyone else, even when Sara, who'd originally taken her to the Den, invited her to a play party.

Kicking aside balloons, Master Alexander carried her upstairs.

Then, keeping her balanced, he pulled back the bedcovers before placing her on the mattress. He undressed, tossing his clothes haphazardly around the room, before ripping open a condom, and rolling the sheath down his cock.

"Later I want you from behind. Now, I just want to look at your face as you tell me again that you'll marry me."

He bent over her and licked her pussy, eating her until she was tossing her head deliriously and whimpering all his honorifics in a single word.

"Tell me what I want to hear," he urged.

She heard the threat. There would be no orgasm until she said the words. "Yes, Master. I'll marry you and be yours in all ways."

"I've reserved the Den for a private weekend with you, if you're agreeable."

"So I heard." He looked at her. "Master Damien didn't know he wasn't supposed to tell me."

"So much for surprises," he lamented.

"Except for the biggest, happiest one of my life."

With that, he knelt between her legs, cockhead pressing against her needy pussy.

He drove into her with a single, hard, fast stroke.

She moaned her appreciation. "Fuck me like you own me, my future husband."

"Every day, if necessary," he said, reaching between them to press his thumb against her clit.

He kept her gaze ensnared. She loved watching him watch her.

With a raised eyebrow, he increased the force of his thrusts, pistoning his hips as he took her fiercely. Then, lips set with intention, he pressed harder on her clit.

She arched and screamed out her orgasm.

Only when she was satisfied did he come.

He collapsed on top of her, somehow also managing to hold her tight. "I love you, Chelsea."

"And I love you, Sir." She exhaled as much as she could with such a large man bearing down so dominantly on her.

"I need to get some arnica on your stripes."

"I'm okay if they stay red for as long as possible," she confessed. Seeing them in the mirror for a few days would be a delicious reminder of their evening together.

He lifted onto one shoulder. "I want you healed so I can tawse you in a few days."

"Oh?" Excitement and nerves intertwining, she ran her fingers through his hair.

"I'll be sure you have as many of my marks as you want. Anything to please you."

If her life never got any better than it was at this moment, she'd be happy forever.

"But first..." he began.

How could there be more? "Yes?"

"To continue your Western theme, you get to be a cowgirl and ride me."

"Really?" In surprise, Chelsea blinked. "I thought men weren't good for a second time so fast."

"Girl, it's going to be a while before I've had enough of you."

She giggled as he moved quickly, rolling them over. He made short work of disposing of the condom and donning another. Heaven above, her man was magnificent. Even though she was already a little tender, she straddled him, taking his cock deep as he held her waist between his strong palms.

"We're going to do this more often."

"Mmm," she approved. She liked it, too.

"Be a good girl and sit up straighter. Show me those beautiful breasts."

Following his command, she arched her back slightly as she drew her shoulder blades together. Everything he asked of her made her achingly aware of her femininity, and that added to her confidence.

"That's it."

With that, he took hold of her nipples, pinching and twisting, driving her to distraction. On a loud scream, she orgasmed. "*Master!*"

"Fuck *yes*." He growled, a low, possessive sound as he orgasmed inside her, marking her as his. "That's what I wanted to hear." He took her head between his palms and pulled her down until her face was within inches of his. "My sub," he said.

"Yours, Sir."

"Forever." He kissed her passionately, sealing the deal.

Want to see more from this author?
Here's a taster for you to enjoy!

Mastered: Over the Line
Sierra Cartwright

Excerpt

Michael Dayton caught a whiff of spiced vanilla on the night air, and he turned his head to find the source.

The view of the woman passing by walloped him. He only managed a brief look at her face, not enough to make out her eye color, but on a primal level he noted the softness of her mouth and the sexy pout of her beautiful lips.

She kept moving in the direction of the Den's firepit. Fascinated by her beauty, as well as her confidence, he didn't look away. How could he? She was tiny, compact, with blonde hair tumbling over her shoulders, the strands an untamed riotous mass. She walked with determination, her hips swaying seductively as she navigated the uneven flagstone patio. Her grace was all the more remarkable given the unyielding leather dress and her crazy-high stilettos. Even though the shoes added extra height, she didn't look tall. In fact, he doubted she'd reach his chin.

A need to protect flared in him. The sensation was as unexpected as it was unwelcome.

Several times a year, he attended BDSM play parties here at the Den, a mountain retreat owned by his friend

Master Damien. On occasion, Michael scened, and he'd been sexually attracted to many of the subs he'd played with.

But he'd only had this kind of visceral reaction one other time in his three decades. Recklessly he'd ignored his intuition and the warnings of others and had ended up married within three months.

A few years later, he and his bride had been in court, and he'd spent most of his inheritance to hold on to the Eagle's Bend Ranch. The two thousand acres had been in his family for over eighty years. If he'd lost it to some scheming bitch, his father would have haunted him from the grave. The lessons Michael had learned while rebuilding his life and fortune had made him harder, smarter, and significantly more cautious.

He adjusted his cowboy hat and continued to look at the blonde. She had joined a group of people near the fire. Her figure-hugging dress did as much—and maybe more—to arouse him as nudity would have.

Until this moment, he hadn't missed having a woman in his bedroom, tied to his rustic four-poster bed, arms and legs spread wide as she lay there for him, willing and waiting. Last night he'd gone to bed alone after masturbating to ease the day's tension. Tonight, he hoped things would be different. He was glad he hadn't simply tossed away the invitation to the Den's summer party. Although, he admitted, if he took this woman home, he'd wish for a longer night rather than a longer day.

As if sensing his perusal, she glanced over her shoulder. They made eye contact for less than five seconds, but it was enough, more than enough for him.

He heard someone say, "She's trouble."

Michael blinked and reluctantly turned toward the newcomer, Gregorio, the Den's caretaker.

"Don't go there," Gregorio advised, coming to a stop in front of him.

But Michael was already thinking about her, despite the fact she didn't resemble the women who generally caught his eye. He preferred a more rounded, feminine form—a woman who could withstand the rigors of ranch life as well as his Dominant demands.

"Her name's Sydney Wallace," Gregorio said.

Michael was aware of Gregorio's voice, but his focus was elsewhere. *Sydney. Unusual name.* He let it roll around in his mind. *How will it sound when I say it aloud as I command her to her knees?*

"She used to dance nude in a cabaret in Vegas and has a boa constrictor as a pet. It killed her last Dom and dragged him out to the backyard. She's on the run from the law. We heard she's wanted in ten states and two Canadian provinces." Gregorio snapped his fingers near Michael's face, jarring him from his reverie. "You listening to me, Mike?"

"What?" He shook his head and looked at Gregorio.

"I figured you weren't listening, otherwise you'd have decked me for calling you Mike." Gregorio chuckled. "Seriously, if you want to play, there are a number of subs here tonight—they're wearing the house's purple wristband. That means they're available for a scene, they know the rules and they follow them. Any one of them would be much better for you than Sydney."

Gregorio, as Damien Lowell's right-hand man, knew things. Gregorio understood human nature and, since he tracked all the membership applications, he had insider knowledge of everyone at the Den. He served as a house monitor and sometimes participated in scenes. Because he was so well respected, Doms and subs alike listened to him. Those who didn't often regretted their decision.

For the first time, Michael wanted to ignore Gregorio's unsolicited advice. "I didn't see a collar around her neck." He took in the people she was standing with. "And she doesn't seem to be here with anyone."

"She doesn't have a Dom."

"I'll bite. What's wrong with Ms. Wallace?"

"Other than the snake and the problems with the law?"

"What the hell are you talking about?" Michael asked, taking a sip of his energy drink and looking back at her. A waiter approached with a tray full of sparkling water, and she snagged a flute. Her back was to him, and he couldn't drag his gaze away from her shapely derrière. "Is she a Domme?" He'd bet money she wasn't.

"She's a sub," Gregorio said, giving the answer Michael wanted. "But one with no real interest in a relationship with a man."

He blinked. "She's gay?" Please God, no, not now that he was imagining her legs wrapped around his waist as he drove into her wet pussy.

"She likes men just fine. What I mean is, she'll start playing, if a guy interests her. If he bores her, she bails."

"Meaning she'll leave in the middle of a scene?"

"It's happened a handful of times." Gregorio folded his arms across his chest. "She's earned the name 'Brat' around here."

Something he could handle. "Challenging."

Gregorio laughed. The sound was both ominous and sympathetic. "A few other Doms have felt the same way," Gregorio said. "Sydney has a history of battering hearts and egos. And she never plays with the same person twice."

Water in hand, she walked around to the far side of the firepit and stood there alone. He responded to the unspoken cue. After finishing his beverage, he crumpled the can and passed it off to Gregorio. "Wish me luck."

Gregorio shook his head. "You'll need more than luck, my friend."

Michael moved toward her.

Perhaps hearing his approach, she looked up and waited for him.

"Evening, ma'am," he said, as he stopped near her and tipped his hat.

"I was hoping you would be brave enough to come and talk to me," she admitted with a smile that could roll his socks down. "I saw you talking with Gregorio. No doubt he tried to frighten you away with tales of how terrible I am."

"And are you?"

"I suppose there could be some truth to it." She shrugged easily. "But a good story is always better than the truth."

She smelled potently dangerous — vanilla blended with unadulterated pheromones. The combination created a cocktail he couldn't get enough of. "Either way, not much scares me."

"A man among men."

"Michael Dayton. Master Michael." Although the sun hadn't completely vanished behind the distant mountain peaks, torches were being lit, adding to the ambience and catching streaks of red in her hair. He wanted to touch those strands, to curl them around his fist as he held her down and made her scream.

"Sydney Wallace," she said, returning the formality.

"May I call you Sydney?"

She rolled her glass between her palms. With a tease in her voice, she said, "I'm hoping you can be considerably more creative than that."

He tipped back the brim of his hat to get a better look at her. She intrigued him. "So name calling is not on your limits list."

A server, this one a woman in a French maid's outfit that left nothing to the imagination, walked nearby. Though she was curvy with luscious bare breasts, he only had eyes for the woman he was with.

Sydney placed her glass on the tray. He appreciated the fact that she didn't need something to toy with.

When they were alone again, she said, "I understand you're divorced, Mr. Dayton. No kids. You have a ranch you'd like to protect from gold diggers. You scene every once in a while, and you're not looking for a serious commitment."

"Do you know my blood type?"

She gave a quick grin. "No. I only asked about the important stuff."

"You found out a lot in a short amount of time."

"I like being prepared. If I'm going to spend an hour with a man, I want to make sure the time is worth it. I don't think it's fair to either of us if there are false expectations."

"You're mistaken, Sydney."

"About which part?"

"We'll be spending more than an hour together. I can't get you properly warmed up in under sixty minutes, and I intend to keep you on the edge, writhing for an orgasm for much, much longer than that."

Her eyes widened, and for the first time he noticed how blue they were, a shade of ice, a shocking contradiction to the heat she radiated.

"That's a brash statement, Michael."

He captured her chin gently. "Find out for yourself. Let's have an experiment here at the Den to see if we have chemistry. After that, we can head out to my ranch. It's about forty-five minutes from here. Or if you'd prefer, we can go to your place. Wherever you feel most comfortable." He noticed her legs were alluringly bare. He'd always been a stockings man. Or at least he had been. Until now. "Are you wearing underwear?"

"I..."

With his index finger, he stroked her cheekbone. "I asked you a question."

"Yes."

"What kind?"

She hesitated for a moment, and he wondered if she was going to answer or whether she was going to run. He held her lightly enough that her movements weren't restricted.

"Boy shorts," she said.

"Please remove them for me."

"Now?" She blinked. "Here?"

"Maybe you're the one who should be afraid," he said quietly, "rather than me. Gregorio says you often bail out of scenes. I wondered at first if it was because Doms asked too much from you. But I'm thinking they probably don't ask enough. I've known you less than five minutes, but I've figured out you're assertive. You know what you want, but I'm guessing you're not always good at asking for it. Furthermore..." He leaned in closer. "I'm willing to bet you're bored with anyone who isn't as aggressive as you are. Am I wrong about that?"

She shivered. Since the Colorado evening was mild and they were standing near the fire, she couldn't be cold. So something he'd said had hit a nerve.

Surprising him, she unflinchingly met his gaze. "You're right about the fact I get bored easily." She curled her hand around his wrist. "And you're wrong if you think I'm afraid of anything."

"Fair enough. In that case, I told you to take off your panties." He released his grip on her chin, and she let go of him. He stayed in place, physically and figuratively refusing to give her space.

He offered his arm, and she held on to it while precariously balancing on her heels.

Finally, she straightened and looked at him as she dangled the pretty pink material from her index finger. Too late he realized he'd made a mistake by not asking to see them on her first. The material had probably stretched across her derrière, highlighting her butt cheeks perfectly.

He accepted the proffered underwear and stuffed the lace and nylon confection in his pocket. Who would have suspected that she wore something so tantalizing beneath black leather? "What are your limits?"

"I haven't found any," she said.

"Then you've been playing with the wrong Doms."

She shrugged. "That's possible. But maybe I'm tougher than you think."

"Perhaps." He met her answer with a great deal of skepticism. His ex-wife had let him believe she wanted things raw, but the moment the ring had been placed on her finger, the figurative collar had come off her throat. "Humiliation?"

"I don't have a lot of experience with that."

"No one has made you stand in a corner with your nose pressed to the wall when you misbehaved?"

She stiffened.

Have I hit another nerve?

Her lips parted for a moment, just long enough for him to wonder how she tasted. He loved anticipation, enjoyed getting a woman so turned on she lost her inhibitions, but now, with Sydney, unaccustomed impatience nipped at him.

"I don't misbehave." She returned his volley with an impish grin.

"Of course you do. Enough to be called the Brat."

"Oh." As if bored, she yawned. "That."

"Scares some people away, no doubt."

"But not you?"

"No. I understand that you're looking for something you haven't found."

She heaved a soft sigh. "I'm not open to being psychoanalyzed. Since it's unlikely we'll never see each other again, can we skip the bullshit and spend an enjoyable evening together?"

Before it formed, Michael hid his smile. "I don't rush. That's the first thing you need to know, Darlin'. I just want to know you better before we play together."

"Really? You like wasting time?"

"You can be certain..." He leaned in a little closer, only to be transfixed by the sexual vibes she radiated. "I'll give you what you need, not just what you want."

"That's as unlikely as it is arrogant."

"Find out for yourself," he challenged.

She scooped up a handful of hair and eased it back from her forehead, revealing her annoyed frown. "I was hoping that since you're a divorced man who doesn't want to go through that nonsense again, you'd be fine with taking what I offered."

"Ouch."

"Do you want an apology for your tender male ego?"

"With me, you don't have to watch your words. I prefer honesty."

"Do you, indeed?"

"I'll return the favor. I'm not against having a relationship. I'm not, in theory, against marriage." Passing the land to his heirs would be nice. He had one sister, who had two girls, but none of them had shown any interest in running the ranch on a long-term basis.

"Are you looking for something permanent now?" Trepidation wound through her tone.

"No."

"Then if you'd like to play, I would, too." Seductively, sexily, she placed her palm over his crotch.

Heat seared through the denim. Except for lovers he'd been with a long time, no woman had been so bold. He wanted to cave to his baser instincts and take her here, now. Instead, he captured her hand and moved it away.

She pulled back, breaking his grip. *Feeling rejected?* What man in his right mind would have stopped her? "Don't take it personally," he said. "In the future, you may be welcome to do that. It's not that I don't want you. On the contrary, I want to be buried balls-deep in your hot pussy as you cry out my name."

Her eyes opened wide. She seemed more intrigued than shocked. "What are we waiting for?"

"We need to clear up a few things."

"Right. I have no STDs, I have no physical limitations. Oh, yes, and I have condoms in my purse — large." She shot a quick, sassy grin. "And medium, just in case you need them."

Did she eat men's egos for breakfast? Rather than responding, he changed the subject. "Why do you scene?"

"More attempts to psychoanalyze me?"

"If you'd like to scene, you'll answer the question You've thought about it, surely?"

"Regular sex is boring."

"Hmm."

"And I like to transcend my limits."

When he nodded, she went on. "I thrive on physical challenges. I guide water river raft excursions. Completed a triathlon last week, and I'm competing in an upcoming mud race. You know, running up a mountain then doing obstacle courses, under barbed wire, over a wooden wall. My team is doing it for charity."

He looked at her with a new-found respect. When he'd first seen her, he'd had an urge to protect and care for her. But she could hold her own. Which only fed his instincts. "What's your safe word?"

"Everest."

Of course it is.

"You don't need to know why."

"Okay." He figured he already knew, but he looked forward to her telling him tomorrow morning over coffee. "How about a code for slowing down?"

"I don't believe in that."

"In that case, we'll use the word caution."

She sighed. "If I have to have one, how about we use the word turtle?"

He thumbed his hat. "You trying to insult me, brat?"

"Not at all. That would be rude. I'm just saying that turtles are slow."

Not only was she attractive, but quick-witted and intelligent. It had been a long time since a woman had appealed to him on multiple levels. "How do you feel about public play?"

She hesitated for a second. "I've never tried it."

"Are you willing to?"

"I suppose."

"I prefer a yes or no answer," he told her. "Unless you'd rather talk about it?"

"No. I mean yes."

"Yes, Sir."

"Yes, Sir," she dutifully repeated.

"Good girl."

He saw her grit her teeth, but she said nothing. He'd hit a nerve demanding she conform to the smallest of courtesies, and he'd remember that. "What kind of impact play do you prefer?"

Before he could ask further questions, she said, "I find an open-handed spanking to be really pleasurable. I also like belts." She glanced at his waist.

Oh, yeah. He'd happily lay the leather across her sweet, sexy rear.

For a moment, she was quiet. A bit discombobulated, perhaps?

In that moment, an air of vulnerability ghosted through her eyes. But then she blinked and smiled. If he hadn't been paying attention, he would have missed it.

"I'm also fine with a shoe or a ruler." She rushed the words together, filling the sudden silence. "Anything, really. Feel free to be creative. I'm okay with a flogger, open to trying a bullwhip or cane. There isn't a position I'm averse to, over the knee, or a table, or a bed. Standing, kneeling over a spanking bench. Did I miss anything?"

"The Sir at the end of your sentence."

"Of course. Sir." She gave him another of her sunny smiles.

She seemed so guileless, he'd bet it would be difficult for some Doms to hold her accountable. "Clamps?"

She nodded. "The harder the better. As you're probably gathering, I find it easier to get off when there's erotic pain involved."

"Anal plugs?"

She fidgeted then said, "If you insisted, I'd try it."

"No one has claimed your ass?" he asked, stunned.

"No."

That he would be the first to place something up there made him even harder, and his erection pressed against his jeans. He wanted to readjust his cock, but he reminded himself to focus on her. There were a few other things he needed to know before they got started. "Handcuffs?"

"Any kind of bondage," she said.

"I haven't lassoed a woman." He paused. "Yet."

Her eyes widened. "Sounds interesting."

Michael was glad he'd ignored Gregorio's advice. The thought of dragging a helpless Sydney toward him was a thrill. If she were barefoot and naked, it would be all the better. "I'm gathering you're open to sex."

"Like I said, I have condoms. In assorted sizes. In addition to having nothing communicable, I'm on birth control. Anything else you need to know?"

"That will cover it," he said wryly. "Likewise, I have a clean bill of health, but I also believe in exercising caution. We'll use condoms."

When he said nothing else, she gave a little flip of her hair and turned away, heading toward the house.

"Where are you going, Sydney?"

She stopped and looked over her shoulder. With a puzzled frown, she said, "Inside." She moistened her lips quickly then added, "I thought that was what you wanted."

"Did I say so?"

"No." She returned to stand in front of him. "I apologize."

"I'm going to spank you over there." He nodded toward a short metal fence in the distance. It bordered the grassy area beyond the horseshoe pits, far enough that they'd have some privacy. Still, since it was lit by a number of solar lights and torches, anyone who wanted to watch could.

She glanced around, and he waited patiently.

At least a dozen people were outside, a small group gathered on one side of the firepit. Some stood around high tables. Elsewhere, a woman sat on a porch swing while her male sub licked her boot.

Another evening at the Den.

"I think you need reminding that I prefer to be called Master Michael or Sir. When we play together, Sydney, I make the rules. I will be sure you understand them and agree with them, but once that happens, they will be enforced. Do you understand?"

"Yes, Sir," she whispered.

"Do you agree to address me the way I prefer?"

She nodded.

"Please pull your dress up to your waist."

She couldn't have taken more time. He didn't complain, though. Still, seeing her obey his wishes was its own reward. She was softness and sensuality all wrapped in a beautiful, tough package.

"Ah," he said when she was exposed. "Such a pretty little pussy. I like that it's shaved." He looked at her expectantly.

"Thank you, Sir."

Interesting—since he'd drawn harsher boundaries, she seemed softer, more compliant. "Please put your hands behind your neck and bring your chest forward."

She did. "Would you like me to take the dress off entirely, Sir?"

"I'd like you to do as you're told. Nothing more. Are you able to comfortably spread your legs a little farther apart? You can take off your shoes if you need to."

When she was in position, more open, he slid a hand between her legs. Her response delighted him. "You're damp, Sydney."

He kept his hand still, but she moved her hips a bit, sliding herself against him. "I generally won't mind if you come without permission. In fact, the more you orgasm, the more I get into the scene." He lowered his voice to an inviting purr. "But not tonight. Tonight I want you more aroused than you've ever been." After she released a tiny moan, he pulled his hand away. Without giving her a chance to react, he spanked her there.

She screamed and pitched forward slightly. He caught her and held her against him, liking the way they fit together.

For a moment, she stayed there before drawing in a deep breath and moving away. "*That* was unexpected. And unbelievably hot, Sir."

"Turtle?"

"No." She shook her head. "More like that, please."

"Stay where you are. I'll be right back."

He went inside. Brandy, a sub who regularly helped with house functions and parties, fetched him a blanket and two separate cuffs.

"My pleasure, Sir," she said when he thanked her.

When he returned, Sydney was still in the same place. She was shifting from side to side a bit nervously, but she'd yet to bail out of the scene. "Are you doing okay?"

"Feeling a little exposed," she admitted. "Sir."

"Seeing you when I came back outside pleased me."

She exhaled. "Did it?" Her words were breathless.

"Indeed." Was he affecting her as powerfully as she was impacting him? "Would you like to continue?"

"You don't think that scared me off, do you? Sir?" The words were sassy and confident, but her voice wobbled, maybe betraying some nerves.

Interesting. "When you're ready, walk over to the fence." Then he scowled. "Are you okay in those shoes?"

"I could hike in them."

We'll see about that. "I'll stay a step or two behind you so I can watch your bare buttocks move."

The view was all he'd hoped for. Her every step was graceful, filled with sultry elegance. Despite her bravado, when she reached the edge of the paved patio, he took her elbow. He helped her over the uneven terrain then draped the blanket over the top rail.

Without being told, she kicked off her shoes and positioned herself, even remembering to spread her legs wide. Sydney Wallace definitely knew what she wanted. And, whether or not she recognized it, by having her beautifully curved ass upturned and waiting for his attention, she was also meeting his carnal needs.

"Use your safe word if it's too much, your slow word if you're uncomfortable or get a muscle cramp. We can get you readjusted."

"Yes, Sir. I understand."

"Your choice—I can secure your legs in place, or I can cuff your wrists."

She answered unhesitatingly. "I'd prefer you fasten my ankles so I can't get away, Sir."

Which meant that sometimes that was an option. "I'll expect you to keep your hands in place."

"Yes, of course, Sir."

He crouched to attach the cuffs, and he inhaled the heady scent of her muskiness. Keeping her turned on without letting her come was going to be exquisitely rewarding.

To test the bonds, he trailed his fingers up the insides of her thighs. She squirmed and pulled and yet she helplessly remained where he wanted her. Sometime in the future, he'd stick a plug up her ass too, to intensify her sensations. "I'm going to warm you up with a few spanks." He fed the words into her ear. "Then I'll make you beg for more."

"You sound sure of yourself, Sir," she said, her voice muffled.

"I am, Sydney."

"You know, Sir, I have never begged for anything my entire life."

"Tonight, brat, you will." *You've never been spanked by me.* "I promise you."

"We'll see about that..." Then, after her challenge, she added a saucy, "Sir."

About the Author

Born in northern England and raised in the Wild West, Sierra Cartwright pens books that are as untamed as the Rockies she calls home.

She's an award-winning, multi-published writer who wrote her first book at age nine and hasn't stopped since.

Sierra invites you to share the complex journey of love and desire, of surrender and commitment. Her own journey has taught her that trusting takes guts and courage, and her work is a celebration for everyone who is willing to take that risk.

Sierra loves to hear from readers. You can find her contact information, website details and author profile page at https://www.totallybound.com

Home of Erotic Romance

Sign up for our newsletter and find out about all our romance book releases, eBook sales and promotions, sneak peeks and FREE romance books!